"We've all wondered just how well we know our children—or if we paint them in our minds with broad strokes to see them as the people we want them to be. *Early Leaving* is a sensitive, beautifully crafted story of one mother's abrupt awakening to the truth that our relationships are never what they seem to be."

—Jodi Picoult

"Judy Goldman's splendid new novel, *Early Leaving*, is even better than her accomplished first novel, *The Slow Way Back*. There is a great luminous beauty to her writing that delights me. Few American writers have ever written with such passion and insight about the joys and great peril of family life."

—Pat Conroy

"*Early Leaving* is one of those novels you know you'll remember forever—the wisdom, the compassion, the absolutely brilliant portrait of motherhood. Judy Goldman has painted every parent's worst nightmare, illuminating denial and everyday mistakes in a way that makes the reader shudder with recognition. Moving, heartbreaking, and ultimately a testament to hope and survival, *Early Leaving* is an extraordinary novel."

—Jill McCorkle

"As in her first novel, *The Slow Way Back*, Goldman once again displays a keen eye for the character-defining detail."

—*Washington Post*

"Haunting questions of parenthood ripple through the pages of this thoughtful second novel."

—*Seattle Post-Intelligencer*

"That Goldman is a poet is evident throughout this page-turning second novel . . . . [She] has increased her fan base with this one."

—*Charlotte Observer*

"Goldman's brutally honest dramatization of a dysfunctional family makes for provocative read."

—*Booklist*

"Judy Goldman's extraordinary new book, *Early Leaving*, is the story of a mother who does everything almost right, with utterly dire consequences. Goldman's Kathryne Smallwood is at once disarmingly honest and deeply self-deceptive. I felt she could be someone I know, if not someone I am. I read with increasing horror as her life unraveled, and with relief as she ultimately remade it. A totally absorbing novel from page one onward."

—Josephine Humphreys

ALSO BY JUDY GOLDMAN

FICTION

The Slow Way Back

POETRY

Wanting to Know the End

Holding Back Winter

EARLY LEAVING

JUDY GOLDMAN

HARPER PERENNIAL

NEW YORK • LONDON • TORONTO • SYDNEY

HARPER ● PERENNIAL

A hardcover edition of this book was published in 2004 by William Morrow, an imprint of HarperCollins Publishers.

P.S.™ is a trademark of HarperCollins Publishers.

First Harper Perennial edition published 2005.

Designed by Cassandra J. Pappas

The Library of Congress has catalogued the hardcover edition as follows:

Goldman, Judy.
    Early leaving / Judy Goldman.—1st ed.
        p. cm.
    ISBN 0-06-059458-6 (alk. paper)
        1. Parental overprotection—Fiction. 2. Separation (Psychology)—Fiction. 3. High school students—Fiction. 4. Mothers and sons—Fiction. 5. Teenage boys—Fiction. 6. Murderers—Fiction. I. Title.
    PS3557.O3688E37 2004

                                                            2004040208

ISBN-10: 0-06-059459-4 (pbk.)
ISBN-13: 978-0-06-059459-6 (pbk.)

05 06 07 08 09 ❖/RRD 10 9 8 7 6 5 4 3 2 1

For my twin granddaughters, Lucy and Zoe. Double joy.

ACKNOWLEDGMENTS

W ITH LOVE and gratitude for my family:

Husband, Henry Goldman (who helped me so much, the book cover should say *by Judy and Henry Goldman*); son and daughter-in-law, Mike and Brooke Goldman; daughter and son-in-law, Laurie and Bob Smithwick; their daughters, Lucy and Zoe. My second mother, Mattie Culp; brother, Donald Kurtz; sister and brother-in-law, Brenda and Chuck Meltsner; sister-in-law, Ruth Cohen. Nieces and nephews: Sasha Kurtz, David Meltsner, Brian and Tonya Meltsner, Scott Meltsner, Danny and Diana Meltsner, Steve and Tina Cohen, Jeff and Sherry Cohen, Doug and 'Leen Cohen, Adam Cohen and Cooper Heins, Tracy Seretean.

With love and gratitude for those who seem like family:

Marly Rusoff—every writer's dream of the perfect agent; my editor, Claire Wachtel, whose vision and insightful editorial skill made all the difference; her hardworking assistant, Jennifer Pooley; my resourceful publicist, Angela Tedesco; attentive production editor,

Joyce Wong; eagle-eyed copy editor, Marty Karlow; gifted jacket designer, Bryce Taylor; everyone at William Morrow who saw me through. Careful readers: Dannye Powell, Christina Baker Kline, Dwight Allen, Mary Hunter Daly, John Vaughan, Abigail DeWitt, Rosa Shand, Peggy Payne, David Cashion. Contributors of useful information: Jennie Ness, June White, David Mills, Carmen Lord, Bev Armstrong, Lindsay Reckson, Eben and Leslie Rawls, Tony Scheer, Lew Powell, George Daly, Eric Levinson, Tony Giordano, Tate Cohen, Maggie Meltsner, Dylan and Sam Cohen, Nick Cohen. Friends who encouraged and sustained: Judy Pera, my breakfast group (Ann Haskell, Bobbie Campbell, Laurie Johnston, Clarissa Porter, Dannye Powell, Mary Hunter Daly), Marilyn Perlman, Debbie Rubin, Mary Fenster, Paula Reckson, Kathryne Perrill, Betsy Rock, Marilee Sanders, Nancy Watson.

This project was made possible in part by a grant from the North Carolina Arts Council, a state agency, the Arts & Science Council-Charlotte-Mecklenburg, Inc.

EARLY
LEAVING

From *The Charlotte Observer,* page one, Tuesday, June 6, 1987:

TOP RANDOLPH ACADEMY GRADUATE CHARGED WITH MURDER

An honor student and varsity athlete was charged Monday in the killing of a young Charlotte man whose charred body was found in the trunk of a smoldering Mazda off Harper Church Road, south of Charlotte. The victim, William James Campbell, 19, had been shot once in the head.

Investigators say Earl David Smallwood, 18, son of prominent attorney Peter Smallwood, killed Campbell only hours after delivering the commencement address at Randolph Academy, a private school in southeast Charlotte.

The victim's mother, Ethel Campbell, demanded the death penalty for her son's murderer. "He burned up William," she said from the courthouse steps, "and he should burn in hell for what he did.

"I don't know what happened," she went on, breaking into tears. "All I know is it would not have happened if my boy was not black."

Minutes later, District Attorney Andrew Wheeler and Donald Sanders, an attorney for Smallwood, left the courthouse. "Early Small-

wood is an outstanding young man who has a lot of family and community support," said Sanders. "His record is unblemished."

"There are aggravating factors here that would support a life sentence," District Attorney Wheeler said.

A farmer checking on his animals found the burning car Friday before daylight. Smallwood was arrested and taken to Mecklenburg County Jail later that morning. Few details were available as police continued to investigate.

ONE

SOME MEMORIES we ignore. Others, little half-stories, we tell again and again, trotting them out for friends— and even people we barely know—like scrubbed children. We love what they say about us, the rosy image they project, exactly what we hoped and imagined our lives would be: bringing the baby home from the hospital, making up silly jingles about the shops and people we passed, turning everything into song. The baby's first lopsided smiles, definitely not gas, real smiles. Steadying him, that day in the park, as he took his first steps, the rolling Charlie Chaplin gait, the sun playing around us in the grass like a goldfish. The time we were at the lake and skipped rocks across a clean, calm surface. Later, when he dove in, water quickly erasing the path he'd taken.

See how the events of a child's life can appear no more complicated than photographs in silver frames?

Early's sentencing is October 6, tomorrow. Our lawyer, Donald

Sanders, worked out a plea to second-degree murder with the district attorney, and Early agreed to take it. Which means that tomorrow morning, our son will plead guilty.

Donald says we have to prepare ourselves for the possibility that Early could get the maximum sentence. Life, with eligibility of parole.

It's also possible, Donald says, that Early could get a lesser sentence, fifty years, forty, maybe as low as fifteen years. The sentence is up to the discretion of the court.

Prepare ourselves for a life sentence? Life is what is given to a child by his mother. Not a judge.

If he gets forty or fifty years, I probably won't be around when he's released. Fifteen years? He'll be thirty-three when he's set free. That's almost as many years in prison as he's spent with us.

Just for tonight, I'm going to stop being terrified. I'll sink into the past, let memories fold over me, haphazard and slow. Not just the ones I tried to believe in all those years. The ones I tried to forget, as well. If the truth makes my reflection stare back at me, I'll tell myself, Get an eyeful. I realize that if I go deep, I might find that I should have seen the end coming. Which raises the question, Was there a point where I could've come between my son and the things that lay in wait for him? Should I have paid closer attention? Stepped in, instead of holding back? Or is it all just a matter of choices and chance, the way every one of us drifts close to danger but only some get sucked in? The question I don't want to ask myself: Was I the cause?

At five, Early's favorite bedtime story was the one I made up about the night he was born. I'd lie slant across the foot of his bed and say that on May 7, 1969, mothers and fathers from all over Charlotte rushed to the hospital to get a baby. I'd lightly squeeze his toes through the blanket, clear my throat to build suspense, and keep going. We heard there were dozens of newborns available for pickup in the nursery, I'd say. But instead of each set of parents choosing a baby in a levelheaded, orderly fashion, there was a huge ruckus. Mothers started shoving mothers, fathers punching fathers—everybody was red-faced and yelling—because we all wanted the same baby. And you know who that baby was (my exact words, Early's favorite part).

When the battles were finally over, I'd tell him, we'd beaten out the Dunhams, who begrudgingly settled for the baby one bassinet over, a howler named Chip. The Jacksons had reluctantly taken Eddie and gone home. The Todds sulked off carrying Steven, but not yet resigned to the idea of Steven. (I would keep going until I'd named all his friends.) Yes, your dad and I were clearly the winners, I'd say. We paraded through the halls of that hospital, out the front door, across the parking lot to our car, holding our sleeping baby aloft, like a trophy, for everyone to see and admire.

Over and over, Early would ask me to tell the story. The second or third time, I'd escalate the drama a notch—wrestling one of the mothers to the floor, her shoes flying off like in a cartoon, arms and legs in the air like a bug, her cries: "Okay, okay, take Early! He's yours!" My sweet son would sit straight up in bed and wiggle with excitement. The idea of his birth causing such commotion! Imagine how much that little baby was wanted! His sheet and blanket would rustle, his head bob. That full head of fair hair he got from me.

Then I'd tuck him in, making sure the covers were snug under his arms and along both of his sides. The pin-oak leaves out the window would be moving slightly, causing the moon to crack into pieces and fall over his shoulders like silver confetti.

Finally, Peter would take over. He'd pat Early on the arm—Peter believed it made a boy "soft" for his father to kiss him—and say in his no-foolishness-about-it way, "Now go to sleep." My husband, setting limits.

Peter's a formal person, self-contained and private. A patent attorney with the oldest, most respected law firm in Charlotte. Board of trustees at the Y. Head of a million committees. Franklin G. Caldwell Award for "outstanding service to the community." All his life, a star. Handsome, with that straight hair falling naturally into place, giving the impression it's just been combed. Fit, five-ten, strong and compact, his muscular arms veiny. Nothing wasted, no extraneous anything. He looks like one of those men who are already seated in first class when you're passing through the plane to coach, the way they're so settled in, comfortable, even though you know they boarded just minutes before. They appear *entitled,* reading their *Wall Street Journal*s, sipping their hot coffee.

Of course, Peter got excited when Early walked at nine months. When he learned to catch a ball at two. When he was three and taught himself to read. "Pilot Survives Crash" was the headline he read out loud, phonetically, one morning at breakfast, perched on a kitchen stool, gazing at the morning paper folded on the counter— "pie-laht" is the way he sounded out the syllables. As though the word had been sitting on the edge of his tongue. We had no idea he could read!

And oh, how that boy worked to make his father proud. In the backyard, he'd climb to the top bar of the swing set, hang by his knees, head dangling, cheeks pink. "Look at me, Daddy!" he'd call out. "Watch this!" Then he'd drop to the ground, rubber-sole it up the sliding board, twist his agile body around, and slide down head-first. He seemed to know that Peter's approval depended on what he could do, not who he was.

Peter said I spoiled Early, that I was too involved in his life. Overprotective is the word he used. Maybe when your husband is *under*-protective, you move in to fill the void. I thought I was doing a good job, though—I modeled myself after my own mother. Some people spend their lives railing against the way they were raised, every action a reaction to their parents, a fierce determination to do the opposite with their own children. I idolized my mother, tried to make my voice the same as hers, adopted her handwriting, even memorized the way she held a cigarette. (If you could look in on my dreams when I was in my twenties, you'd see me always holding a cigarette—my first two fingers graceful and straight, last two fingers curled under—even though I'd never smoked a day in my life.)

Peter's childhood? When he was nine, everything that was right turned wrong. He went from being raised by loving parents to living with two unmarried aunts, his life suddenly threadbare and cramped. Where would that leave him, years later, as a parent? He'd learned to survive a grim situation. Not just survive. He'd navigated his childhood as though it were a boat whose controls he'd had to take over. Now he firmly believed that going through tough times gives a child self-confidence. Let a kid flounder so he can see for himself that he'll survive. It's not so much what happens to us in life as what we do with it, he'd say. Then he'd say it again. *It's not so much what happens to us in life as what we do with it.* As though repetition turned it into a gold-plated, hand-polished, embossed plaque.

I believed we should make things easy for our children, help them glide through life. I wanted to give Early all the love he deserved. That was my job, to give him love and make him happy. I lived to hear that lilt in his voice. I didn't think I was so different from other mothers. After all, we promise our children we'll keep them from harm. We know the world is always waiting to hurt them. Sometimes, though, it's hard to judge when we should do a little more of this or a little less of that. There are so many ambiguities we haven't counted on. My closest friend, Joy, who raised three wonderful children on her own—her husband died before I met her—used to say we're only as happy as our unhappiest child.

Peter and I never argued about any of this; arguing is just not something we did.

The real story of Early's birth: an immediate, profound attachment between the two of us. A reverberation that was private. That baby and I had our own code. A code my husband could not crack.

May 6, 1969, after a spaghetti dinner at home, Peter drove me to the hospital. I'd brought two plumped-up pillows from our bed to cushion my sides and was concentrating on breathing deeply and evenly through my mouth when each contraction hit. And they were hitting. Closer and closer together. I thought I'd deliver any minute. The traffic light at the corner of Ridge Avenue, our street, and Providence Road turned green just as we got to it. Most people speed up when the light is green, especially when someone in the car is in labor. Peter slowed down (not one to ever come close to breaking a rule, he always slows down at green lights). He looked both ways, gave his horn a quick toot to warn the one lonely driver going straight on Providence Road, who'd already come to a complete stop, not to dare run the red light. Then Peter turned left in the direction of the hospital, stopped at the next intersection for a yellow light (the same carefulness for yellow lights), waited for it to turn red, then green.

I needn't have worried about delivering in the car. I was in labor for thirty-six hours. The baby was angled the wrong way—sunnyside up, they said, though there was nothing sunny about it. Early was faceup, instead of facedown. Open to the world and whatever it dished out. Wide open, even in the womb, and vulnerable.

Hour after hour, contractions cut through to my back; my cervix refused to dilate; my hands crawled over my stomach. I desperately wanted Peter with me, in that pain-thick labor room, not out in the family waiting area. I wanted him to be the type of husband whose presence would make everything okay, certain. He could be that. At times.

But the hospital had a rule about this, and he was not allowed in because he hadn't gone through the Lamaze classes with me. We'd attended the first session together, but I knew I'd lost him when the instructor—an earthy woman in her thirties, who'd had three sons using Lamaze—held up the uterus she'd crocheted, drawing it in and pushing it out with her fingertips to demonstrate how we were expanding ("a tiny bit every day"). It looked like a bird taking breaths, preparing for flight. I heard a low groan from Peter when she hit the switch and put the room in darkness to show the home video her husband had made during her youngest son's birth. While the film jerked along, she pointed with her pen: "Here. Right here. If you look carefully, you can spot small hemorrhoids forming." She said this as casually as if she were directing our attention to a mountain range on a map. "Just behind my vagina. See where the baby's head is crowning? Next to that."

So, except for the nurses, I was alone. Not even my obstetrician was there. He didn't come until my thirty-third hour of labor, as if he were saying, *You want natural? I'll give you natural.* I found out later he was opposed to natural childbirth, even though during my pregnancy he'd acted as though he was its biggest advocate. I loved the idea of natural childbirth. I believed that if I were awake, if I were *there,* I could make sure nothing bad happened to my baby.

After all those hours, Dr. Bowles, still in his weekend clothes, stood in the doorway across from where I lay. Straight as a spear, a sheaf of charts tight under one arm, that perfect crease in his khakis. His first words were "Is this what you'd call a beautiful experience?"

He changed into scrubs, examined me, then returned to his spot across the room, leaning against the doorframe, although with his stiff posture it was more like a tilt.

"This 'natural business' is not working, Kathryne," he said. "You're only two centimeters dilated. We have no choice. We're going to have to give you a little injection." Why do doctors have to refer to themselves in the plural? I wanted to ask. As though they're more than one person. As though they're a whole team, for heaven's sake. And why do they call everything "little"?

Three hours after the sedative, I came to, just as Early had turned himself and was ready to be born. In that half second, everything cracked open: Dr. Bowles was by my side, his chin jutted forward with interest. I was shifted onto a stretcher, rails clicked into place, wheeled down the hall into the brightest room I'd ever seen. Draped, swabbed. Nurses, like a flock of mothers, sponged my forehead, my eyes, and when my buttery baby slipped out—that human sound crossing the space between us—it *was* a beautiful experience.

Seconds after he was born, I held him, his puckered ear against my heart. I counted fingers and toes, traced the sweet curve of a wrist bone.

We named him Earl David Smallwood, after Peter's father, and called him Early. Our little joke, since he'd taken so long to get here.

For weeks after we brought him home, I stood over the crib, with its fresh-laundered, blue-elephants-tossing-balls-in-the-air cotton sheet pulled tight. I couldn't get enough of that baby. His pinched eyes, glowing skin, the way he cocked his head as if waiting for my voice. I'd stand there for hours, just watching him sleep. Sometimes I'd wake him up to play. When I was ready to lay him back down, I could always quiet him—nudge him back to sleep—by stroking his eyelids lightly with the tips of my fingers. I'd brush those lavender, cellophane-paper eyelids all the way down to his puffy cheeks, as though I were raking with the world's gentlest comb. His eyes would close as my fingers passed over them, but then they'd open, wide and defiant, furry lashes fluttering. Over and over, I brushed. Over and over, his eyes closed, then opened—a rhythm he and I settled into like a duet. Soon his eyes would open more slowly with each sweep as he struggled against sleep. Until finally, his milk-sour hands, his legs, his perfectly shaped head, his whole body would give in and he'd let himself fall asleep, as naturally as curtains in an open window go limp in summer's warm breath.

TWO

I N THE BEGINNING, we were the perfect family. Married in 1967. First and only child born two years later. Like other young, married couples in Charlotte, North Carolina, we watched the evening news, but the unrest on college campuses and in big cities was far from our leafy, well-mowed world. In August 1968, the week of the Democratic National Convention, Peter and I flew to Chicago for a cousin's wedding. One night we wanted to take a shortcut through Grant Park and asked a policeman if it was safe to walk there. "Yeah," he said with a sneer, "if any of those hippies give you any trouble, just throw a little soap at 'em and they'll run the other way." I remember thinking that with that attitude on the part of the police, the city was going to erupt.

The first year and a half of our marriage, we rented a one-bedroom furnished apartment. Just before Early was born, we rented a two-bedroom duplex and bought furniture—a brown, black, and white plaid sofa, easy chair, étagère, French Provincial bedroom suite, dinette set, crib decorated with dancing lambs, a changing table, painted chest of drawers. I happily gave up my full-time job reviewing movies for the *Observer* and started writing monthly reviews for *Charlotte Magazine* so I could stay home with the baby. Mornings, while he slept, I worked on a review, read magazines, talked on the phone. After his nap, I'd take him on long, luxurious stroller rides; we had our two-mile loop past the 1920s bungalows and cottagey front-yard gardens in the neighborhood. Sometimes, if we were feeling lazy, we'd skip the walk and play in the Pawleys Island rope hammock strung between two redbud trees in the backyard. My days were all the same and I loved that they were the same. The only thing that changed was the number of hours Early napped. Which made for good conversation when Peter called. I'd tell him, in great detail, about the two-hour morning nap, how the skin around Early's mouth was tinted orange from too many Gerber carrots, how I could get him to stop crying by holding him in front of the oven and flicking the light on and off, how he'd found his foot. When I told my mother these things, her response was always the same: *I'm telling you, Kathryne, there's nothing that boy won't be able to do, if he puts his mind to it.* Sometimes I called her or Peter with fast-breaking news: Early turning the pages of a book—when other babies his age were teething on them. Early beginning to crawl—only he seemed to be moving backward instead of forward.

I was learning to cook and would start dinner in the middle of the afternoon. We'd have a protein—chicken divan, hamburger pie, tuna noodle casserole with canned onion rings on top. A starch—baked potatoes or rice. Something green—canned peas. Fruit Jell-O for dessert. During dinner, we'd place Early in his yellow plastic infant seat in the middle of the round table in the kitchen. He was our centerpiece. He'd suck on his pacifier, look around, take in the world. When we pulled the pacifier out, his wide yawning grin made him look like the MGM lion.

We directed our conversation *through* him:

"Does Early's daddy want more water?"

"Could Early's mommy please pass the butter?"

There was no way we could top this baby. Which is one reason we decided not to have any more children. Actually, Peter and I never really discussed it. I just started taking my birth-control pills again and never really stopped. If I'd been honest with myself, the real question for me was: Is there room left in my heart for anyone but Early?

W E DIDN'T EAT OUT very often, but when we did, it was at one of the inexpensive places in town. Olde Hickory House Barbecue Restaurant, in north Charlotte, was our favorite. It was what we could afford in those days, and the food was good. The address seemed to be a symbol for the way things were taking shape for us: Gloryland Avenue. As simple as our life was then, there was an ease to it. A good-natured hopefulness.

One night, Peter and I sat across from each other in one of the red vinyl booths lining the knotty-pine walls, the lamp between us a little covered wagon. Early sat in an old wooden high chair at the end of the table.

The waitress brought our sweet iced tea, her fingernails clicking as she set the wet glasses in front of us. "And how old are you, you cute little thing?" she asked Early in a drowsy voice. Her accent was a mixture of southern and something else, maybe Appalachian.

He laughed, drawing his whole body up. I answered for him, the way mothers do, like a ventriloquist, "I'm eighteen months old."

"Cu-u-ute!" she said, pulling a pad and pencil from her skirt pocket. "You look like your mama. Same pretty, heart-shaped face, same green eyes and blond hair. Ooh, and that creamy skin y'all both have . . ."

"Thank you," I said, grinning. I was always glad for people to notice how much he looked like me. I had a snapshot of myself at the same age, standing on tiptoes in my footie pajamas, kissing a giant pink-and-white giraffe my mother had won at the county fair when she was a teenager. The baby in the picture could've been Early. The same coloring, same afterthought of a nose—so tiny.

Peter took the two mimeographed menus from the metal clip on the side of the paper napkin holder and handed one to me. I opened and closed it without reading and ordered my usual: chopped barbecue pork with crispy end pieces thrown in, Brunswick stew, french fries, and tossed salad (a slice of iceberg lettuce with Thousand Island dressing). Peter ordered the same. I asked for a glass of milk and small plate for Early so I could give him food off my plate.

"All you get is a drink and an empty plate, dollbaby?" she said to Early, smiling that kind of smile where your lips disappear and your gums show. He stared at her mouth for several seconds and then wrinkled his nose and turned his lips out to show *his* gums, like a mischievous monkey.

"I see your teeth, cutie! They are shiny as can be," she said, touching his chin with the tip of her fingernail.

The barbecue was especially good that night, woodsy and sloppy. Early was his usual contented self, munching french fries, chasing the barbecue around his plate with his spoon. Peter had good news: the following Monday he'd be moving into a larger office at work, one with a window and a view of the pond out front. "Windows are key," he was saying, "and a window with a view is even *more* key. We're on our way, sweetheart!" He'd been getting better and better cases and was receiving a lot of attention within the firm. The week before, he'd been interviewed by a reporter at the paper, for the "Profiles" column on the business page.

As we talked, I noticed Early making eye contact with a woman seated with her family at a table close by, out in the room. It was a black family: the woman, her husband, and their son who was about four years old. The woman wore a white turtleneck top and had slim shoulders and perfect posture. She mouthed to me, "He's adorable," meaning Early.

"Thank you," I mouthed back. I pointed to her son and nodded to let her know he was adorable, too.

Early gave her a smile, raised his eyebrows, and widened his eyes as if to say a big hello. As soon as she smiled back at him, he averted his gaze, buried his chin in his chest. He was flirting with her!

Music played in the background, a fast-paced country song about somebody cheating on somebody else. Early bounced a little and his high chair squeaked like a fiddle.

"What're you looking at?" I said in a teasing, baby-talky voice. "You see that lady over there?"

Now she was waving at him. He put his hand next to his face and curled his fingers in a tiny cupped wave. Then he quickly buried his chin in his chest again. This time his eyes stayed on her, his eyebrows raised, lips pursed in a funny smile.

"Say hi," Peter said, smiling and winking at the woman. "Say hi there!"

"Hi there," Early said to Peter.

"No, I mean say hi to the nice lady!" He was making sure the woman heard him.

"Hi to nice wady," Early said to Peter.

Peter and I started laughing. It wasn't really that funny but we were feeling so light, so happy, so in love with each other and ourselves, we could've cracked up over the list of side dishes on the menu. The more we laughed, the more Early repeated himself. "Hi to nice wady. Hi to nice wady." Then he threw his head back and laughed as though he were in on the joke, but because he had no idea what the joke was, his laugh was big and fake. He had barbecue sauce on his face. His hair—straight and long because it was so pretty I hated to cut it—was damp, dark with sweat around the rims of his ears and the back of his neck. On top, it fluffed out like feathers. Peter took off his glasses and wiped a tear from his eye with a corner of a napkin; that's how hard he was laughing. Then he leaned across the table and kissed me on the forehead.

The little boy at the other table was talking. He'd been talking nonstop since they'd sat down. In the middle of all his chattering, I heard him ask his father, "How do your eyes stay in your head, Daddy?" The father didn't answer, but the mother draped her arm around the boy and gathered him closer, an affectionate gesture— maybe a protective gesture.

Then the boy said in a stage voice, definitely louder than before: "Now, Daddy, I'm going to tell you a story about the big bad wolf. Once upon a time, the big bad wolf had an idea. He decided he was going to be nice . . . *not* mean." It didn't seem to matter that the father wasn't listening, the boy kept going. "And the wolf did *not* blow down the pigs' houses, he just *played* with the pigs . . ."

I noticed the boy sat very straight, like his mother, even with his feet dangling. He held his fork like an adult and his napkin never moved from his lap. Such good manners, I thought. So much personality. I also thought how nice it was to have that lovely family over there—and this lovely family right here. *Yes, yes, yes,* the music was saying.

For the first time, I took a good look at the father. There was a shadow over his face. He was square-shaped, his head and shoulders and chest blocky. He seemed to take up more than his share of space. Even while he was eating, his left hand was in his pocket jingling change. While I was looking at him, trying to find a place for him in this picture, he lifted his free hand in exasperation and directed a bellow toward his son: "You know what your problem is?"

The boy shook his head; it wasn't exactly a *no*. It was more a small, nervous movement. So small I wasn't sure I'd seen it.

The father got right in the boy's face. "You know what your problem is?" His voice rose with temper and desperation. "You're hardheaded and you talk too damn much!"

Everything came to a halt in the restaurant. I'm sure the music didn't actually stop, but it felt as if it did. Waitresses disappeared. Customers stopped chatting—the easy tinkle of their voices. All the pinging, clinking noises you hear in a restaurant suddenly silenced. The four-foot saws, scythes, ice-block tongs, guns and holsters decorating the walls were practically vibrating.

The father kept screaming at the boy. "Sit up straight! Stop slumping! And eat! I'm sick of your goddamn jabbering!"

The boy and his mother were hunched over their plates. She hid behind her iced tea, the boy, behind his milk. Her arm was still around him. I could see her nervously squeezing his shoulder. Instinctively, I reached for Early, patted his cheek, smiled at him. A smile that said nothing at all is going on and let's just have a nice time.

Peter leaned out of the booth, twisted toward the man, a little like a flirty woman, and said good-naturedly, "Look, buddy, let's keep it down, okay? We're trying to have a quiet dinner here."

The man pushed back his chair so abruptly he almost tipped over—a sound like a rusty saw shrieking. He spoke to Peter in a fixed, but enraged voice: "You got a problem, mister? You got a problem? This is none of your business, you know." Then he turned to his wife; "Let's get the hell out of here. I don't need this crap."

The three of them got up and walked out, the father half a room ahead of the others, the mother pulling the child by the hand, trying to keep up with the father.

And then they were gone. Like that. The restaurant was silent. It felt like the split second after lightning, when you know a bolt struck close. Clipped a tree next door. Maybe even one of your own.

Early burst out crying. A burned, wounded kind of crying. Within seconds he was crying so hard he could barely catch his breath. Between sobs, it sounded as if he were gagging. I thought he might vomit. I tried to slide out of the booth—quickly—so I could pull him out of the high chair, nestle his head in the wing of my neck and shoulder, reassure him. But my skirt caught on a vinyl tear in the seat, and before I could get to him, Peter started patting him briskly on the back, as though something had gone down wrong. Surprisingly, it worked. The gesture was too businesslike for my taste, but I have to admit, Early was now hiccuping the way children do when their crying is coming to an end.

I ran my finger over the dimples on the back of his hand. I thought how much pink there was in his skin and how much I adored him. I touched each dimple. As though they could bring back the comfort of a few minutes before. As though those dimples could bring us all comfort: Peter, me, our supersensitive Early, everyone eating barbecue in that restaurant, including the father, the mother, and their hardheaded, talkative son.

I CAN ONLY GUESS at why I remember such an ordinary, unimportant incident. At the time, I looked on the evening as one that started out soft and full of possibilities and ended up tight and narrowed down. I had no way of knowing it was a preview of our future, the way everything would end up so off course. We were good at beginnings. We just ran into trouble trying to maintain. That night the problems were external, outside our tight little family unit. Later the problems would be closer in. Our perfect family would become less and less perfect with every passing year. Our perfect evenings would have a way of turning.

Now I see that the other family in the restaurant was a shadow of us: the father wanting more than his son could give, Peter a couple of years away from his own version of that, not nearly as harsh, but still in the same vein. Two mothers so in love with their sons.

And race—was it an issue at all that night? Peter and I believed in our righteousness. Peter and his volunteer work—all those meetings around polished tables trying to come up with programs to lift the lives of the underprivileged. My history—beginning in 1956 when I was fifteen and the University of Alabama admitted its first black student. I remember crying myself to sleep after watching the images on TV: Autherine Lucy, the straps of her slim leather purse over her arm, the white hat and conservative suit, serene smile. As she walked to class, white students and townspeople and groups bussed in from out of state pushed in, threw eggs, yelled, "Let's kill her! Let's kill her!"

Years later, when I was a sophomore in college, I testified in court as a character witness for the black waiter in my sorority house, T.R., who was accused of breaking into our sixty-five-year-old white housemother's bedroom in the middle of the night and raping her. The only way "Aunt" Ruby was able to escape with her life, she informed the court, was to tell him, "This will be our little secret. You can come back every night." There was no proof of rape because she claimed that she douched when it was over. Yes, my action was chancy, at the University of South Carolina in 1961. But I believed T.R. was innocent. My testimony would show "Aunt" Ruby's attitude (extremely prejudiced) toward "coloreds," as she called them. I remember taking the stand and seeing her in the front row, blinking and shaking her head "no" over and over, determined to feed me answers. Her lawyer tried to discredit me, saying that wasn't it true I'd not had any experience "handling help in the kitchen" and that maybe someone who had high standards might appear harsh in my eyes? And wouldn't my friends say that I was "nice, maybe sometimes too nice, *unrealistically* nice," especially to people less privileged? T.R. was given something like fifteen years, which, to my way of thinking, meant that he was innocent but they couldn't let a black man go free. When school was out, I was so depressed I went home and did nothing the entire summer.

That night in the barbecue restaurant, Peter and I were busy being polite to the other family. We were busy being open, demonstrating to them our openness, doing everything but coming right out and telling them our long history with civil rights. Later our son would find himself in a situation where race would become a young man's identity. There would be an angry outburst. And another promising evening would have its own upside-down conclusions.

THREE

I'M SITTING HERE, at the kitchen table, a pitcher of half-dead mums I picked from the yard three weeks ago in the middle of the table. I'm waiting for Peter to come home. He's late, but with the sentencing tomorrow, he's probably working ahead so that he can be out of the office all day. I don't want to read the paper or watch TV—the news these days is like a current of dark water running beneath my life. Overwhelming—unbearable—to see your family discussed in hard type on the front page and in fake-quiet voices on every local channel.

Tender is the word I would use to describe Early. There's good in his face. If he'd had his portrait painted, it would be in pastels. I suppose, though, there's always something that doesn't meet the eye.

I'm trying to think of a word, the name of the law in science that explains the existence of opposites. What I remember from college physics is that both the particle and the antiparticle, with its opposite charge, are present in everything around us. If the two collide, they destroy each other, releasing energy. Positive and negative—tender, not so tender—elbowing around inside each of us. More often than not, there's a collision. We rarely come through intact.

For the first two years, Early was as easy as a baby could be. He ate, played, slept. That's it. No crying. When he did cry, it was because I hadn't read him right—maybe I'd put him down for a nap before he'd gotten tired, snapped him into his car seat when he'd wanted to be free.

Then, just before he turned three, he began having temper tantrums. Not your run-of-the-mill two-year-old tantrums. These were intense, glass-rattling fits that persisted until he turned four. If you'd witnessed them, you would agree they were the opposite of what anyone would have expected from him. How could those soft features turn so angular? That face become so sour and secret?

One night, Peter agreed after much pleading on Early's part to play a game of Candyland with him. Early was three. Ever since his second birthday, Peter had been growing reserved with him. Distant. No more LEGOs on the den rug while I cooked dinner. No Saturday baby-sitting while I ran out for groceries or shopped for clothes. "Just take him with you," Peter would say. At a time when we should have been choosing our battles—saving our *no*s for when it really mattered (small hands discovering an electric outlet or a kitchen cabinet)—he was constantly saying no. No, son, don't touch my newspaper. No, hold your spoon this way. No, try harder, don't be afraid of the ball. Just as Early was becoming his own person, Peter was carefully retreating, coming close only when he wanted to push him in a particular direction, toughen him, as though Peter's only job as a father was to mold his son's character, create a boy who'd be strong and make his father proud.

In the beginning, I accepted Peter's closed-down behavior. My own father had hidden behind his silences, so I thought this was the way things were supposed to be.

But this evening, Peter and Early were sitting cater-cornered at the kitchen table, bent over the game like two old men studying the stock-market pages in the newspaper. I was picking dead leaves off the philodendron beside the French doors in the den, thinking what an ideal, all-American family we were—exactly my image before I got married of what a family should be: the father and son playing a game after dinner, the mother doing small, neatening chores around the house. I could imagine someone passing by outside, stopping to look at us with envy—the brass lamp in the window, faint light catching the back of our heads.

I stayed close to the kitchen so I could hear the smallest sound. Early was winning. Peter landed on Molasses Swamp and, turn after turn, could not draw a red card to get him out of the swamp and back on the path. Meanwhile, Early kept picking cards that allowed him to take shortcuts, with names like Rainbow Trail and Gumdrop Path. He was moving ahead quickly.

In between all the laughy teasing, Peter said, "You're playing tough, son!"

Early echoed, "I'm playing real tough, Daddy!"

Peter picked a red card, then the Queen Frostine card, which meant he could jump way ahead, almost to the end.

Early picked Plumpy, sending him all the way back to the beginning. He let out a scream. I went running.

Just as I got in the kitchen, he flipped over the whole board. It landed on the floor with a dull *thud-splat*. The gingerbread men and all the cards went flying. He reared up and threw him*self* on the floor. He lay there, facedown, sobbing, banging his little fists and kicking both feet on the hardwood. The energy! I couldn't believe it. I tried to put my arms around him, gather him up, but he was too much for me; his arms and legs were like weapons.

"Early! What's gotten into you? It's only a game. Sweetie, it's okay. Come on, Early," I said. Anything to get him to stop.

I looked up, toward Peter, still seated at the table as though the game would resume any minute. His face was absolutely tranquil, even approving. It said, *Leave him alone. He'll be fine.*

I kept trying to talk to Early, calm him down: "Honey, you'll win next time. In fact, look at Daddy. He wants to finish *this* game. Who knows, you could still win this one, couldn't he, Daddy?"

Peter didn't say a word. Finally, Early let me pull him onto my lap. Over and over I whispered his name in his hair.

Later, after Early was in bed, Peter told me he didn't think it was so terrible for a child to feel frustrated every now and then, that it was absolutely normal for two-year-olds to have tantrums, and anyway, Early's anger showed he had backbone. That's the exact word he used. Backbone. I told him Early was three, not two, and that he should not have been beating Early in the first place—why on earth would he want to compete with a three-year-old? Especially his own son. Peter said competition was good for a child, that it introduced him to the real world. I said the real world could be kind and humane and let's show him that one.

Time passed; more and more, Peter held himself aloof from Early. The tantrums multiplied. Early turned four. Any little thing could set him off.

Then it was his first day at Myers Park Episcopal Nursery School. He was sticking to me, his sad little right leg attached to my left leg, as though we were in a three-legged sack race.

"I don't like it here," he whimpered. "I want to go home."

I picked him up and held him in my arms. "It's all right," I said, "it's all right."

The teacher, who had that kind of soft, doughy appearance the really good, old-time teachers have (I'd handpicked her), spoke to him very sweetly about the "fun things" (that's how she talked) they were going to do. She reached to take him from me, but just as I was helping her loosen his grip on my sleeve and peel him away from my body, she had to leave us—quickly—to tend to a little girl who'd wet her pants. Early started crying and screaming and whipping his body around until he scrambled out of my arms onto the floor and ran toward the door. He was trying to leave, but couldn't get the door open. He kept working the knob and getting more and more agitated until he darted over to the piano, which the music teacher had just rolled into the room (she rotated among the classrooms), and he heaved at the piano as though he could push it over. He nearly succeeded! When he saw that he was not strong enough to actually topple it, he started spitting on the keys. Luckily, the teacher was in the bathroom with the girl and didn't see any of this.

What's wrong with my son?—my first thought—quickly turned into *What could I have done to avert this behavior?* I wished that I'd anticipated how overwhelmingly frightening the first day of school could be. I should have engineered things better, read him books about boys and girls starting school, brought him in for a visit *before* opening day.

I whisked him outside, and we sat in the swings next to the sandbox on the playground. Yellow leaves floated past, and the air was crisp and blue. I talked and talked. He asked, "What if they have a fire drill and I'm in the bathroom?" I told him his teacher would make sure he got out with the other children and that I knew it was scary to go to a new place, but the teacher was very nice and she'd take good care of him, and if she didn't, he could tell me when I picked him up and we would change to another school. He asked, "Will they call it recess, when we go outside?" I told him that whatever they called it, I was sure it would be fun, and if he'd just stay here for a little while, I'd come back when school let out and we'd go to the toy store to buy some new race cars. Finally, he said he would go back into the classroom if I would carry him. I handed him over to the teacher and she signaled me away. One week later, he was completely settled in. But that morning, after I left him, I sat in my car in the parking lot, the blood pounding in my head, and cried.

Before Christmas, that same year, the teacher called me. She said she'd had to clear the room—send the children into another classroom—because Early's behavior had been so extreme. He flipped over the aquarium, she said. When she tried to restrain him, he almost bit her.

"He's bright and capable," she said, "but he worries too much about being right. He can't stand when he isn't the first to finish something or when his work isn't perfect. I've been teaching for thirty years and I've never seen a tantrum like that. It was off the charts."

Why would my son get so hysterical? Was this normal? I wondered if she was such a good teacher, if it had really been necessary to make the other children leave the room. After all, that would be humiliating for any child. Why couldn't she have handled the situation without involving the rest of the class?

I didn't tell Peter right away. I told my mother. I also told her about Peter's lack of involvement with Early. She listened the way she'd always listened. Every time she uttered an *oh* or a *my, my,* it felt like she was scooping me up into her arms. I wanted to take my son and go home. Where there'd never been any contradictions. Where I could count on things being the way they were supposed to be. I wanted safe and predictable.

Christmas vacation came. Then it was January. I still hadn't told Peter. February, Early had his last tantrum. I'd bought him a pack of construction paper with a big heart printed on every sheet, thinking he was old enough to make his own valentines. One minute, I left him at the corner desk in his bedroom, beginning to work—scissors, caramel-colored glue, crayons picked from the box and lined up. The next minute, he was tearing the paper to shreds, lobbing crayons and scissors and glue out into the hall, crying, shrieking at the top of his lungs, totally out of control.

He hadn't known what he was supposed to *do* with the heart, what was expected of him: Should he color it in? Write his name inside the heart? Color around it? I decided I'd made a big mistake. I should have shown him what to do. I could've made the first one, then let him copy me. That minute, I vowed to pay closer attention, not leave him alone to struggle with problems that were too big for him.

But then, as abruptly as the tantrums had started, they stopped. He was now the agreeable, easy child he'd always been. The tantrums had obviously just been a stage. Like when your child has a cough and then it deepens, goes bloaty—you scare yourself to death thinking it could be some fatal illness. But it turns out to be nothing more than a cold. Your worst fear is that your child's temper tantrums might be permanent, a sign of some deep-rooted problem. But just as you're wondering if something is terribly wrong and you should consider taking him to a specialist, the child moves out of that phase. Into another, totally different phase.

That's how I talked myself into believing none of it was noteworthy.

FOUR

I BELIEVED my own mother was a genius at doing whatever had to be done to set things right—the small comment, the generous gesture that provided me with a sense of safety. I remember how it was—and then suddenly she's here, walking back out of memory, falling into step with me:

I'm in the fifth grade. Making a map of the world. Almost ready for the contest where we'll vote for the best. I'm sure I'll win. Not only can I draw girls' faces, I also make great maps. I may have a bad sense of direction, but that doesn't stop me when it comes to drawing a map. (Four years later when I get my driver's license—age fourteen in South Carolina because of farm children needing to drive tractors—I can't find my way from one place to another without first returning home, my starting point.)

Almost finished. Not satisfied with the eastern shoreline of the Philippines. I draw, erase, draw again. Still, it doesn't look right. I raise my hand.

"How does this go?" I ask Miss Neely. "The Philippines, I mean."

"Like this," she says. Miss Neely is bony and has a stiff back and a sharp, pointy nose. When she bends over, she looks like one of those fuzzy toy birds you place next to a glass of water and tip to get started—the bird drinks, stands up straight, drinks, stands up straight.

Miss Neely pencils in the outline of the Philippines, which is as far away from my hometown, Rock Hill, as anything can be. Now I'm ready to color it in. A soft tangerine shade. Miss Neely goes back to her desk. After a while, the student teacher walks by my desk. Our school is a laboratory school for Winthrop College, the state teachers' college, so we have student teachers in most of our classes. "Good job," she says. "Except for the Philippines. It curves *that* way." She traces it with her forefinger.

I erase the old pencil outline, leaving a bad graphite smear, and draw a new outline. Then I begin coloring, but the waxy crayon only makes the smear worse. The student teacher moves on. I keep coloring, hoping that, layer by tangerine layer, I can make it neat again.

"Kathryne. I thought I showed you how the Philippines are supposed to be." Miss Neely again.

"But she told me it went like this, so I changed it," I say, waving my crayon in the direction of the student teacher, who's now helping someone on the other side of the room.

At this, Miss Neely's face turns as red as my Mexico. She grabs the map, balls it up, stomps to the front of the room where the whole class can see her, stuffs my map in the metal wastebasket, squishing it down into the mesh with her long, skinny foot. Then she goes to the art supply cabinet in the cloakroom, brings out a clean sheet of poster paper, and deposits it on my desk with a slap, saying in a loud, angry voice, "Why did you question what I told you? Going behind my back to ask the student teacher if I was right or wrong! If you know so much, you can just do the whole thing yourself!" She marches back to the front of the room, to her desk, where the student teacher is grading papers.

At first, I just sit there, thinking this has to be a joke. But Miss Neely turns around to glower at me, her dark eyebrows a straight line across her face, and I know it's not a joke.

I wait.

When she turns her back to whisper to the student teacher, I sidle over to the blackboard, sign my name under GIRLS in the bathroom column, and slip out of the room.

I hurry down the hall, past the music room, past arithmetic, past the half-open door to the art room, where I see Christmas-tree-shaped Miss Latimer stirring paint with a stick. I walk as fast as I can without running. When I get to the bathroom and the heavy wooden door gasps shut behind me, I begin to sob, heaving sobs, my whole body rocking.

After a while, the bathroom door opens. I make myself stop crying. I'm afraid it's Miss Neely.

But it's the school nurse, Mrs. Patrick. She takes one look at my red, wet face and says, "What in the world is wrong, sweetie?" She pulls me close. Her soft, white skirt smells like rubbing alcohol. My heaving begins again—now I'm shivering and can't catch my breath.

I finally get the story out.

She takes me to the office and calls my mother.

There is never a question in my mind whose side Mother will be on. My version of any incident is the only version that matters. If someone hurts me, that person hurts her. The expression on her face always shows that she *feels* my heartbeat. The shape of my being is hers.

We live two blocks from the school. She pats my leg the whole drive home.

"Miss Neely's behavior was un*warranted*. What was she *thinking*?"

she mutters. I worm my left leg closer so she doesn't have to reach to pat me. "I'm really upset this happened. Really, really upset."

There are phone calls back and forth between Mother and the school. Later that afternoon she goes to meet with the principal. She comes home and tells me she's had me transferred to the other fifth-grade section. Mrs. Nibarger's class. Mother says that if Miss Neely ever even *tries* to broach the subject with me, I should call home immediately and she'll come get me.

Instead, I avoid Miss Neely, never go near her classroom; if I pass her in the hall, I study my shoes.

The class votes on the maps. Oddly, my map is still in the running, and my friends tell me I come in second. The best artist in the class, Marilee Rock, wins, but I know that my map—at least before it was wadded up, thrown away, then tacked up on display with the others in the lunchroom for the whole school to see—was better than hers. But it is a mess now. The Philippines are a blur. There's a tear across Alaska, separating it into North Alaska and South Alaska. Spain is so wrinkled you can hardly make out its border with Portugal.

A FEW YEARS into our marriage, Peter and I were at a neighbor's house for dinner. We were telling funny stories about our children and school, and I ended up telling my map story.

The wife said, "Oh, that almost makes me cry! It's so hard to be a kid."

Her husband laughed and said, "Lord love our mamas and how they look out for us!"

Then Peter weighed in: "The interesting thing about this story is what it says about borders. And I'm not talking about Spain and Portugal! How about the border between mothers and children?"

I remember the wife immediately lifting the platter of roast beef and passing it to Peter; behind me, I saw a blurred image of the husband reaching over my shoulder to refill my wineglass. I didn't like what Peter said or the fact that he said it in front of other people. He was making a point and passing it off as humor. Husbands and wives do this sort of thing, though, when they have a hard time being honest with one another in private.

FIVE

WHEN EARLY WAS A BABY, I had the same dream again and again:

I strap him in his infant seat and set him on the trunk of the car so my hands are free to open the door. I get in, start the engine, use the sideview mirror to back out of the driveway, then head up the street, trying to remember everything I need to buy at Harris-Teeter: paper towels, mustard, Virginia baked ham. Anything else? Orange juice? Is the container in the fridge almost empty? Suddenly I remember. The baby. On the trunk. Nowhere in sight. Sliding off. Hitting the asphalt. Under the wheels. Nothing to protect him. Except a dream, holding him in its shifty arms.

How can we keep our children safe? Happy? We worry about something awful happening to them. All night long, we grind our teeth, the moon through the window a clock's face. Awake, we pay close attention every single minute so that when it's necessary, we can act quickly and efficiently. Take our children out of a situation that's not good for them. Put them into a better one.

My son went to three different schools between the beginning and end of kindergarten. It's what parents did in those days. The school system was changing, and for the first time we had choices. It was when parents—mothers in particular—were beginning to believe that if we could find the right school for our child, he'd be assured of the right future.

Early started kindergarten at Myers Park Elementary, our red-brick, white-columned neighborhood school. He was already reading on a third-grade level; his classmates wouldn't even learn to read until the following year. At our first conference, the teacher told us that Early always finished his work before the others and then would go from desk to desk telling each child, "Good job! Keep it up!" or "You're doing great!" This was not what I wanted to hear; we weren't sending him to school to be a cheerleader.

That same September, a new, very progressive public school opened, Willow Elementary Open School, geared to the needs and abilities of each individual child. The idea, according to the article in the newspaper, was "to replace authority with freedom, to teach by appealing to the child's natural curiosity and spontaneity, without using punishment or homework or exams." The child would help decide what he learned and how he learned it. This sounded perfect for Early. He could just vault ahead. A parallel goal of the school was to achieve a racially balanced student body. Court-ordered busing had been in effect in Charlotte since 1971, and the plan was that Willow, originally a black inner-city high school, would have such an appealing format, along with the best principal and teachers in the system, that white students would want to be bused in. Peter and I were eager to show our support. The school's motto: *All Children Are Equal, Each Child Is Unique.* Unfortunately, this proved to be an omen. A comma separating two sentences? A school with a punctuation error in its motto?

Students at Willow were chosen by lottery. We applied for second semester, but weren't accepted. I was glad the school was such a success, but upset that Early's name was not picked. I told Peter we should talk to Adam Lobell, his golfing buddy and a member of the school board. Adam would get us in.

"I'm not comfortable doing that. Imposing on a friendship," Peter said, grinding his chin in to ease the starched collar of his blue oxford shirt away from his neck. "Let's just go through the proper channels."

"Proper *channels*?" I said. "This *is* a proper channel if it means getting our child in the right school. We do whatever it takes."

"I'd rather work within the system," he said. "Anyway, the idea of Willow may appeal to us, but it might not be in Early's best interest to switch him from school to school."

"I don't care if it takes ten schools! It's our child!" My basic philosophy.

"I'm not going to do it, Kathryne." His final words.

I made a few phone calls and found that if we could prove our child was having problems in a traditional school—if a psychologist wrote a letter—the school board would grant a transfer to the open school.

Charlotte-Mecklenburg Schools' Student Application Center sent a list of child psychologists who'd been approved for the testing, and I made an appointment with Dr. Kusz, whose office was in one of the new buildings downtown. To my surprise, he answered his own phone. I explained what we needed, that our visit was simply for the purpose of testing Early. I made it clear we were not coming for therapy.

The wall-to-wall carpeting in Dr. Kusz's reception room was gray

with maroon and teal flecks. There was a chair for a receptionist behind the painted gray counter, but no receptionist. Just as I was
wondering how long this psychologist had been in practice, he appeared and greeted us, whisked Early away, leaving me in the reception area. I felt a little reassured; he looked about my age.

I didn't feel like reading, so I just sat there, listening to the music—was it a harmonica? Anyway, it was loud enough to keep me
from hearing what was going on in the next room. I counted chairs,
chrome with nubby maroon upholstered seats—four on one side of
the room, four on the other. The wallpaper was gray with a streaky
texture, resembling tree bark. A lamp beside me flickered. *How did
maroon, teal, and gray become the color scheme of choice for doctors' offices?*
Even the framed, slightly-Japanese-in-tone posters on the walls were
in shades of maroon, teal, and gray.

The testing took almost an hour. Then they came out, Dr.
Kusz's hand holding the back of Early's neck, as though he were
steering him. Early was smiling his polite smile and tidily tucking his
hands in his pockets. For the first time, I noticed how dark Dr.
Kusz's eyebrows were, almost black, quite a contrast with his
copper-colored hair and beard. He wore a faded gray suit, white
shirt, and maroon tie.

"Wait here, son, while your mom and I have a little chat in my office," he said.

"Yes, sir," Early said. He picked up a *National Geographic* from the
table, and slipped behind me into the chair I'd left.

Dr. Kusz's private office was warmer and cozier than his reception room. Sort of a 1940s feel, with oak file cabinets and glass-
fronted bookcases. He motioned me to the sofa and backed into the
leather chair behind his desk. He spun in little half circles, left, then
right, until he found the exact spot he seemed to be looking for.

"A nice young man, your son," he said, running his thumb over the top of his desk. "I'll be happy to write a letter stating he has an exceptionally high IQ and could easily become frustrated in a regular classroom. No problem. No problem at all."

I said I really appreciated that. He stood. *This was it?* I gathered my jacket and purse to leave. He walked around the desk and came right up to me, touched my elbow, and studied me with his big, fatherly eyes. "One more thing, Mrs. Smallwood," he said. "I was struck with how attuned to other people your son is. Quite an acute sensitivity to the emotional signals he picks up from others."

"What do you mean by that?" I asked. *How can you presume to know so much about my son after one short session?* is what I wanted to say.

"Well, I really shouldn't be commenting, because I haven't spent that much time with him, but I thought you might be interested in my observation. Your son's level of sensitivity is impressive." Now it was sounding more like a compliment. I found myself agreeing. Early *was* sensitive. Empathetic.

D URING CHRISTMAS HOLIDAYS we received word from Charlotte-Mecklenburg Schools that Early had been admitted to Willow for second semester. It struck me that as long as I was in charge, as long as I could just trust my instincts and do what had to be done, my son would get what he needed. The letter said he'd been assigned to Miss Gina Stump's class and the class would combine seven grades—kindergarten through sixth. I understood the theory immediately: the younger children would learn from the older ones, which, of course, would benefit everyone. Very natural, I thought. Organic.

Peter picked up the letter from the mail table in the front hall before I had a chance to fill him in on what I'd done. He didn't say a word.

———

Januarʏ 2, I decided to drive Early both ways rather than let him ride the school bus, which picked up the children in our neighborhood too early in the morning and delivered them home too late. That afternoon I drove fast along Freedom Drive, determined to get to school well before the last bell. The sun flashed with all the cars I was passing. Then, in my rearview mirror, I saw a patrol car signaling me over.

"You know the speed limit?" the patrolman asked, leaning in.

"No, sir, I don't," I answered, restraining my impatience. The speed limit was the last thing I was thinking about. How was Early's first day? *That's* what was on my mind.

"School zone. Twenty-five. Clocked you going forty-one. License and registration?"

I took my license from my wallet, opened the glove compartment for my registration, and before I could think, heard myself saying that a red car had been following me, yes that's exactly what it was, a red Toyota that then cut in front of me and slowed way down like it was trying to block me, then dropped back behind me again, riding my bumper so close I thought it might crash into me, and all the while, the man driving was practically hanging out his window gesturing at me, these awful, obscene gestures. The only thing I did not say outright was that the driver had been giving me the finger. The patrolman got the message.

"I know I was going too fast," I added, "and I'm really sorry, but I was scared and wanted to get away from that man."

I couldn't believe what I was doing. I hadn't planned it. I saw the words traveling from my mouth into the air, acting on their own accord, and there was no way I could get them back.

The patrolman was a short man with a rosy, sympathetic face. "Was it a young fella?" he asked.

I said yes. I hadn't really thought how old the driver might be, but going along with what the patrolman said seemed like a good idea.

"Yep, I saw him a ways back. I know exactly who you're talking about. He was going forty-plus, too. I b'lieve I can find him."

My hands were trembling—from the patrol car's hectic light spinning and flinging blue everywhere, from lying through my teeth, from imagining some innocent young man in a red Toyota being tracked down. The good thing about my trembling, though, was that it made what I was saying seem totally believable. *Of course she's telling the truth,* the patrolman and I both were thinking. *Look how upset she is over what she's gone through.*

"I'm going to give you a warning and let you go," he said. "Next time, you get yourself to a good, safe place like a gas station and call the police."

"I will." Genuineness oozing. At that moment, it all seemed real. The man who'd followed me. The danger I'd been in. My promise to find a safe place next time and call for help.

I drove into the school parking lot—on time, amazingly—but there was no sign of Early. I sat in my car, glad to have a few minutes to gather myself. I had just lied to a patrolman! That's what it was, an out-and-out lie. On the other hand, I told myself, wasn't it necessary to speed a little and tell a tiny white lie so that I could pick up my child on time?

I took a deep breath and rolled my head from side to side, feeling the stretch on the right side of my neck—that wiry cord that gets so hard and tight. The school was old, and annexes spread out from the main building like crab claws. Since it had originally been the largest high school in the county, it was going to take a while for Early to find me.

I watched children, happily chattering, meander out, group by group. Teachers, looking more like potters or weavers in their loose clothing and macramé shoulder bags, headed toward their bedraggled cars. School buses filled and pulled away, coughing.

No Early.

Soon the grounds were quiet. No children, no teachers, no buses. I checked the clock on the dash. School had been out for half an hour. I'd have to go in after him. But his classroom would be empty now. Maybe the principal. Yes, that's where I should go. The principal's office. He'd use the intercom to locate him.

At that minute, I spotted Early. Drifting down the worn granite steps out front. Backpack bumping along behind. Shoelaces untied. Sobbing.

As he climbed into the car, he spoke in a rush, sniffling, "I was going up and down the halls and then I went to another floor and then another floor but all the floors looked the same and I couldn't tell if I was, if I was going up or down, and then I was in the basement where the furnace was and it was real loud and that was scary and I've been trying to get out of the school, I've been trying to get out since the bell rang."

I was steaming. Why on earth would the teacher let the little ones wander around lost? I handed him a Kleenex. He blew his nose.

"Could we maybe stop someplace?" he said. "I'm hungry."

"What'd you have for lunch, honey?" I took his backpack and dropped it in the back.

"I didn't eat lunch."

"You didn't eat lunch?" I realized we were still in the parking lot. I pulled out, headed for the street.

"I couldn't find the cafeteria." He rolled down his window, put his wet face in the breeze.

"Doesn't your class go together? With Miss Stump?"

"No, it's not like that. When you're ready to eat, you just go. I couldn't find it. I tried. But it's real far away." He turned toward me. His long, pale lashes were matted with tears.

"Does Miss Stump know you didn't have lunch?"

"I was going to tell her, but she was busy. There're so many boys and girls in our room you don't get to talk to her much. It's no big deal. I can just eat after school."

"What about the other kindergartners? What did they do?"

"Well"—his nose was stuffy—"some of them got the older kids to help them find the cafeteria, but I didn't want to do that."

THE NEXT WEEK, I stopped by his class, just to check on things.

Books and papers were strewn about the room, and children were walking over them without any thought of picking them up. Some children were lying on the floor reading, curled up in thready tapestries or rugs—wrapped in them, as though they were blankets. A few were silently shaping words, but most were reading out loud to themselves. Others were sitting around in clusters on tabletops and window ledges talking, their voices raucous and worked up. Children were at workstations scattered around the room, holding beakers with soapy liquid up to the light, typing and jamming the keys of old Royal typewriters, building rickety structures with scraps of wood. The room sounded like it was filled with birds—all that high-pitched chirping, tapping, and scuffling about. Miss Stump—a fortyish woman wearing leather hippie sandals and thick socks, her oatmeal-colored hair in braids—was sitting cross-legged on the floor in the far corner of the room, quietly working with a girl, probably a sixth grader, who was lying on her stomach, twirling a pencil over her notebook. The way the two of them were concentrating, so blissfully, the noise in the room like a blessing over their heads, they could've been a testimonial for education in its purest form.

But where was my son?

At that moment, a little boy whose skin was as dark as pencil lead raced up to me—he almost ran into me.

"Whose mother are you?" he asked.

"Early Smallwood's," I said, and bent over with my hands on my knees. "Can you help me find him?"

"He's working on his contract." The boy wore a winter coat that was too heavy for him. He was obviously a kindergartner.

"His contract?"

"That's what we do. We make a contract every Monday with the teacher. Then all week we do our work. Early's contract is maps. He's out there." He pointed stiffly toward the door. His coat sleeve came down to his fingertips.

I walked out of the room and looked both ways. At first, I didn't see anyone. Then, at the end of the hall, off to the left, I saw a boat—a real boat, old, wooden, with peeling green paint, perched on gritty linoleum. Sitting inside was Early. For a second, I pictured him floating away on platinum water. I blinked and saw that he was trying to balance a sheet of poster-size paper on his lap, coloring in a crudely drawn, Xeroxed map of the world. He was making tiny, careful strokes, each no bigger than his baby fingernail, filling in that endless Atlantic Ocean. At the rate he was going, the school year would be over before he'd get to the continents.

L ET'S LEAVE HIM WHERE he is," Peter said that night. "We sure don't need to move that child again. He'll figure out how to get along and the challenge'll be good for him. It just may take a little time. Patience, Kathryne."

"I don't agree," I said. "The school is not set up for five-year-olds. They treat them like they're sixth graders."

"Well, children need guidance, not protection."

"I think we should give Early the best we can afford. I think private school is where he belongs."

"*Private* school? Yes, we can afford it. But do we believe in it? Is that what we want for our child? If *we* don't support public education, who will?"

"What we don't want is to sacrifice our child's education for our principles."

Early had been upstairs listening. He came down in his Big Bird pajamas and begged us to take him out of Willow. He started naming all the things he didn't like: The older kids pushed ahead of the little ones. The older kids teased them. They didn't pick on him, but there was one kid—"the boy who showed you where I was, Mom, when I was out in the hall working. Jamal, that's who they pick on." Early said he wanted a desk and chair like in "real" school, not a boat. He wanted schoolwork, not maps. He wanted homework and tests. He didn't want big kids in his class.

"I want to go to private school," he said. "Like that boy down the street. Send me to his school. Please, Mom and Dad, please."

The next day I pulled him out of Willow and put him in Randolph Academy, a private school in a leafy stand of hardwoods in the heart of white upper-class Charlotte, a school with arched front doors painted blue, where every classroom had students the same age and in the same grade, where the lower grades were separated from the upper grades, where children ate peanut-butter-and-jelly sandwiches brought from home in Disney lunchboxes, where Early and Chip Dunham, who lived four houses down from us, fastened on to each other the very first day.

SIX

EARLY WAS CRAZY about Chip Dunham. Mesmerized. Overrun, really. Chip was a star at Randolph
Academy. Popular. A head taller than everyone else in
the class. Early was small for his age, his head biggish, round, out of
balance with his beanpole body, like a character in a *Peanuts* cartoon.
Once, when Chip was at our house, I looked at his sneakers next to
Early's. They'd left them in a jumble on the brick floor inside the
back door. Chip's could've been the shoes of a full-grown man;
Early's looked like they belonged to a toddler.

Chip was big, all right. To Early, Chip was bigger than life. My son
was like a pin drawn to a magnet. A boy pulled straight to the sun.

Kindergarten, first grade, second grade, third—the two of them
spent long afternoons setting up racetracks for their Matchbox cars,
looping the snap-together plastic over chairs and ottomans, under
the glass-top coffee table, around the legs of the piano. They pulled
cars from the canvas bag that held both of their collections. Some-

times it was matching red convertibles with doors that really opened, sometimes silver Corvettes or VW Beetles. Those cars would sing along the tracks, whip high and wide through the den, and Early and Chip would fall down laughing. Chip's dog, Pepper, who went everywhere with him, would bark like crazy.

Up in Early's room, they'd riffle through shoe boxes filled with baseball cards filed in clear plastic. They arranged the cards in alphabetical order, compared prices in their catalogs. Early's all-time prize card was an autographed Reggie Jackson; Chip's was an autographed George Brett.

They invented board games, spent days constructing the pieces they needed out of cardboard or plywood they'd found in the tool-shed. Then they played, their heads tipped together, making up rules as they went along. "Do you think your dad'll help us patent this one?" Chip would ask. "I bet so," Early would answer.

They kept a running list of knock-knock jokes—pages and pages of them—to enter in *The Guinness Book of World Records.* "We'll get in, for sure," Chip would say. "Nobody else ever thought of *this*!"

They played just about every kind of ball there was—soccer, basketball, baseball, football, tennis, Ping-Pong, Wiffleball.

They drew intricate mazes with pencil on construction paper. Quilt after smudged quilt of dead ends and winding, unexpected turns.

The two of them were never ever bored. In the beginning, their friendship was a pure, unself-conscious delight. I loved hearing their laughter, felt tender pangs watching them race each other out the back door, jump on their bikes, cut across the neighbor's yard on their way to the 7-Eleven.

Chip was robust. Exuberant, perspiry. When he entered a room, you knew it. This was before the word "charisma" was in my vocabulary, but it would've been the perfect word for him. As time went on, I saw that "mercurial" would have been another good word. His mood could change in an instant, in the way a child who's popular knows, regardless of how extreme his behavior might be, that others will go along with him just to stay in favor. It didn't appear there was any strategy on Chip's part; he simply took his own pulse, decided what he wanted, went after it. Spontaneously and at full power. Very different from sensitive, empathetic, deliberate, plan-ahead, under-control Early. Chip was constantly switching things up—one minute he could be laughing hysterically at Early's jokes; the next, he was flying off the handle at some imagined slight. Chip's showy and unrestrained self-centeredness constantly surprised Early, kept him off balance. At the same time, Early was enthralled with his boldness in doing everything out in the open. "You'll never guess what Chip did today, Mom! He talked back to Mrs. Poe!" Of course, my son would never be disrespectful to a teacher.

Chip's risking everything didn't just get him attention—it brought cheers. He was one of those very physical kids who excel in every sport. When he scored, he pumped the air with both fists, his face a fierce, victorious contortion. When he did badly—if it was tennis (one of the tournaments he was always playing in)—he threw and kicked his racquet. In baseball, he slung the bat.

Early didn't have Chip's strength or competitive edge. He understood sports and played with finesse, but he was not aggressive. At the end of a tie game in soccer, when the coach had to select a player for the shoot-out, Early was usually the choice because he could be calm in a tight spot, planted firmly—and it was uncanny how he could tell which way the goalie would commit. But forceful he was not.

Season after season, in every sport, Peter urged Early to get in there and challenge, in a skillful way, of course, not brutish or violent. Surefooted. The way Peter himself had been his whole life. Not just in athletics, in everything. The more he yelled from the sidelines, though, the farther Early positioned himself from the fray.

When the boys were eight, they played on the same Y basketball team. Of course, Chip was high scorer every game, and by far, the strongest on defense. Early's innate feel for the game was not what the coach wanted. Coach Zotti, who had a perm and looked like a brunette Harpo Marx, wasn't looking for self-control. Or calm. He wanted aggressive.

The first game, Early rode the bench and came home sad-faced. "Coach Zotti told me to take lessons from Chip. He said I play like a girl."

"He said that?" I asked. I was already planning what *I'd* say to Coach Zotti. And to the youth director at the Y.

"In front of the whole team he said it. I wish I *was* Chip."

"Nonsense," Peter said, wiggling his chin away from his starched collar. "You can be better than Chip. All you have to do is practice. You ought to be out there every afternoon after school, shooting a hundred layups. Fifty with your right hand. Fifty with your left."

"Okay," Early said, too quickly I thought.

"And practice your foul shots. Shoot thirty-five every day. And your dribbling—get just as good with your left hand as with your right. You should be dribbling at least ten minutes a day with each hand. It's not so much what happens to us in life as what we do with it, son."

"I know, Daddy. I know."

"Now don't go making any phone calls, Kathryne," Peter said later. "Give Early a chance to handle this himself."

The next afternoon, I could hear him dribbling the basketball up and down the driveway. I remember the sound. How it felt. Like it was bouncing inside my ribs. I took him a cup of apple juice and a plate of Fig Newtons. The basketball goal was at the top of the driveway. I stood in front of the toolshed and watched, next to where he'd propped his bike, his blue University of North Carolina Basketball sweatshirt tied around the handlebars. He started on his layups: the initial push-off. The drive across the cracked concrete. The leg drawn up, the shot, then the quick unwinding. The ball angling off the backboard. Going in. Not going in. Over to the side, in the wet grass, were his charts—wavy lines drawn across and up and down the paper, the number of layups and foul shots made that day, how many minutes of dribbling.

Long after I'd gone back into the house, Early was still going through his drills. This was after all the neighborhood children had been called in to wash up for supper and the light was falling.

Later he showed Peter the pages. Dutifully. Peter nodded, said, "You're getting there, you're getting there."

Every afternoon, Early practiced. He did not miss a day.

One night Peter came home early and watched. "Excellent," I heard him say. "You're making good progress."

Still, the coach did not play him. I forced myself to go along with Peter and not report the coach. It took all my willpower.

Then it was the last half of the last game of the season. We were winning by a huge margin. Chip once again was the star; there wasn't a player on the other team who could guard him.

Coach Zotti leaned forward, looked down the straggly row of players on the bench. They raised their faces toward him like birds hungry for seed.

He curled his index finger at Early.

Early tore off his warm-up pants, ran to the table to check in, trotted out onto the court, his too-big jersey hanging down almost to his knees. He was ready. He'd been ready for weeks. Immediately, he positioned himself to run the play the point guard called out, made a break from the boy who was guarding him, yelled for the point guard to throw him the ball—*Jeffrey, over here! over here!*—caught it even though the throw was out of his reach. Started dribbling toward the basket. He dribbled with his right hand, then his left, leaving the boy who was guarding him behind. It was a matter of seconds before he'd make the shot. A clear path to the goal. He drew up his leg, his feet left the floor, the ball dropped through.

Immediately, he looked toward Chip. Early's face was full of wild, reckless joy and excitement.

The referee blew his whistle.

Early had been so eager to get into the game he'd pulled off his shorts along with his warm-ups. And there he was, all eyes on him, in his tight, white underpants.

Chip curled his mouth as if to say, *What's wrong with you?* Then he laughed out loud and turned his broad back on Early, as though he had no idea who the crazy kid was.

The referee said softly, "Son, go on back to the bench and put on your shorts."

Early looked down. I could tell he was turning his thoughts over and over. He yanked at his jersey to make it even longer and ran off the court. It was obvious he believed they'd hold the timer until he could get his shorts back on and return to the game. But Coach Zotti, his face so twisted it looked fractured, said loud enough for everybody in the gym to hear, "Sit down, Smallwood!" Only it sounded like *Siddown, Smaw-wood!* He signaled another player—with that same crooked index finger—into the game.

Early pulled up his warm-ups, sat at the end of the bench, his face colorless. He dropped his head between his knees and I could no longer see his expression. I knew what he was thinking, though. He was humiliated by what he'd done and disheartened that when he'd finally gotten into the game, his playing time got cut short. But his anguish was due to one thing and one thing only—no matter how hard he tried, he could never be Chip.

SEVEN

I HEAR PETER'S CAR in the driveway, picture him walking past the wax myrtle that needs limbing, stopping to wheel around on his heels to check to see if he's locked the car.

He comes into the kitchen, says hello from across the room, just stands there.

"Hi," I say. Then, "What?"

"Donald Sanders called this afternoon." It annoys me that our attorney calls Peter at the office. I know it's a lawyer-to-lawyer thing, but I'd like to be in on the conversation. "He wanted to make sure we understand that if Early receives a fifteen-year sentence tomorrow, it's possible he might serve only three years. Here's how that works: The sentence would automatically be cut in half for good behavior, which will bring it down to seven years and three months. Then, under the One-eighth Parole Eligibility Statute, after he's served one eighth of the sentence, he could be paroled."

I'm trying to do the math, but I can't think. I can't even remember what percentage he just said.

"In other words, it's possible it could be somewhere in the neighborhood of five years, but Donald says it wouldn't shock him if Early ends up serving as little as three. *If* he gets the presumptive sentence."

"What does 'presumptive' mean?"

"Well, let's just say it's presumed the judge will sentence him to fifteen years. But actually, that concept is too complicated to explain. And what it all comes down to, Kathryne, is this—we can't get our hopes up where anything is concerned."

I realize Peter's bringing good news, but it's hard to tell from his tone of voice. Of course, anything less than life is good. And anything less than fifteen years is very good. But. Five years. Three years. It feels as though we're talking about the length of time someone might stay on a job. It's prison. It's our son. The noise in my head is deafening.

"Here," I say, pulling a chair out. "Sit down for a minute."

"I'm really tired," he says. "I've had a long day and I want to go to bed." He pushes my hair away from my face, kisses the top of my head, then is halfway through the den.

"How can you leave, Peter? This is such a big thing you've plopped in my lap. It's our son we're talking about. I need to be a part of it. Tell me what you said again. I'm having trouble remembering. And what else did Donald say?"

"Kathryne, I told you everything I know. We'll talk in the morning, I promise. Good night now."

I say, "Let's just talk for a little while," only to let it drift off.

I USED TO PRIDE myself on being able to remember things. When I was young, I'd invent exercises to improve my memory, like teaching myself to say the alphabet backward. Night after night,

I'd lie in the dark before falling asleep and practice. First I'd work on my accuracy, going over the letters section by section—z up to q, p to i, h to a—until I could recite them perfectly. Then I concentrated on my speed. Pushed myself. Zeroed in on the trouble spots. Faster I'd go, until I was satisfied I could say the entire alphabet backward faster than most people could say it forward.

I HEAR PETER TURNING out his light. Nothing for me to do but lay memories like a stone path. Some seem like leaps to nowhere. But I just keep placing them end to end—with small detours here and there, a memory or two going afield—and hope that I can understand what must have been obvious all along. Everyone knows that the past shapes the present. I'm trying to figure out if the present can shape the past—if I hold up to the light for reexamination what I believed all those years to be true.

So I go backward like a baby learning to crawl. I travel in reverse trying to discover how to move forward:

I'm standing at the kitchen sink, rinsing lettuce for a salad, looking out through the double windows at Early, eight and squatting, poking around in the tall grass, springing back in surprise, then squatting again. He appears serious, intent, his delicate features squeezed into the middle of his face. I keep watching until I see the brown thrasher scrambling in the grass beside him, realize it's a baby bird that tried to make a break from a nest in the half-green hedge that edges the yard.

Early crimps his hands around the bird so lightly his fingers barely touch its mouselike body, then lifts it and guides it through the maze of branches and prickly leaves back into the nest. He turns to come inside. There are muddy circles on the knees of his jeans from the wet ground. Just before he gets to the shadows at the back door, he glances over his shoulder at the gap in the hedge: the brown thrasher has shot out of the nest again.

Over and over, Early gathers it, places it in the nest, turns to leave. Over and over, the bird smacks the ground. I wrap the lettuce leaves in paper towels, squeeze out all the moisture, wipe my hands on a dish towel, and stand there watching, thinking how I love that Early is anything but indifferent. He's the type of child who'll pursue what he believes in. Pursue it patiently and relentlessly, even if the rest of the world turns a blind eye.

Early cocks his head. The bird looks as though it's trying to swivel its small head to stare back at Early. Then he disappears into the toolshed at the top of the driveway. Minutes pass. I glance at the clock over the sink. I can't believe how long he's in there. Any other child would come out dribbling an old basketball or kicking a half-flat soccer ball, forgetting all about rescuing the bird, but I know that bird's helplessness has broken Early's heart.

When he appears in the driveway again, he's holding a dented-in shoe box that Peter's golf shoes came in last summer. Slowly, with a deliberate heel to toe, he picks across the grass to the spindly pine trees in the far corner of the backyard, bends down, gathers a wad of pine needles, and stuffs them in the box. Then he goes back to the bird, still lurching about in the grass. He places the bird in the box and tucks the dry needles around it like a sheet. From the window, I can see a beak poking up and a soft smile on Early's face. He's figured out how to keep that bird from throwing itself away.

EIGHT

I PULL THE CAFÉ CURTAINS across the bay window behind the kitchen table. At the same time, I picture Peter, in
bed, pulling the covers tighter, then the two of us tomorrow morning, waking up, dressing for our son's court date. It's raining tonight. You can feel the weather stiffening. October's like that.
One day you're wearing short sleeves and cotton. The next, there's a
cold, drizzly wind.

One October night when Early was nine—1978—he was spending the night at Chip's. After dinner I called my best friend, Joy, to
find out how her three-day silent retreat had gone. I should've been
writing my review of *Up in Smoke*, an amateurish, low-budget
Cheech and Chong film—definitely not my cup of tea—but instead,
I started reading a biography of Stanley Donen, who directed *Singin'
in the Rain*, my all-time favorite movie. Stanley Donen grew up in
Columbia, only seventy-two miles from Rock Hill, where I grew up.
In 1951, his romance with Elizabeth Taylor was all over the movie

magazines. I cut out a picture of the two of them, side by side on a tufted banquette in a Hollywood restaurant, Elizabeth Taylor wearing a mink coat, Donen smoking a cigarette, a white telephone on the table. I was thrilled that one of South Carolina's own was going with such a famous movie star. I tried to envision him bringing her home to Columbia to meet his parents, memorized the sequence of events played out in *Photoplay* and *Modern Screen:* Taylor's divorce from first husband Nicky Hilton, her fling with Donen, their breakup—all in 1951; then in February 1952, her marriage to Michael Wilding, a man old enough to be her father.

Peter was on the screen porch with one of his bonsai trees, shaving the knobby knuckles of a limb. I'd seen him use weights and copper wires to shape the trunk and branches into a triangle, the way an orthodontist uses braces and bands to straighten teeth. "The idea," Peter had explained, "is to spiral the wires a fraction of an inch at a time. If you don't do it slowly, the bark is so soft and tender you'll end up with scars."

The French doors were closed, not tightly closed, just barely, the curtains open. I pulled the afghan over my feet. From the den, I could see Peter through the glass, in the navy blue jacket I'd given him for his birthday. Navy was one of his best colors, although it was hard to find a color that did *not* look good on him. When we'd first met, I'd fallen in love with his appearance, the way he dressed, the sense of his body. Tonight he was wearing blue jeans, a cotton-knit golf shirt, moccasin-like boat shoes, white athletic socks. His usual after-work clothes.

The doorbell rang, one chime, which meant that it was the back door. Outside, it was dark as midnight. The one lamp I'd turned on in the den was so dim it looked like it was failing. I couldn't imagine who could be coming so late, but then I looked at my watch and saw that it was only seven o'clock. The days were no longer getting shorter gradually, the way they had been; they were just suddenly half gone.

I went to the back hall and flicked on the porch light. At first, all I saw through the chilled panes in the door were moths rising up, like nervous little shadows. Then I saw Chip's father, Thomas Dunham, looking down, to his right. His metal-rimmed glasses had slid to the end of his nose. I turned the key and opened the door. Then *I* looked down. Early was standing there, his red windbreaker turned inside out. He was holding a white dish towel to the left side of his face. Blood was soaking through the thin weave of the towel, running down his arm, like Kool-Aid. Dripping onto the brick.

"My God! Early, what happened?" I said. My voice sounded muffled to my ears. It could've been coming from next door.

"Kathryne, there's been a terrible accident . . ." Thomas's slow drawl. He was taking way too long to say what he had to say.

"Are you okay? Early, are you okay?"

"I'm okay, Mom," he said. "I'm okay."

"Let me tell you what happened," Thomas said. "The boys were playing with Pepper. Early wasn't roughhousing with him or anything like that—"

"Oh my God! *Peter!*" I yelled over my shoulder into the kitchen, hoping he could hear me all the way through the kitchen and the den. "Come out here! Peter!"

"In a minute." I could barely hear him. "I'll be there in just a minute. Let me finish what I'm doing."

"*Now,* Peter!" I yelled back. "*Come now!*"

"Come in, come into the house," I said to Thomas and Early. Before they could take a step, I dropped down, letting my trembling body rest on the back of my heels until I was eye to eye with Early. "Let me take a look at this, honey."

I pulled the towel away, inch by sticky inch, a slow-motion act that seemed to take forever. His face was the wet red-brown of calf's liver. The gash was so deep it looked like it went to the center of him. Started in the corner of his mouth. Curved all the way up to his left eye. His eye! Had it damaged his eye? Could he see out of that eye?

I couldn't talk. Couldn't move. I wanted to stand up and take one step forward to pick up my son—he looked so breakable—but it was as if my shoes were heavy with mud and my arms had hardened into casts.

Chip's father reached down, took my hands, and pulled me up. I saw that he was wearing running shoes, gray sweatpants, a Ralph Lauren sweatshirt. He pushed Early and me into the kitchen. "He's been bitten . . . pretty bad," he was saying.

"Bitten," I said. Pepper was a border collie. Years before, the Dunhams had flown to Missouri to buy the dog.

Thomas held both of Early's shoulders in his hands. His hands were shaking, and for a second it looked as though Early was moving his shoulders to some wild jungle beat. "The boys and Pepper were playing out in the yard, and for some crazy reason, the dog jumped up and bit Early right in the face. I can't understand it . . . Pepper knows Early. It doesn't make sense." Early was just standing there, where he'd been led, not saying a word. I couldn't begin to tell what his expression was, with all the blood.

"Doesn't make any sense at all," Thomas was saying. He took off his glasses and wiped one eye with the inside of his arm. His Rolex caught the light. I never really understood what he did for a living, something in commercial real estate, but I knew he was extremely successful. He and his wife, Barbara, were not involved with their son at all. Vacations, spas, shopping, restaurants—that's what they cared about. Joy told me that Barbara had attempted suicide the summer before Chip started kindergarten. An overdose of pills. He was the one who'd found her. Somehow, he'd gotten his father on the phone and they'd rushed her to the hospital. Joy also told me that Barbara was the type of person who'd grown up poor and now had to have the best of everything. In a sad way, she and Thomas were a good fit: he could afford to buy the best of everything and she spent her days trying to find it.

Thomas was still talking. "I thought about calling a doctor, but then I knew I needed to bring him home to y'all before I did anything. Do you want me to call the pediatrician? I know you use Dr. Duerck, like we do. You just tell me—"

Dr. Duerck. Dr. Donald Duerck. It struck me suddenly what an absolutely absurd name for a pediatrician that was.

"Peter!" I yelled again.

The too-bright light in the kitchen started breaking apart, throwing clots everywhere. My legs felt like tangled strands of rope. The floor softened. I found myself sitting in the chair next to my desk in the kitchen—the carved antique chair from my mother—my head flopped over between my knees. The very minute Early needed me—and I was about to pass out! I gestured for Chip's father to press down on the back of my head while I lifted my head against the pressure of his hand. He was not just keeping me from fainting—he was preventing my life from emptying out through my scalp.

When the room swirled back from darkness, Early was holding the towel to his face again, only now the towel was thick, swollen with blood. Peter was standing beside him, both arms dangling at his sides, like he was carrying heavy buckets. Thomas's glasses were again down to the end of his nose, about to fall off. The three of them looked as though they were outlined in thin, shaky, unreliable pencil, badly drawn by an amateur artist.

We did not call the pediatrician. Peter, taking charge now, his arm around Early, said in that voice I'd fallen in love with years before, "Come on, Kathryne. We need to go to the hospital. And we need to go now."

Thomas stood in front of the toolshed, waving us off, as we scraped the low spot at the bottom of the driveway before turning up the street. I hadn't thought to grab a jacket and was cold. Early was still wearing his windbreaker, with the seams and label showing. I held him in my lap. He spoke only once.

"Mom," he said, "all I did was pet him. I didn't think I was doing anything wrong. Is Pepper going to be all right?"

I told him that, of course, he hadn't done anything wrong; for some reason, Pepper had reacted in an uncharacteristic way, that dogs can do that sometimes and for him not to worry, everything would be okay. I adjusted my blouse so the buttons down the front wouldn't dig into his face.

At the emergency entrance, they rolled him away in a wheelchair. I sat in admissions with Peter, trying to do what we'd been told: sit and wait. I was concentrating on being calm, but the waiting room felt like it was shrinking and the smell of hospital expanding. *Why was I sitting there? Where was Early?*

After five full minutes, which felt like five lives, I told Peter in my most reasonable voice that I had to go to the ladies' room. He was filling out admission forms on a clipboard, marking endless Medical History boxes with careful, sensible *X*s.

As soon as I was out of his sight, I charged down the hall. *Where had they taken my son? Was anybody with him, comforting him?* When I got to the cafeteria, on my left, I slowed down, as though I might be stopped for speeding in that high-traffic area. I looked to the right, toward the main entrance: the wide-open marble expanse, people sprawled on sofas and chairs as though they were lounging around in a luxury hotel. A shiny grand piano off to the side. An aquarium-like glass box filled with live birds in citrus colors—like miniature oranges, lemons, and limes being tossed about. *Why was so much money spent on hospital lobbies?*

Go. Faster. Near the end of the hall, a door was open to an of-fice. A young woman behind a desk, tapping her pen against her fingers. Her phone book was open to the Yellow Pages, to a full-page ad for "Boudoir Photographer."

"Would you help me find my son?" I said, more shrill than I'd intended. Her lips were glossy, her earrings hearts. I decided to give her so many details she'd want to help me. "Earl Smallwood," I said. "We brought him in with a dog bite. To the emergency room. His best friend's dog bit him. A dog he's known forever! We were all shocked. Really shocked. They took him back here somewhere. Would you know where?"

She pointed toward the hall with her pen, casually, charmingly. Nothing in this world will ever go wrong, her face said. "He's probably in a room near admissions. Where you were. Follow the carpet until it ends. Take a right at the first corridor, in front of the elevators. You'll see somebody at a desk on the left. They'll tell you where he is. Now don't you worry. I'm sure he'll be fine."

"Thank you," I said in my sugary voice. *How would she have any idea whether I should worry or not?*

I followed the carpet, took a right. Radiology ahead. Physical Therapy to the right. On the left, a large plate-glass window overlooking a lighted brick courtyard. Teak benches and huge pots of geraniums, this late in the season still a feverish scarlet. Did she say a right or a left at the first corridor? I turned to retrace my steps, my shoulder bag flapping against my hip, but when I found my way back to her office, the door was closed. Locked. Had she given me bad directions or could I just not follow what she'd said?

A hospital aide pushed past me, catching my heel with the corner of the food cart she was wheeling.

"Sorry, dear! Coming through!" she said cheerily. The gluey smell of picked-over mashed potatoes and gravy filled the hall.

Maybe Peter was with Early now.

Just get back to Peter.

I found the lobby, and from there, the emergency-room waiting

area. Peter was holding the clipboard to his chest, the forms filled
out. He raised his eyebrows at me and touched my bag.

"Where were you for so long?" he asked.

"It took me a while to find the bathroom. I'm sorry. Have you
heard anything?"

"I'm waiting for them to come get these."

I was about to sit down when a large, bosomy woman in a red-
and-turquoise flowery dress walked over. She took the clipboard,
unclipped the forms, stapled them together with two loud claps, like
castanets, and said, "All right, then. You folks can come with me. I'll
take you to your son."

IN TIMES OF CRISIS, I know I can take on what Peter used to
call my "hospital personality," but there's no way I can stop myself. Suddenly I'm convinced I have to pay close attention to every
single detail. If I don't, if I turn away for half a second, terrible
things will happen. Like Shirley MacLaine in *Terms of Endearment,* in
the hospital scene when she goes to the nurses' station and demands
pain medication for her daughter, who has cancer. She knows it's up
to her to keep everything from falling apart. She can't count on another soul. The fate of the world rests on her shoulders. The reality
is, in spite of all she does, her daughter dies anyway.

We were directed to a large room with steel equipment shining like
sterling silver under the lights. Early was on a gurney, his eyes closed,
an overwashed white blanket pulled up to his chin. His face had been
cleaned with something mustard-colored, giving him a jaundiced
look. I could see that the gash did not actually reach his eye.

In the corner, a doctor was washing his hands. He was short. If
we'd been standing face-to-face, he'd come up to my nose, and I'm
not even five-four.

"Hello." His back was to me. "I'm Dr. Lomax."

"Hi." I waited a few seconds, a reasonable amount of time. He turned around. "I have to ask you, Dr. Lomax, are you a plastic surgeon?"

"An emergency-room physician. Don't worry, Mrs. Smallwood, we'll take good care of your son." Now he was drying his hands. Where was Peter? I thought he'd followed me in.

"Well, do you think a plastic surgeon should be called? Since it's his face and all?"

"No, I really don't think we need a plastic surgeon. We stitch plenty of folks up. I assure you, we can handle it." He pulled on one rubber glove, then the other. "Your son will be just fine."

"I *know* he'll be fine, but I believe we need a plastic surgeon." I was trying to make my voice sound sweet. It wasn't working. I sounded like Shirley MacLaine, when I wanted to sound like Shirley Temple.

"Really, Mrs.—"

"Smallwood."

"Mrs. Smallwood. I've been doing what I do for a very long time." He looked like he was twenty-five. "Your son won't be any problem."

"Dr. Lomax, I *know* he won't be any problem. This isn't about my son being a problem. He's never a problem. I would simply prefer a plastic surgeon. I'm not saying I don't have confidence in your abilities, but in this situation, I'd like a plastic surgeon."

I was not going to let this doctor get near my son. Sure, he might sew up a gash on an arm or a leg. But he was not going to sew up my son's face.

He threw his gloves in the sink, excused himself, said he'd be back in a minute. The door squeezed shut. I could hear a squall of rushing around at the nurses' station outside, phone calls, hushed conversations—thin-lipped, frenzied words when they forgot themselves and raised their voices loud enough for me to hear: *but she said she wouldn't let Dr. Lomax do it, I don't care what she said, can you believe, get doctor so-and-so.*

I pushed in beside Early on the gurney, half sitting, half leaning. His eyes were closed. Had they given him something to relax him? I patted his arm, didn't say anything, hoped he was sleeping. Every now and then, I thought I saw a weak little smile aimed in my direction. Where was Peter? I certainly wasn't going to leave Early to go find him. *Breathe,* I told myself.

I don't know how much time passed, but after a while, a different doctor came in. His legs were long and he covered the length of the room in a couple of strides.

"I'm Dr. Ferguson, young man," he said to Early. Early opened his eyes, smiled that same weak smile, managed to say, "Hi, Dr. Ferguson." My son never forgot his manners.

The new doctor, probably in his fifties, smiled back, an all-out smile, a basket weave of wrinkles surrounding his eyes. "Let's see what we have here," he said.

He bent down to Early's level, looked at his cheek, a gentle and confident expression on his long face. Then he straightened up and said tenderheartedly, convincingly, "I'm a plastic surgeon, Mrs. Smallwood, and I'll take care of your son." He held out his hand. I shook it. Strong. And nice. "Now, I must ask you, are you sure you want to stay in here?" He'd taken me by the elbow and was pointing me toward the hall. "Let me tell you how I'm going to repair your son's face." We were outside the room now. "The wound is deep, so I'll have to reattach muscle and tissue first. Your son is fortunate in that the tear does not go all the way through his cheek, but I'm going to have to work in several layers. It'll be a long, tedious process. Why don't you relax in the waiting area and we'll come for you as soon as we're done?"

"How many stitches?" I asked.

"I don't know exactly."

"A dozen? A hundred? Can you give me an idea?"

"Could be fifty, maybe a hundred. There's no way to tell at this point. However many it takes, when I'm finished you won't see anything but that handsome face."

A hundred stitches! My stomach felt like I was in an airplane that had suddenly lost altitude. "I'll stay," I said, heading back into the room, Dr. Ferguson a couple of steps behind.

He and the nurse scrubbed, gathered their instruments, began their work. I sat on a low stool on the other side of Early, holding his hand. I heard myself jabbering. About school. Baseball cards. Playing ball. Words, words. Anything I could think of to take his mind off what was being done to him. He lay perfectly still, never even flinched. I watched Dr. Ferguson closely and asked him to tell us when he was a third of the way through, halfway, close to the end. That was back when I believed we can endure anything if we know how long it will last.

A T ONE POINT I spotted Peter out in the hall pacing back and forth, looking like anyone else moving through that grim place. I've always known this about him: there are times when he can rise to the occasion and do what has to be done, his face to the wind—and there are times when he simply keeps his distance. He and I were like scales. Those rare instances when he weighed in, I lightened up. When I stepped forward and took over, he floated off.

A FTER DR. FERGUSON FINISHED and walked out, Peter came in. I told him I had to go to the bathroom and would he stay with Early until they brought the discharge papers.

"Sure," he said. "Hey, buddy," I heard him say to Early as I left the room.

"Hey, Daddy," Early answered. "I was real brave."

I waited a few seconds in the hall.

"I know you were, son. I know."

"Have you talked to Chip? He won't have to give Pepper away, will he?"

Inside the ladies' room, I realized that my fingers, hands, forearms were freezing; I was up to my elbows in cold. I felt so cold my teeth ached. I stood in that overheated room, holding out my arms, trying to absorb the warmth. Then I tore off a paper towel, fished through my pocketbook for a ballpoint pen that worked, pressed the paper towel against the cracked wall and scribbled every four-letter word I could think of, words I never say out loud: DAMN!!!! SHIT!!!! FUCK!!!! Then I balled up the paper, stuffed it in the too-full trash can, tore off another paper towel, scratched out the same words—those fat, ugly letters—and balled up the paper and threw it away. My arms, hands, fingers were feeling warmer. Something about writing those rocky consonants on rough brown paper against the uneven wall was as soothing as transcribing psalms on vellum might be for a religious person. My own version of praying, I suppose. Saying to God that I was scared and didn't understand why something like this was happening to people like us. Sometimes I've wished that I *were* religious; it would make everything so simple. But my rational mind keeps me from believing. I was raised in the Episcopal church. Peter and I went to church now and then when Early was small, mostly on Christmas Eve and Easter. Then we stopped. It's not that we had any dramatic change of heart. We just ended up going less and less until we weren't going at all. More of a dwindling than a decision.

Now I needed to get back to Early. Take him home. Get him healed.

Then we'd deal with the dog.

———

THE ONLY CHOICE for the Dunhams was to put Pepper to sleep. I could not accept anything less. Peter said he didn't think it was up to us to voice an opinion, that this was the Dunhams' decision. But I knew that once a dog bites, you can never be sure he won't do it again. You're dealing with the unpredictability of an animal. We were also dealing with parents who did not pay enough attention to the dangers our children face.

Naturally, Early begged me not to say anything. "If I hadn't been bitten, Chip would get to keep Pepper," he said.

"Honey, it's not your fault that dog bit you," I said.

"Then can we buy Chip a new puppy? Another border collie?"

"Well, I think that's something his parents might want to do."

Thomas and Barbara did not buy their son a new puppy, and soon it seemed that Chip was doing everything he could to make Early feel guilty. He stopped calling. Stopped coming by. It was at least a month, maybe two, before he and Early were back to normal, spending the night at each other's house, riding their bikes to the 7-Eleven.

Later, I wondered if we should have bought Chip a new dog. All I'd been concerned about was Early and his face; I hadn't really given Chip much thought. Maybe he *wasn't* trying to make Early feel guilty. Pepper had been his shadow, always there, licking his ear. Maybe Chip was just sad, having lost the one member of his family who was fully for him. Maybe he'd been just too sad to come around.

EARLY GREW MORE AND MORE self-conscious about the ragged scar, the shape of a long comma, that curled from the corner of his eye down his cheek. I told him I could barely see it. He said he could see it. I told him the plastic surgeon had said that when he got older and started shaving, the scar would fade. But it *was* a thick red ridge embroidering his face. I told him he looked like Clint Eastwood. A gentle version of Clint Eastwood. It gave him charac-ter, I said. He had the face of someone who'd had *experience*. He said it made his face look like wadded-up paper. He began standing that particular way, like Jack Benny, his right hand cupping the elbow of his left arm, left hand flat on his cheek, covering that side of his face.

When the scar was brand-new and rough and at its reddest, I'd sit on the side of his bed at night, the room too dim to see the sports pennants he'd tacked all over his walls, but not too dim for me to see his face, lit by the stars fixed to the ceiling. I'd smooth in vitamin E oil, telling him to concentrate with me and visualize the scar fading, the same way we'd wished away the warts that had appeared on his smallest finger the year before. I honestly believed he and I together could wish away any bad thing that came along.

NINE

ALL THAT WAS GOOD in the world gathered itself in my mother's expression. She had remarkable eyebrows, perfectly shaped and symmetrical. A pointed chin, which Early and I both have. Small fingers. I used to love to watch her play the piano, the way her hands moved over the keys, graceful as palms. When I was young, I'd come home from school, have my chocolate-chip cookies and milk, then dance to her music—arabesques, piqué turns, tour jeté leaps through the air. As though helium spun through my veins.

Every Sunday night, she'd wash my hair at the kitchen sink. I'd bend my head forward, my face buried in a folded washcloth. She'd pour cups of warm water through my hair until the last bubble of shampoo became a thin line in the porcelain. Later we'd sit together on the sofa in the den and I'd lay one skinny arm across her knees, then the other, and she'd tickle, a gentle *scritch-scratch* from my shoulder down to my fingertips and back again. Eden Terrace was the perfect name for our street. It was safe there. African violets lined the windowsills; white tulips circled the dogwood tree in the green, green front yard.

My parents had planned to have only one child, my brother, Billy. Then, four years later they had me. Definitely an accident. My mother turned this into something wondrous. "Thank goodness, you were born!" she'd say. "What in the world would we have done without our Kathryne?"

She raised me to take life easy, to glide. She told me not to work so hard in school, that B's were just as good as A's. "Don't push it" was her favorite expression. When I was in college, she wrote to me, saying I wasn't spending enough money. "Go out and buy something you don't need," she said. She acted as though the whole world were a purse she could reach inside, taking out whatever I needed.

People in Rock Hill loved my mother, and she loved them. She especially loved attractive people. Charmers. Stars. Appearance mattered. I can see her walking over to some pretty young woman at the register in the Winn-Dixie. My mother would ask her what on earth she did to have such a lovely complexion, or she'd go on and on about the girl's marvelous posture. Mother was generous with her attention and compliments. People stopped her on the street to have a conversation with her. I watched them touch her hand, study her perfect face. I knew they envied me because I was her daughter.

PETER USED TO SAY that I only remember what I want to remember. I wanted to say, Isn't that what everybody does? The way the days reach back and forth—who can be absolutely sure we're remembering everything we should remember?

WHEN ROCK HILL celebrated its centennial in 1952, I was eleven. My mother had a dress made for me that was absolutely authentic. Long, with a flouncy hoop skirt. Lavender cotton, white eyelet trim. Matching bonnet. Lavender-and-white parasol with silk flowers woven through the spokes. Every Saturday for weeks, I stood on the splintery wooden platform in Mrs. Gaddy's living room while she measured, chalked, cut, fit. I'd turn slowly as she pulled pins from the tomato pincushion strapped to her wrist. She'd hold a pin in her tight lips, thread a second one through the soft material. She sewed nickels into the hem to "make it hang right."

It was hard to find anyone in Rock Hill who was not involved with the centennial. Months ahead, men were letting their beards grow ("brothers of the brush," they called themselves); women were cooking and filling their freezers ("sisters of the swish," they were called, because of the old-fashioned gowns they'd wear); every would-be actor in town was spending long hours in rehearsal—with a director brought down from New York!—for the outdoor drama to be performed in Confederate Park.

The afternoon of the centennial, I sat in the back of our Chrysler, my skirt spread over the seat, while my father, Abraham Lincoln–ish in his beard and black suit, and my mother, in a chintz gown covered with sprays of pink and white flowers, talked animatedly in the front seat. We were as excited as we'd ever been about anything. Even my father. There was something in the air around us. I wondered what my friends would be wearing, imagined us posing for snapshots in our costumes, a lineup of laughing girls, the day framed in silver.

The drama in the amphitheater was the opening event. I sat with my friends in the front row, applauded when the covered wagons

pulled by horses and filled with waving women and children rum-
bled across the grassy stage. We covered our ears when the men following on horseback fired real rifles into the air. After they'd all
settled in, the men lit campfires and the women rattled tin pots and
pans as though they were making dinner. Halfway through the meal,
Catawba Indians, who'd been off to the side in bark-covered round-
houses, whooped and hollered across the grass, their faces painted,
black circle around one eye, white circle around the other, curly
snake tattoos on their shoulders. We booed until we were hoarse.
Until our side won. Until recorded patriotic music filled the southern sky.

After the play, the grown-ups headed up the wide gravel paths
to the armory to browse through a photography and map exhibit
and hear lectures by Winthrop College professors on the history
of Rock Hill. The children stayed in the amphitheater and took
turns going on hayrides in a wagon pulled by an old limping horse.
We bobbed for apples in oak barrels, did the egg toss. Physical-
education teachers from the two elementary schools helped us elect
captains (I was one) and pick teams for games that children back in
the 1850s would have played, games using antique wooden balls.

Next, we ran races. During the relay race, my heel caught my hem
and ripped it loose. Nickels spilled out as if somebody had hit the
jackpot. I tried to keep going but ended up tripping over the eyelet.
Soon my whole hem was hanging, the skirt dragging the ground like
an old ragged sack.

By this time, the grown-ups had come out to watch. My mother
took one look at me and pulled me aside—not with anger, but with
a seriousness of purpose.

Before I knew it, we were back at the seamstress's and I was up on
the platform again. Painstakingly, Mrs. Gaddy rehemmed my dress.
By hand. While the dress was still on me. Mother sat on the stool beside the sewing machine, one leg crossed over the other, the hem of

her gown gathered in one hand above her knees. The air from the oscillating floor fan pushed her bangs back from her face as she watched me take the same little bird steps I'd taken the first time Mrs. Gaddy had hemmed my dress, turning in a slow circle so that she could pin the hem, then make her baby-size slip stitches. The fluorescent face of the clock on the mantel gave the whole room a sad glow.

By the time Mother drove me back to the park, my father had gotten a ride home. My friends were gone, all the games over. I'd missed having my silhouette cut out of black construction paper. The fried chicken, casseroles, corn bread and biscuits, cakes, pies, and cookies had been laid out on the picnic tables under the arching trees, and eaten. Musicians had played their looping sing-along songs and packed up their instruments and left. Fireworks had etched their lights in the sky, and vanished. Lawn chairs were flattened and packed away in car trunks. A cleanup crew—their heads bowed—were fanning out over the grounds in the dark, filling huge metal garbage cans. I did not say a word to my mother. I was too much in love with her to complain. Even though I'd been dreaming about the centennial for months and had ended up spending more than half of it in Mrs. Gaddy's living room. Even though there wouldn't be another celebration like this one until the year 2052.

WHEN SHE WAS SEVENTY-TWO, my mother was struck by a car. She'd talked my father into taking ballroom dancing at Winthrop College, and instead of parking on campus, they parked on the street, opposite the college. My father ran across Oakland Avenue first. When he called her to follow, a car seemed to pull out from nowhere and swerve into her. She was killed instantly. My father replayed that scene a million times. "Why didn't I wait for her?" he'd ask no one in particular, over and over, his face buried in one big open hand.

Sometimes I think I'm still reeling from that accident. I thought my mother would always be there for me. She was so much a part of me I couldn't acknowledge even the most natural mother-daughter tensions between us—much less the tremendous hold she had on me. She was so much a part of me—like my spine—that I believed if I lost her, I might not be able to stand.

M Y FATHER WAS INTELLIGENT and bookish, and with-drawn. I used to think I could never say anything smart enough to capture his attention. But when I got older, I realized it was just that he was self-absorbed. I'd talk to him and he wouldn't answer. As though I were sending out words and they failed to land. Or maybe my words remained in the air, aimlessly drifting about, held in a contrary breeze. I remember thinking, *Okay, try another subject. Surely, he'll be interested in this.*

He was a lawyer, well known in Rock Hill for his fairness. Well known in our family for fairness. (Think Gregory Peck in *To Kill a Mockingbird.*) Once, my mother gave me an old boxy camera she'd had as a girl, the kind you hold below your waist and look down into, the plastic strap around your neck. I was twelve; my brother, Billy, was sixteen and knew I was never going to take pictures. He was dying to refurbish the camera and use it. He asked if he could have it. I hesitated. True, I would never use it, but I was sentimental about my mother and kept everything she ever gave me, especially things she'd had when she was young. My father heard Billy ask for the camera, saw me having trouble hammering out an answer. He said, "Billy, you have the right to ask. And Kathryne, you have the right to say no." This was my father at his best. Making sure Billy did not feel selfish for asking, making sure I did not feel selfish for refusing.

Fairness, however, is not always compassion.

The problem was, my father felt free to pick and choose what he responded to. He was the one who decided whether to honor you with a reply; it had nothing to do with how important the subject might be to you.

My mother adored my father, though. And he adored her. In the entrance hall of our house—on the gateleg table, right by the front door—was a photograph of their twenty-something-year-old selves kissing passionately. You could hardly tell where his army khaki ended and her printed cotton began. Not only was he kissing her, she was returning the kiss. He was dipping her backward, as though they were dancing. I remember standing in front of that picture, studying their greedy eyes, that war-movie kiss, wondering why his embrace hadn't broken her back. Wondering if people as old as my parents still had sex. Wondering if old age—or something else— made married couples stop having sex.

DURING THE FIVE YEARS between Mother's death and my father's death, my father mellowed unbelievably. As though he actually *became* my mother. He began to listen intently when you talked to him, and to answer with what had to be called compassion every time, not just when he felt like it. Peter joked that after my mother died and my father went through his transformation, you could hardly get off the phone from him. My father asked questions, then asked follow-up questions. He was interested in everything you had to say. The last five years of his life were like beginning again.

A LITTLE MORE THAN two months before he died, on December 26, my father walked out to get the morning paper, fell in the driveway, and broke his left femur. I had him transferred from the hospital in Rock Hill to Charlotte Memorial for the surgery. I thought that if he was here, I could make sure he received the best care possible.

New Year's Eve, Early was at a middle-school dance, and Peter and I were going to a party at Joy's. The theme was Mardi Gras; all the guests were supposed to wear masks. I found some old, close-up, black-and-white photographs Billy had taken of Peter and me the last time we were in New York, and I had them enlarged. I cut them out, mounted them on cardboard, stapled them onto wooden sticks, thinking it would be funny to use our own faces to create an illusion.

On our way to the party, Peter and I stopped by the hospital to check on my father. The evening before, the doctor had changed his pain medication. My father told me on the phone that morning he'd been hurting all night, even after the change in medication.

I kissed his stubbly cheek and immediately buzzed the nursing station.

"Could you send someone to room five thirty-two? My father's in pain," I said.

No one came.

After ten minutes, I buzzed again.

"My father, in five thirty-two, is in pain and needs stronger medication," I said, a little bit louder, more insistent, bordering on demanding.

A few minutes later, a nurse, whose body was as wide sideways as it was across the front, threaded her way into the room and looked at me as though she'd sized *me* up: another annoying family member, she was obviously thinking, who's not only pushy but believes she knows more than the nurses and doctors.

"I just gave him his medicine," she said. "Right before you came. It'll take effect soon." She smelled like breath mints.

"How long do we wait?" I asked.

"If he's not feeling better in an hour, come get me."

"An hour?" As though she'd said a month.

Peter caught my elbow.

The nurse turned to leave. She positioned herself to slide sideways through the door.

"Listen," she said, now in the hall, "I understand your concern, but I've got a lot of other patients on the floor to take care of, and we're short-staffed. It's a holiday, you know. Let's give the medicine a chance to work."

Why do they have to say "medicine"? Is it codeine? Morphine? Why couldn't she treat me like an adult and call the medication by name?

Peter walked over to my father. "Dad," he said quietly, "how about getting up for a while, maybe sit in the chair and give your back a rest? You know you're not supposed to stay in bed too much."

"Okay, sure," my father said in that pleasing way he'd had during the years since Mother had died.

Peter helped him sit up and swing his legs over the side of the bed. I lay across the foot of the bed. My father's legs were the legs of an old man: hairless, yellowish, like beached fish, especially right above his ankles where tight dress socks over the years had worn them to a shine.

Slowly, Peter walked my father and pulled the IV pole to the chair in the corner of the room. Peter could be gentle and strong at the same time, especially when the patient was someone other than our son. I felt such a rush of admiration for him that my eye started twitching. He pulled up a chair for himself, next to my father. We sat like this for a while, Peter and me telling my father about Joy's party, showing him our masks—only I held Peter's and Peter held mine, which got a laugh from my father. He told us in a breathless voice about the awful supper he'd had *at four-thirty*—and he was beginning to tell us something about the nurse. In the middle of his sentence, he stopped talking and seemed to be staring at the dense shadows out the window.

"I see shapes," he said, his voice now dreamy and distant, cottony.

"What kind of shapes?" I asked.

"See? There. Your mother." He raised his eyebrows and smiled. "Hey, darlin'!" he said brightly, as though he were sitting at the kitchen table back home on Eden Terrace, eating a bowl of cornflakes and bananas, and my mother had just walked into the room.

Then, even more brightly, he said, "Look! She's playing the piano! She's playing 'Humoresque.' She has on those real high heels and her blue dress, the one with all the lace at the bottom. Oh, what a stunning woman she is, your mother . . ."

I strained to see her in the darkness.

Then, as suddenly as my mother had appeared, I could tell by the slope of my father's shoulders, she was gone.

He closed his eyes. The corners of his mouth drooped.

After a few seconds, Peter asked him, "Want to go to bed?"

My father opened his eyes, turned toward Peter, grinned. "Not tonight, dear. I have a headache."

It was the first off-color joke he'd ever cracked in my presence!

Peter and I began to laugh. Then my father laughed, a strong and healthy laugh. Soon we were laughing and crying—all three of us— big, heaping, messy sobs. We were laughing and crying so hard we couldn't stop.

The nurse came in, her wide hips filling the doorway again. She was carrying a Styrofoam pitcher of ice, paper cups, and a bouquet of flexible straws. She looked surprised, then disapproving. Yes, definitely disapproving. But for the life of us, we couldn't stop. We laughed as though my father had said the funniest thing in the world. We cried as though he'd said the saddest thing in the world.

Two months later, at home in Rock Hill, he went to sleep in the carved mahogany bed he and my mother had shared for forty-five years and never woke up.

TEN

I KNOW NOW that it was Early's friendship with Chip that realigned Early's life. Even more so after they got to high school. It was not just one incident. And it was not sudden. In fact, things happened so gradually I couldn't see what was happening under my nose. It was easy to fool myself into thinking my son was living the life he was supposed to be living. Like the summer I lost a whole bed of black-eyed Susans. Every July for years, the area around the lamppost had brimmed with yellow. Then one summer, a few empty spaces popped out. I absentmindedly reminded myself to up my watering. More spaces appeared. I noticed, but barely. By August, all that was left was dirt. Rabbits—those creatures that win our hearts with their furry cuteness—were devouring everything that attempted to bloom around the foundation of our house.

When Early was in tenth grade, I had enough questions about what was going on to listen in on a few of his phone conversations with Chip. The first time, I'd just walked into the house after previewing John Hughes's *The Breakfast Club*. I always went to the movies in the afternoon. I loved sitting alone in the dark, dreaming my dreams in the midst of all that magic: the actors' wide eyes and wide mouths, plots that consoled because I could believe, for two hours, that my life was the same as theirs, or because I could believe that, thank goodness, my life was nothing like theirs.

The editor of *Charlotte Magazine* had asked me the week before if I'd be interested in a change, and a promotion. There was an opening for managing editor. I said no, that all I wanted was to review movies. At least until Early left for college. This job suited me perfectly.

I eased the phone off the hook downstairs about the time Amorite, the man who took care of all the yards on our street, cranked up the leaf blower outside Early's room, where Early was talking.

Chip was saying, "Today was a real bummer. When I woke up this morning, I tried to fake sick, but my mom wouldn't go for it. And I'd already written an excuse for myself for an orthodontist appointment yesterday. God, I yawned all day." I could hear music in the background, the stress on a relentless first beat, *da*-duh, *da*-duh, *da*-duh.

Then Early said, "You know, you skip so much, somebody's going to catch on. I mean, nobody goes to the orthodontist as much as you say you do. You could get an in-school suspension. Or worse. They're not stupid. They know you don't go every week."

In the movie I'd just seen, Judd Nelson played a disturbed teenager named Bender, who was doing everything he could to get into trouble. Emilio Estevez—what was his character's name?—got really angry at him. I remembered Emilio Estevez's exact words: *You know, Bender, you don't even count. I mean, if you disappeared forever, it wouldn't make any difference. You may as well not even exist at this school.* But Early clearly was not angry with his friend. I don't think he ever got angry with him.

"You don't understand," Chip was saying. "I truly despise school. I swear, first period goes so slow, I seriously don't think time *moves* in that class. And another thing, Julie's a bitch. After homeroom this morning, she and Paco were really going at it. She was all over him. They're probably fucking their brains out."

Julie Cauthen had been Chip's girlfriend the year before. Now she had a new boyfriend, Tom Furr. Chip's code name for Tom was Paco, which, I happened to know, came from when Chip spotted him at SouthPark, followed him into Belk's, spied on him while he bought himself a bottle of Paco Rabanne cologne.

"Listen, you've got to get over her. She likes Paco. Anyway, you'll find somebody better than Julie." This was Early, sensible and kind Early.

"Yeah, well, maybe, maybe not. I gotta go. I hear my mother." Then, as he was hanging up, he yelled at his mother, "Don't call me again! I said I was coming!"

I waited for Early to put down the phone before I hung up. Easy. Early and Chip never heard me. By the time Early came downstairs, I was at the kitchen table with a pad of yellow paper. Reviewers don't usually write their own headlines, but I was jotting down what I thought was the perfect one for *The Breakfast Club:* PEEVISH AND PASSIONATE TEENS COPE WITH PRESSURES.

In some ways, the conversation had been reassuring. Early did have a good head on his shoulders. But what about Chip's forged excuses, missed classes, his foul language? Who was this kid, my son's best friend?

Days later, Early asked me to hang up the phone for him in the den. He was going up to his room to talk.

"Got it, Mom!" he called down.

I clicked the button once and stayed on, holding the phone to my ear without allowing it to touch me, the bottom of the receiver turned away from my mouth, pointed toward my shoulder.

"Okay," Early was saying. "I'm back. What's up?"

"Today sucked!" Chip's nail-file voice. Like a grinding of brakes and gears. "I'm letting all this Julie-Paco stuff bug the shit out of me and I shouldn't, but I can't help it. I just wish I had a definite answer as to whether or not they're together."

"Look, here's the deal. They *are* together. You've got to . . . you've got to get over it . . ." Early's voice trailed off. He was trying to talk sense into Chip, but didn't want to run the risk of upsetting him.

"You're wrong. I don't have to get over anything, because Julie tends to play a major role in my life. I've written a song about her every day since school started."

Early murmured an automatic "yeah" or "well." He was retreating, backing off.

"Forget it. You don't understand. Anyway, this has gotta be short 'cause I spent the whole damn study hall not doing shit and I have an English test tomorrow, and so far, I've got a C in there. Hey, are you going to the senior class play Friday night?"

"Yeah. Everybody's going. Eddie, Steven, Brian, Amy, we're all going together. I thought you were, too."

"What about *The Rocky Horror Picture Show*?"

"I don't think my dad'll go for that," Early said. "Mom will. But Dad'll talk her out of it."

My heart was beating quickly and heavily. *Mom will. But Dad'll talk her out of it.* I knew I was the sympathetic parent. But when had sympathetic turned into pushover?

"Well, work on your dad. Make up something. I wanna go. Damn, I had a weird dream last night. I dreamed Julie came over to my house with Paco and gave me a card that said, 'I love you.' Like a valentine. It was weird because when I got it, she told me in front of Paco that she'd been using him the whole time just to make me jealous. God! Too bad that dream wasn't true!"

"I know, I know. Listen, I'll see what I can do about the movie.

Do you want my mom to drive us to the play? We could pick everybody up." I hated hearing Early scrambling to get back in Chip's good graces. I lifted my hand and saw that it was shaking.

"I'll let you know," Chip was saying. "I gotta go study. As if it'll do any good. I'm not a fucking brain like you."

"Go over your notes from class. And my notes that I gave you. You'll do fine."

"Gotta go."

"Later."

Two nights later, around nine, Chip called. Early answered the phone in the kitchen. He asked me to hang it up so he could take it in his room. Same routine. Click the button. Stay on the line.

"Okay, Mom!" Then: "Listen, I'm sorry I couldn't call you tonight, but I got home after eight and had a ton of homework to do." I happened to know that Early had called Amy Whitley the minute he got in the house, before he started on his homework. Early wasn't telling Chip this.

"I waited for you to call. I can't believe you couldn't take one goddamn break and make a phone call. It was important."

"I'm sorry, I—"

"I have to figure out my life."

"Figure out your life?"

"Yeah, what do you think about this?" Music played in the background. It sounded like the same *da*-duh, *da*-duh, *da*-duh I'd heard before. "I called Julie because at school she told me her dad was really sick, so I called to ask how he was. We talked for one minute at the most. It wasn't that she was being mean, she was just being herself. Okay, so she *was* being mean. She was being a real shit. She hung up on me!" A tight laugh. "But maybe she did have to go, her dad being sick and all."

"What'd she say?"

"I don't know. Nothing."

"You could find somebody else, you know. A lot of girls like you."

"You think? Who? Shit, you're the one they like. I know Amy Whitley likes you, for sure."

"Hey, wait a minute, you hear something?"

I put my hand to my lips and held my breath.

"What do you mean?" Chip, annoyed.

"I don't know, like somebody's on the phone or something."

I sucked in my stomach. I could hear the static of a fly somewhere in the room, the way every sound becomes amplified when you want quiet.

"I don't hear anything. Anyway, I was thinking, I don't care how much I love Julie, there's gotta be a stopping point to everything. I know I haven't reached it yet, but she *has* gone a little far in the amount of times she's hurt me. I don't plan on taking this from her much longer."

"Good. You really ought to forget about her. There are a million girls out there."

"Yeah, but she's the one I like, so I'm not going to give her up so fast."

"I know, I know. Not to change the subject, but I'll be at school for as much of the cross-country meet as I can tomorrow afternoon and then my mom's taking me to get a haircut. You going to the meet?"

"I've got tennis practice. Well, I may not go to tennis. But that's another subject and I don't really want to talk about it. I'm probably gonna quit."

"Quit tennis? You're kidding! Who gets to be number two in the state and quits?"

"Maybe not. I'll see. You know, Early, all I want is for Julie and Paco to break up and I'll be happy. That's all I want. That's not asking too much, is it? Uh, I'll call you later."

There was also Chip's note that I found in Early's jeans pocket:

> *Julie Cauthen*
> *is a*
> *snob*
> *freak*
> *asshole*
> *bitch*
> *fuckhead*
> *etc.*

Don't think all I did that year was listen in on my son's telephone conversations or go through his pockets. Because I didn't. The phone calls I did listen in on made me tired deep in my body. I was eager for details, but the details drained me. I wondered if my mistake was in looking for the hidden. Maybe it's better to assume everything is fine, I thought, and not root around beneath the surface. Early sounded mature, trying to get Chip to see things realistically. But why did Early like him so much? Why would Early want to be friends with someone who was so troubled?

THERE WAS SOMETHING ELSE. Something I don't like to think about. A letter Early wrote to Chip that I'm sure he never gave him. I found it in Early's room. I wasn't looking for it. I actually went in to get his dirty clothes. It was a Monday, the day I do the wash. I always check pockets because I hate to pull a load of clothes from the washing machine and find soggy strings of Kleenex or paper stuck to everything. Peter's good about emptying his pockets before he puts his clothes in the hamper. Early's dirty clothes were usually where he left them when he took them off. Jeans beside his bed, each leg a rumpled column squished down to the floor. Boxers dropped just before he opened the top drawer to pull out a clean pair. Socks, inside out, beside the door, limp.

Why would Early write Chip a letter? They saw each other every day of their lives. It's not like Early was the type to write about his experiences or feelings. He never kept a journal, as far as I know. Wasn't a big letter writer. He *was* good about thank-you notes. Wonderfully expressive notes to Joy thanking her for the gifts she brought every Christmas and birthday, toys when he was little, clothes as he got older. Thank-you notes to my brother, Billy, and his wife, Lily, who sent magic kits, T-shirts with team names on the front, baseball caps. Billy always knew the right team. Even the right-size bill. Early would then shape the bill to get the right curve in it.

But the letter. I read it, stuffed it back in his jeans pocket, left the jeans where I'd found them, the note in the side pocket balled up, like a rock.

Dear Chip,

I'm supposed to be doing my homework for English. We have to write an essay on something that happened to us when we were young that changed our life in some way but then I started writing this stupid letter.

I guess I just want to know if you remember what you did. Granted, it was a long time ago. I think we were 11. We were at your house after school listening to tapes up in your room. I remember you said something like, hey, want to do something cool? And I said, sure. You dropped your pants and you had a hard-on. I couldn't believe it. You told me to touch it. I didn't want to but I guess I tend to do everything you tell me to do. I had a sick feeling in the pit of my stomach. I was scared to death. But I didn't want you to know how scared I was. You were just standing there in your T-shirt. I remember thinking how much taller you were than me. You looked like a grown up, not a kid. And then you told me to put it in my mouth. I remember I said, do what? And you said it again. Put it in your mouth, you said. I felt like I was going to throw up. I said I can't do that. You said why not? I said I just can't. Why don't you put your clothes back on, I said. Let's do something else. But then you said okay, just put your hand around it and I'll show you what to do. So I did. I didn't want to act like a total wimp and I didn't want you to think I was too big of a nerd. And then your mother came in the front door and called up to you and you yelled at her to shut up and leave you alone. You went in the bathroom and closed the door. I just stood there not knowing what to do. I waited but you didn't come out. So I went downstairs and your mother started making conversation with me which was really embarrassing after what had happened. Then I went home.

Do you remember this? What do you think about it? I know we're not queers. We both like girls. But what do you think about all this? That's what I want to know. Because after that day you never said a word about it. And neither did I. It was like it never happened. But it did happen. And I just want to know if you remember it.

I know I'll never give you this letter. I'm not sure why I'm even writing it in the first place. Maybe some day I'll get up enough guts to ask you.

Early

Everything turned to pattern. Blue and orange and green and gold and red, the colors of the sports pennants covering the walls, taking over. I held on to the dresser with both hands, leaned against it, pushed aside the soccer trophies, and pressed my face to the cool glass covering the top surface.

I felt like I could vomit.

Like I was choking. The words in that letter were caught in my throat.

What else did I not know that had happened to my son?

My first impulse was to call Chip's mother. Tell her what kind of son she had. Demented. Sick. Tell her that if he ever called Early again or tried to see him, I would take out a warrant for his arrest.

I went for the phone. But wait. How would I explain why I'd read a letter I found in Early's pocket? What if it got back to him? He would never forgive me. Was it worth losing my son over?

I could tell Early not to see Chip again; I could put an end to the friendship. But would that make Chip even more appealing to Early? Would I be handing my son something to rebel against? If I stepped in, it could backfire in a big way.

Peter. He'd know what to do. But—oh, my God, this would kill him. And what if he insisted on calling the Dunhams? Wrong, wrong, wrong. This was not something to be openly discussed.

Anyway, I thought, in the context of childhood these kinds of things happen. Boys—and girls—experiment with their sexuality; of course, this is common. There are many different versions of "playing doctor."

I remembered my brother and me sitting on the floor of my mother's walk-in closet, the legs of my mother's silk slacks brushing my bare arms like insects. Billy, two of the neighborhood kids, and I were playing strip poker. Billy's idea. The other kids were my age, eight or nine years old. Billy was twelve or thirteen and the only one willing—no, eager, to take off his clothes. He was standing there, completely naked. And he had an erection. I remember looking at the hair beginning to grow in his groin. I was mesmerized. Hair! There! I had no idea.

He walked around that little square-shaped room, stepping over Mother's shoes, stopping to stand in front of each of us. A few seconds per person. First, the girl from next door. Then the boy who lived behind us. Then me.

"Touch it," Billy said.

I was the only one who did what he said.

ELEVEN

I HAVE NEVER LIKED answering machines. People leave messages and don't tell you enough. Or they tell you too much.

Once, I came home to a nub of a voice saying, "Sorry, wrong number, but remember, Jesus is Lord." This was a case of someone not telling you enough and telling you too much at the same time.

Nineteen eighty-five, Early's sophomore year, an afternoon in April—I stopped by the grocery store for chicken, baking potatoes, salad fixings. Early was at baseball practice, Peter at the office. I came home to a message that was so long I couldn't understand why the machine hadn't cut off in the middle. Leave it to Peter. He would never be careless about anything. He knew when he left the message that I'd be home before Early. No chance of anyone else hearing his words. No chance, either, that I'd ever forget his words:

"Kathryne, I know this is cowardly of me and I apologize, but, well, this is very difficult to say." A pause. It sounded like the beginning of a practical joke, but Peter didn't play practical jokes. "I've felt for some time that things aren't, well, things aren't right with us. Something's missing. Maybe it's that something's missing inside me." A short silence. I could picture him grinding his chin in to ease his collar away from his neck. "I believe that on the outside looking in, we're the perfect family. On paper it probably looks like we have it all. The Smallwoods and their perfect marriage. The Smallwoods and their perfect son." He stopped again. "I suppose you could say I've been successful in my work. I try to give something back to the community. And you. You're a charming, beautiful woman, people love and respect you, you're a fine movie critic. And Early . . . well, he does well enough in school and is a good student, although he could be at the top of his class if he applied himself. He's a decent athlete. Not the most aggressive. Adequate. But that's not what I want to talk about. Not what I want to talk about at all." Quiet again. "What I want to say is, things are *not* perfect. We've been deluding ourselves for quite a while. And now . . . well, now I've done something I had no business doing, and I'm afraid I've hurt you. Hurt our marriage. I hope it's not irreparable." Again, he stopped. "I'll be home after a while to explain. Kathryne? I'm sorry. But I need a little time to figure things out. You and Early go ahead and eat without me. I'll get something on my own. I'll be home late, at nine-thirty." Then he added, "All right." As though he were answering himself.

TWELVE

PETER USED TO SAY, "It's just that we're so different from one another." I didn't like when he said this. Why do people have to focus on differences? Who is not different from someone else? Name any husband and wife who are alike. My mother and father, for example: all those years, one so openly affectionate, the other so reserved. Name any two people—period. Even close friends. As much as Joy and I have in common, we have our differences. She's an artist at heart, a visual person; I can't visualize at all. When I put away leftovers after dinner, there's no way I can tell what size container I need until I spoon the food in. I end up shifting rice or squash or mashed potatoes from one piece of Tupperware to another until I finally get it right.

And Peter? How would I describe him?

A star. Everything going for him. Looks. Brains. No need to tinker with the polished structure that was his life. No wonder I fell in love with him. I'd always been drawn to men who were stars. Charmers.

When I was young and single, I made it a point to date good-looking guys so everyone would think I was something special. Joy used to say that when she was young, she never liked to date good-looking guys. Although she was pretty (I'm sure she was—she's pretty now), she didn't want anyone saying, "What's a guy like that doing with a girl like *that*?"

At the University of South Carolina, my big love was movie-star-handsome John Moody. John was pre-med and president of the student body (and practically everything else there was to be president of at the school). His hands were smooth and hairless, spongy, like a girl's. He had the kind of crooked smile, with deep dimples, that could talk women into doing anything he wanted. And he smiled all the time. We met at Homecoming, after I was crowned queen. With that self-important air of his, he marched right up to me and started talking, right after the halftime ceremony, minutes after the quarterback had escorted me off the field. Later that night, he removed the bobby pins from my piled-up hair, one by one, carefully, precisely, like the surgeon he planned to become.

We went together my junior year. That summer, before my senior year, he stayed in Columbia for summer school, and I went home to Rock Hill to work in my father's law office. John invited me down for a weekend in July. Not all the sorority houses were open during the summer—mine, Chi O, was closed—so he arranged for me to stay at the Tri Delt house.

As I unpacked my suitcase in the largest bedroom, on the third floor, I noticed an eight-by-ten photograph on one of the dressers. Of John! Why would anyone have a framed eight-by-ten of my boyfriend? Another girl, a Tri Delt, was staying in the room, but I knew she was engaged. Her two roommates were away for the weekend. No matter where I stood—beside the three single beds lined up like in an orphanage, beside the pitted oak desks and chairs—the John in the photograph seemed to be looking in the opposite direction.

Sunday morning, over fried eggs at the Toddle House, I asked him about the picture.

"Maybe somebody cut it out of the school paper," he said.

Possible, I thought. Being president of the student body, he was in the paper pretty often.

But an eight-by-ten? Did that make sense?

I drove home to Rock Hill that afternoon, wrote him a letter that night. Not a long letter. Not a short letter. And not gushy. It was important to strike just the right note. I wasn't ready to give him up.

I did not hear back from him.

It was a long summer; I grew sick of hope.

When I returned to school in the fall, he was hot and heavy, as my mother would say, with one of the girls who'd been away the weekend I'd been there. John's fraternity brother told me this. She'd had no idea he'd invited me down, had no idea I even existed. Of course, I hadn't known about her either. The entire year before, he'd managed to date us both at the same time.

My senior year stretched long before me. All I did was go to class and study. The seasons passed: leaves dropped to the ground, windows in the classrooms frosted over, azaleas untied their blooms like ribbon. I graduated with honors and moved to Atlanta to teach high-school English.

And met Buddy Blankenship.

Buddy was in the management-training program at Rich's Department Store. He had turn-and-stare good looks. His brown eyes were spaced far apart, giving his face a somewhat puzzled expression. He ended almost every sentence with "Okay?" I was crazy about him, crazy about being seen with him. By September, we were thick.

Mid-October, his father died unexpectedly, and he had to move back home to Gadsden, Alabama, to the house where his mother and grandmother lived, to run the family department store. He wrote to me, though not often. I figured he just wasn't the type to write. He'd already invited me to Gadsden the weekend before Christmas, so I knew we were okay.

When I got off the plane in Gadsden, though, it was clear we were not okay. I waited for him to talk to me, to notice I was there. He focused somewhere over my shoulder.

All weekend he kept leaving me to talk on the phone. I could hear the low, mumbled drawl of his voice, knew he was cupping the receiver with both hands. His mother, grandmother, and I sat in the overheated, damask-curtained parlor, which smelled like roasted meat, trying to keep a conversation going, though we could hardly make each other out in the dimness.

Back home in Atlanta, a mutual friend, one of the other young teachers at my school, told me she'd heard that Buddy had a girlfriend in Gadsden, and the day I'd arrived at his house was the day she'd told him she was pregnant.

The rest of that school year I did not date. I spent a lot of evenings in my terry-cloth robe and fuzzy slippers watching TV, the curtains on the picture window in my apartment drawn. The loneliness was immense and unsettling. Men had always found me attractive, wanted to date me. They'd complimented me on my green eyes, the shape of my face ("like a valentine," Buddy had said), my figure (thin arms, big breasts). Why was I so alone?

It never occurred to me to question the type of man I was attracted to. I'd been taught by my mother to put looks at the top of the list. When other mothers were advising their daughters to find someone "with substance," my mother was asking, "Is he cute? Exactly how good-looking *is* he?"

In May, she called to say she thought I needed a change, that I should consider moving to New York. My brother was there, she said; it would be a good thing. (He'd lived in Manhattan since graduating from Princeton.) I could tell she was worried about me.

In June, I packed my Samsonite suitcase, took the Southern Railway train to New York City, moved into the Barbizon Hotel for Women at Sixty-third and Lexington, and got a job as a production assistant at Filmex, a company that produced television commercials. After a month, my neighbor in the Barbizon (a tall and narrow, beautiful girl from Teaneck, New Jersey, who was an administrative assistant at *Mademoiselle*) and I rented a newish, no-personality shoe box of an apartment on Seventieth between First and Second.

At work, I booked film crews and tended bar in the president's suite when advertising-agency copywriters and art directors came to the studio to film. I also acted as a nonspeaking extra in commercials. For the closing frame of one sixty-second spot, I held a bottle of Top Job cleanser. You'd never know how heavy a bottle of Top Job actually was until you had to hold it with one hand, elbow bent, for an entire afternoon. That's how long it took them to get the shot they wanted. My arm would start to quiver and the bottle would slowly keel over. "Cut!" the director would yell, and they'd start again.

During lunch, I relieved Madeline, the British switchboard operator. I'd sit at her desk in the reception area, and when there was a call for anyone in the studio, I paged that person over the loudspeaker. Weeks into the job, I found out that my first day, the production guys actually called over and over, asking for one another, just to hear my South Carolina drawl echo through the halls of that hollow brownstone.

After six months, I decided that even though the men who worked in film were glamorous, with their safari jackets and heavy gold watches, they were also a little rough around the edges. They never even bothered to learn my name. It was always "honey" or "sweetheart" or "the chick in the studio." I started noticing the copywriters from the ad agencies. They were educated, clever, smooth. I decided I was better suited for writing than show business. I left Filmex for Ogilvy & Mather Advertising and a job as copy secretary, which I understood was the route for a woman on her way to junior copywriter and copywriter.

All along, I did not see my brother much. The weekend I'd moved to New York, Billy was off photographing the Grand Canyon. I'd always thought he used his hobby as a way to be involved and not involved at the same time. He could take pictures at family events and not have to talk to a single person. Soon after his trip out west, he met Lily. They got engaged after only two dates, and then I really didn't see him. If you'd asked if he and I were close, I would've said yes. After all, our mother wanted us to be close, so I assumed we were—which meant I had to be willing to forget what had happened between my brother and me in her closet. The truth is, Billy kept his distance from everyone, especially women. I was used to men keeping their distance. When I look back on my dating years, were the men I met so unlike Billy or my father? I kept assuming, though, based on no evidence whatsoever, that each new man in my life would be different.

Lily introduced me to a guy in her building named Michael Kaye, who was a talent agent for William Morris. Michael's job was to escort celebrities appearing on the Johnny Carson show, which meant that he'd pick them up in a limousine, keep them company in the Green Room, then deliver them back to their apartment or hotel after the program. I was dazzled by the names he tossed around—the most famous actors and actresses in movies and on TV. He was a true New Yorker, born and raised in the city. He wore expensive suits, had a gravelly voice and a bull neck. His chin was strong enough to support a piano. For my birthday, he gave me a gift certificate for a makeover at Kenneth's Salon. It was 1966, the year

Jackie Kennedy made Kenneth's famous. I knew that if I didn't make myself over, Michael would be out the door. I had the make-over—they straightened my hair, teased it into a bouffant helmet, taught me how to use smoky eye shadow and false lashes—and Michael left anyway.

Before our last date, I decided to make him jealous by sending myself seven long-stemmed red roses. I wanted to send a dozen, but that would've been too expensive. I signed the card, *Now am I forgiven, Southern Belle? All my love, Al.* The roses were to be delivered while Michael and I were at Jones Beach; the super in my building would hold them until we got back. The temperature that July day must have been a hundred and ten degrees, and the super's basement room was not air-conditioned. By the time we returned and Mr. Zumaya answered his buzzer, remembered where he'd stuck the box, handed it to me, and I opened it in front of Michael, the roses were brown and limp. Michael's only comment: "Who the fuck sends seven dead roses?"

Stars. Golden boys who've been the center of attention all their lives. You can never control them. Or predict how long they'll stay. Which is part of what makes them so charming. They're charming when you meet them, not so charming when they leave you for somebody else. Once they're gone, they never double back.

I finally fell in love with and married Peter, the biggest charmer of all.

I'd turned twenty-five and was beginning to wonder if I would ever meet the right man. I'd study the girl next to me on the subway, in the deli, on the elevator at work, and check out her left hand. If she was wearing an engagement ring or wedding band, I thought, *How can she find a husband when I can't?* If her ring finger was bare, I felt relieved; I had time. I'd bought the misty promise of the 1950s: husband, house, children. No, that's not quite it. Perfect husband. Perfect house. Perfect children.

Since moving to New York, I'd dreamed that a guy wearing jeans and a plaid flannel shirt with sleeves rolled above the elbows, someone strong and handsome and resourceful, who lived in an apartment one floor up, would knock on my door and ask if there was anything I needed done. I'd say yes and he'd come in and change the lightbulb in the kitchen, move the ficus plant that had grown too heavy for me to lift, fix the burner on the stove.

Peter was the man of my dreams.

We met at a Thanksgiving dinner on the Upper West Side. I hadn't dated anyone seriously since Michael—gruff, cocky Michael. Peter was southern, soft-spoken, courtly. He listened when I talked, laughed when I said something funny, expressed himself beautifully—not with flash, but with quiet self-assurance. He was in Manhattan visiting a law school buddy who gave the dinner (my roommate's boyfriend), and even though there were fifteen other people in that high-ceilinged, velvet-and-brocade apartment, Peter and I spent the evening—from turkey and beef Wellington to fruit and Roquefort cheese—talking to each other. As if we were sitting on a tip of the room that broke off.

He may have been charming, but he was not an operator. He didn't have to work at being charming. He just was. People hung on his voice, then quoted him to others. Men wanted to be like him. Women wanted to be with him.

We were married that summer in my parents' home in Rock Hill, a small wedding with thirty guests—aunts; uncles; cousins; Peter's law-school buddy and my roommate, who'd introduced us; a few other friends. The ceremony was in the living room, with lunch afterward on the screen porch. My mother had had an air-conditioning unit installed on the porch and the screens lined with clear plastic. It was the hottest August 5 on record, but inside that porch, we were as cool as the quivering Jell-O salads dotting the buffet. Mother's Christmas card the following December was a photograph of Peter and me at our wedding lunch. My veil is off my face and we're both looking up, faces bright, smiling our hearts out. This was just before I disappeared into my childhood bedroom to change into my going-away outfit—red linen sheath, matching navy patent heels and purse, short white cotton gloves. Just before we ran down the front steps to drive away for our honeymoon, rice flying for the camera, the two of us believing that day was a conclusion.

THIRTEEN

OF COURSE, there was Ann. But I understood. Anyone who knew the details of Peter's childhood would understand.

How, for years, his parents had wanted a baby, but were unable to conceive. Finally, when his mother was forty-one, she became pregnant with Peter.

His parents were sweet, gentle people, very loving. The three of them lived in Atlanta, in a stucco bungalow with a wide porch across the front. The type of house people become so attached to, they hang its portrait over the mantel.

When Peter was eight, his father was diagnosed with a malignancy in a minor salivary gland. By the time they found it, the tumor had metastasized along the nerve, and his voice box had to be removed. He communicated by scribbling messages on a tablet he kept in his shirt pocket. He had to suction out his own saliva. Six months after the surgery—Peter had just turned nine—his father choked to death. When Peter's mother told him his father had died, Peter didn't cry. Later that day, the little girl next door—Ann Cole, his best friend—said to him, "Peter, you've got to cry. Your daddy's never coming back."

Eleven months after Peter's father died, Peter's mother, who'd never been seriously ill in her life, dropped dead from an aneurysm. Peter found her on the kitchen floor, dressed for bridge club, in her stocking feet, gripping a slice of buttered toast.

After a lot of back and forth among various relatives, Peter's two unmarried aunts in Valdosta, Georgia, took him in. He used to say that Valdosta was the ugliest name ever invented. He'd lost both of his parents, and moving to that town cost him Ann, his best friend.

Peter thought his aunts were ancient when he moved in with them, but they were only in their forties. One was so shy and modest she never spoke above a whisper. Her hair was thin and dyed tar black; Peter said you could see her dandruffy scalp when she lowered her head, which was most of the time. She collected red pincushions and dolls from foreign countries, and they covered tables and chests all over the house. She owned the two-bedroom house she, her sister, and her brother (Peter's father) had grown up in; she still slept in her and her sister's ruffled childhood bedroom, hung her pink girdle to dry over the shower-curtain rod in the hall bathroom. The other aunt had been living in London for twenty years and moved back home to Valdosta to help raise Peter. This aunt was big-boned, no-nonsense, a strong golfer, even played from the men's tees. Because she took the master bedroom, Peter slept on a metal cot in the living room, as his father had done when *he* was growing up. Peter kept his clothes in the cupboard in the small dining room—underwear in a neat stack in the drawer with the straw place mats and cotton napkins, pants and shirts on top of the silverware. Every morning Peter folded up his cot and rolled it into the coat closet in the front hall. His pillow and blanket went on the shelf. Every night he unfolded the cot and made it up in the living room.

Home was such a hard, indifferent place that Peter concentrated on his studies. But because he was so athletic, his English aunt introduced him to golf, paid for lessons with the pro at Valdosta Country Club. Soon he was winning junior tournaments. Fall of his senior year in high school, he won the club championship. She made sure, though, that he always worked. He started with a paper route when he was twelve, waited tables at the Elks Club through high school, washed dishes and bussed tables in his fraternity house during college. He graduated first in his high school class, won a full scholarship to study engineering at Georgia Tech, graduated Phi Beta Kappa, decided at that point to become an attorney, did exceptionally well on his boards, left for Harvard Law, which he paid for with student loans, and never called Valdosta home again.

Peter had to achieve. He said it would have been ungrateful if he hadn't tried to repay his aunts for all they did. They gave him a home. Devoted their lives to him, even though the lives they offered were scant and bony. He believed he owed them his success.

During his first year at Harvard, the house in Valdosta burned down, with his aunts sleeping inside. Like Peter's parents' deaths, the aunts' deaths were stitched together. Every winter for years, after we were married, we drove to Valdosta on the anniversary of the aunts' deaths to visit their graves, side by side in the overgrown cemetery on the outskirts of town, beneath the scaly branches of the oldest live oak in the county.

I understood how much it meant to him when Ann found him— a couple of years before he left that gaping message on our answering machine. Ann Cole, with her soft manner, tortoiseshell combs holding her light hair back from her lovely oval face. Ann Cole, who never married. They were born one day apart. Not only had they been inseparable when they were young, their mothers had been best friends, too. Peter and Ann wrote to each other all through elementary school and high school, but after he left for Georgia Tech and she for Sophie Newcomb in New Orleans, they lost track.

When she finally found him, after searching for years, she was able to tell him a million details she remembered about his parents. How on summer evenings after dinner Peter's father would take Peter and Ann to the Dairy Queen and they would all get vanilla; "So basic," Peter's father would say with a wink. How Peter's mother was forever trying new recipes: peanut-butter fudge, candy apples with a glaze that could break your teeth (the only way to bite into them was to first crack them over the back of a wooden bridge chair), chow mein before most people in the south had even been to a Chinese restaurant. How Peter's father built a pond in the backyard, pouring cement, like sticky cake batter, into the hole he'd dug, lining it with flagstone, taking Peter and Ann to Woolworth's to select the fish. The scales of those fish were as bright and translucent as mica in the pond's brown water.

In all the years Peter lived with his aunts, they never mentioned his mother or father. And he was afraid to ask. He didn't resent this; he knew his aunts didn't want to make him sadder than he already was. Ann brought Peter back his early childhood. A time that had been totally erased.

Of course, Ann was drawn to memories of Peter's parents as much as Peter was. Both of her parents had been alcoholics, and she'd never felt she belonged in her own family. She spent more time at Peter's house than her own. His parents adored Ann, called her their "adopted girl." She'd been devastated when Peter's parents died and he moved away.

I understood. At first, there was the phone call. Ann was living in Atlanta and had called Information in random southern towns, hoping to find Peter. Out of the blue, she tried Charlotte. In the beginning they had long, consoling telephone conversations. Then, to my surprise, she bought a house twenty minutes away. She took a job as assistant principal in a new elementary school in southeast Charlotte. She said she'd been ready for a change, Atlanta had grown too big. Right after she moved, we invited her for dinner. That's when I heard all the stories. Peter had told me very little before this.

She sat across from me at the dining room table, Peter between us at the head, a smile so broad it seemed as though it might be fixed forever on his face. Ann wore tan wool slacks, a white blouse, and a pine green cardigan sweater tied around her shoulders. She was careful to include me in the conversation, looking me in the eye even as she and Peter reminisced. The only jewelry she wore was a man's antique watch with a brown alligator band; I wondered if it had been her father's. It crossed my mind that it might have belonged to Peter's father and he'd left it to her, but I didn't ask. Even though the watch had a large round face, it appeared stylish and even feminine on her small-boned wrist.

I'd wanted to keep the dinner casual, not a big deal, so I'd set the table with country French place mats rather than a tablecloth. No candlesticks, only a loose arrangement of red camellias I'd picked from the yard when it had finally stopped raining. During dinner, I noticed they were drooping with the weight of water.

EVERY NOW AND THEN, Peter and Ann went out alone. Lunch on Saturday. An occasional dinner. Peter was very upfront about this. Once, when she came by the house to drop off some old photographs, I saw him kiss her on the lips. A quick kiss, but definitely on the lips. I would never kiss anyone *but* Peter on the lips. I also noticed he cupped the back of her head with his hand instead of just lightly touching her shoulder or arm—a gesture that made the kiss seem even more intimate. Still, such an attractive woman so obviously crazy about my husband—I talked myself into believing this said something good about me.

I didn't like it when Joy said, "There are no accidents." Implying the friendship between Ann and Peter might be more than friendship. She'd spotted them through the front window of an Italian restaurant in southeast Charlotte late on a Friday afternoon. But Peter had already told me they were meeting there for about an hour to go over some old letters Ann had found. Joy said I lacked a "built-in shit detector," that my best trait was my worst trait and the very thing that drew me to the magic of movies was what made me gullible and unrealistic in my everyday life.

"The more clearly we see the world, the better we can deal with the world," she said, quoting one of those books she was always reading.

Joy and her New Age thinking. Her brassy bangle bracelets, beaded necklaces, dangly earrings. Her herbal tea steeping in the sun. Juice fasts. Weekend silent retreats. She saw connections everywhere. Believed in synchronicity and closure. Believed in the planets—or maybe it was the stars—lining up in the universe, causing certain things to happen, or not to happen. She used to look me square in the face, her well-intentioned, unlined face earnest. "Kathryne, dear Kathryne," she'd say, "you must open the door of your own awareness."

FOURTEEN

E ARLY CAME IN from baseball practice after seven. We sat down to chicken, twice-baked potatoes, and salad. I picked at my dinner, wasn't hungry, made myself eat. He had seconds. Told me about school and practice. I brightened, hearing his details. He went upstairs to study, saying he wanted to turn out his light at nine (he'd been up early that morning for a yearbook meeting). I scraped the dishes, washed the pans, spooned leftover chicken and potatoes into a Pyrex dish that turned out to be too big, but I wasn't in the mood to transfer everything to a smaller container and then have to wash the Pyrex.

The phone rang. Unusually loud. It was the Mother's March of Dimes wanting to know if I'd collect door-to-door next month.

I sat down in the den to wait, tried to concentrate on the morning paper. The lead story was about a man who was quoted as saying, "I didn't rape the eight women the cops said I did. They counted it as rape if I had sex with a woman I didn't love."

I thought about the idea of truth in the world, this matter of facing reality. How two people can view the same incident so differently. "You did such and such," one person will insist. "I did nothing of the kind," the other person argues. Maybe it all comes down to this: We witness life's events as though we're seated several seats apart, which makes it seem as though one person has a blind side, when actually, the angle for viewing may simply be different from the next person's.

The clock in the hall cleared its throat. Nine-thirty on the dot. Then, Peter's key in the lock. The dull clunk of the bolt.

He looked tired. His tie was loose, collar wilted, yellow oxford shirt open at the neck, which, I noticed, was reddish and irritated looking—different from the way his neck looked in the morning after he shaved, when the skin was slightly chalky. He walked over to the sofa; his kiss brushed the top of my head, a grandfather kind of kiss. He sank down in the cushions of his brown leather chair. My eyes scanned the table beside his chair: the stack of bonsai books, the ceramic rooster lamp, my collection of glass paperweights.

Now he and I were staring at each other. Like two people sizing each other up on a blind date. He crossed and recrossed his legs. I focused on his leg muscles stretching the dark fabric of his trousers.

"Hey," he said.

"Hey," I said back.

"I suppose you heard my message."

"Well, yes. I'm not sure I understand it—"

"I should not have started this conversation on an answering machine, I know," he said quietly. "I know."

We stared at each other again. Now it was more like two people who'd come through a bout of amnesia, trying to remember who the person across the room was and why he or she seemed so important.

Finally, he said, "For a long time I've been in . . . knots."

My lips were dry. The kind of dry you get before a speech you're not the least bit ready to make. My throat felt dry, too. I cleared it. Rubbed my hands together. They were dry. Papery. They needed lotion. I wanted water. I wanted lotion. I wanted Chap Stick. I wanted *not* to know what was coming next.

But I knew.

"My parents," he was saying, "they were the parents you'd have if you could design the perfect parents. I had as idyllic a life as a child could have. Whatever made me happy made them happy. Oh, I had limits, but they were always fair and reasonable. My parents never had to discipline me because I would never want to disappoint them, in any way."

This was about his parents?

"I knew how much they loved me and believed in me, and I would not let them down. Then it was over. Like that." He snapped his fingers. "And my life changed as much as a life could change. That's when I suppose I . . . shut myself off. I had to stop feeling because otherwise, it would have been unbearable. The first nine years of my life were all about love. The last thirty-four have been about duty. All I have left are my responsibilities. I've taken them seriously and fulfilled them. I live, eat, sleep responsibility." He was gesturing with his hands, making slicing motions to punctuate "live," "eat," "sleep." "And I'm tired of doing that."

This was about work? Had he done something—unethical maybe—in the office? Impossible.

"In fact, this is what I've passed on to my son. Duty. Not love. I've done the same thing to Early that Aunt Edith and Aunt Mary did to me. Love may be what fuels that acute kind of ambition for one's child, but all the child sees is a frightful monster—and its name is *d-u-t-y*."

Spelling that word must have been like putting a period at the end of a long sentence. He stopped talking.

We stared at each other again. Maybe I didn't know what this was about. He looked as though he was surprised at what he'd said, too, and that maybe he had no idea what was coming next.

"Is all this about Early?" I asked. A subject I did not mind talking about—how Peter had made mistakes as a parent. Maybe he'd come to realize I was not overprotective, that my way of raising Early was correct. That he'd been too strict with him, his expectations unrealistically high.

"Well, no," he said. Nervous eye motions. Well-groomed head perfectly still. "It's about us."

Dryness again. Lips, throat, hands. I licked my lips, tried to swallow, ended up making a gulping sound. I had the feeling that whatever was coming next would be too big for me.

"Kathryne, what I'm saying is . . . I've done something I'm very ashamed of . . . something that is extremely hurtful to you . . . and I have to tell you about it. I can't keep it a secret any longer."

I did not like secrets. My belief was, if you had to have a secret, then you should just keep it. Don't go spilling it all over the place. Too dangerous, bringing things to light. "Are you sure you have to tell me?"

"I don't want to continue living a dishonest life—"

"Some things are better left unsaid, you know."

"I need to get this off my chest—"

"If you—"

"See, the thing is . . . Ann and I . . . well, what I want to say is . . . she . . . I . . . I slept with her."

I heard his words and know that it sounds crazy and naive and maybe just flat-out ridiculous, but in my mind, I flipped them over to mean *all they did* was sleep together. Two adults—like teenage girls at a spend-the-night party—sleeping in the same bed, out of necessity. Not enough beds to go around. They simply shared sleeping space for a night.

But no, as much as I wanted that to be the case, it was not what he was saying. I tried to concentrate, tried to hold on to the meaning of his words, as though I were taking my own face in my hands and forcing myself to look.

"You slept with her?" I said, determined to be real. Not slide away from this moment we were in.

". . . to you and me," he was saying at the same time.

"Wait. Say what you just said again. I couldn't hear."

"You couldn't hear? At what point did you stop listening?"

"It's not that I stopped listening. I just stopped being able to hear. What did you say when I asked if you actually fucked her?" There. Use the word you would never normally use. Call a spade a spade. Talk straight to this man with the strong morals, whose whole life has been about rules and doing the right thing.

"What I said is, there's no way I can justify what I did." His voice was thick and low. "It happened . . . well, it happened only one time, and that is the absolute truth. But I was dead wrong, and I feel sick about it. I suppose I believed, down deep, that Ann could help me develop the part of my life that collapsed when my parents died. She could be my ticket out. Or in, I suppose I should say. I wanted my happiness back. I wanted what was taken away from me. She was my link to my parents. She represented . . . all those lost years."

"And how would sleeping with Ann help you get those years back?" His explanation sounded like the world's scrawniest excuse. I was furious. But at the same time, I didn't want to *appear* furious. *Calm down*, I told myself. *You don't have to look like a squinty shrew.*

When I think back to that conversation, a number of things bother me, not the least being that my husband was telling me he'd slept with another woman and I was concerned with how I looked!

"Well, I understand now that I can't rely on another person to hand me my life," Peter was saying. "I've got to do that myself. It's not so much what happens to us in life as what we do with it."

The familiar pattern. The comfort and promise of people we know very well repeating themselves. I felt myself softening.

"Before I came home tonight, I stopped by Ann's—"

He was just there! In her house! I knew that house. Not long after she'd moved to Charlotte, I'd driven past, just to see.

Now I was picturing him driving there: Partridge Circle. All the brand-new brick houses with their fake Palladian windows, perched on small hills like a fake San Francisco. So different from old, established Myers Park, where we lived. I imagined Peter driving his silver Volvo up Ann's steep driveway, engaging the emergency brake, the hoarse groan of it. He'd walk across the newly planted grass, past a newly planted sapling, to the newly painted pea green front door— did he use that door or some side door? Or did he use the back door? Did he have his own key?

"... and I told her this was not going to work—"

"This? What's *this*? *What* is not going to work?" Her or me?

"Being in contact with Ann is not going to work." He got up from his chair and came over to sit beside me on the sofa, close, our hips touching. I drew my legs to my body. He put his arm around me. His hand fell on my shoulder, heavy, as though he were showing me the effect of gravity, how the weight of something can make it fall.

I felt his closeness. I felt my nerve endings—their delicate network—closer than normal to the surface of my skin.

"I want to stay married to you," he was saying. "All I can do is ask for your forgiveness. I'm sorry. I'm deeply sorry for what I've done to you. For what I've done to our marriage. Ann understands why it happened, and she agrees it cannot continue. She's thinking she might move back home to Atlanta. When school is out. As far as she's concerned . . . being in Charlotte . . . seeing me . . . going over the details of her childhood and my childhood is what she was after all along. Although she didn't know this when she moved here. Now that she's gotten what she came for, she's ready to go back home and put together a new life for herself."

"She's gotten what she came for?"

"I didn't mean that the way it sounded," he said. "What she came for was a reconnection to her own past. And now she's ready to begin again. I need to do that, too, only I can do it right here." He was weaving the fingers of his left hand through the fingers of both my hands. My hands were cold; his were colder. "I love you, Kathryne. This is the only real, permanent home I've ever had. This is my home. With you."

I remembered a recent Ann Landers column. A woman had written in about her husband "straying"—which always sounded to me more like a dog than a person—and Ann Landers advised her to forgive him. At the time I thought the woman should tell her husband to take a hike. What right did he have to destroy their marriage, break promises, ask for forgiveness? How could the wife be sure it wouldn't happen again? I was furious with the husband for what he'd done to his wife, furious with Ann Landers for giving such bad advice. Wake up and smell the coffee, I wanted to say to Ann Landers and to the woman.

But sitting there beside Peter, hearing his voice, seeing his face, I knew what my answer would be. He did, too. It was the only answer I knew how to give.

FIFTEEN

T HE MOON through the window was bright as chalk, and full. A blue moon. I always liked knowing what that means—that there's a full moon twice in the same month. Something returning, coming back for more.

Peter was asleep in our bed; I was in the den. Two in the morning. Hours since our talk. The house so still I could feel it settling.

I wanted the two of us to stay together. The couples you see walking hand in hand—I wanted that. And, I wanted everyone to *think* we had that. I felt that I was born to be successful. If Peter left me, it would mean I'd failed at marriage, failed my son. I couldn't go out and admit I'd failed. Didn't want people to look at me and whisper behind my back, "Oh, she's divorced." I believed Peter when he said it wouldn't happen again. This time I knew we'd get it right. And anyway, I wanted Early to have a mom and a dad; Early needed us. I had every confidence Peter would wake up one day and say he was glad he'd stayed.

A S UNLIKELY AS IT SEEMS, right after our conversation Peter plunged into his files and papers at the kitchen table. I went to bed, listened to the bats cutting zigzag paths across the backyard, their oily voices. It wasn't long before I heard Peter in his closet, hanging up his tie and blazer, folding his pants over a wooden hanger, then in the bathroom, flushing the toilet. I was still awake when he pulled the down comforter over himself. I lay there, not moving, facing away from him, the clock on my bedside table humming, the huge expanse of sheet between us. I knew I could not sleep in the same bed with him. Not that night.

When I heard his breathing deepen, I threw off the covers and quietly slipped out of the room.

I curled up in his leather chair with a book I'd checked out of the library, a biography of Katharine Hepburn. I opened it to the chapter on *The African Queen,* to a description of the actual filming, most of which took place on location in Uganda, on the Lualaba River. The author even quoted my favorite line from the movie, spoken by Rose, Katharine Hepburn's character: *Nature, Mr. Alnutt, is what we are put in this world to rise above.*

At that point, I wondered how it would be for Peter and me to have sex, wondered if we would ever have sex again. Even before this happened, we were going weeks without it. He'd always had a strong sex drive, but mine was beginning to dwindle. I'd experienced menopause early and had decided not to take hormones (I don't believe in taking even an aspirin unless it's absolutely necessary), so everything was going dry. Unless I used lubricants with names like Replens or Astroglide (surely a man invented that one!), making love could be painful. Now that I thought about it, Peter had been less interested, too. I wondered how those two young people who, in the early years, used to fall into each other wherever they happened to be—in the shower, on the living room floor, in the kitchen of that one-bedroom furnished apartment across Park Road from Billy Graham's birthplace—how we got to this: thinking of love as a once-a-month event, having to use a cream so sticky it made my fingers clump together like a mitten. I still wanted the intimacy that sex brought, being held close, skin to skin. The warm, comforting broth that sex was.

Would we ever have sex again, now that I knew about Ann?

Peter and Ann. My thoughts sprinted wildly when I tried to picture the two of them together. In bed. Naked. Kissing. His veiny arms around her delicate shoulders. Legs over legs. When I tried to take it further, my mind switched off. Legs, sheets, stop.

What would it be like with Peter now?

Would he find me desirable? Was I as pretty as Ann? As sexy?

I thought of a time my faithful, steadfast father had not been so faithful and steadfast. I don't know that the incident meant that much, really, but it opened possibilities I didn't want to see open. I was ten. It was a Sunday night and my family was watching Ed Sullivan's *Toast of the Town*. My father and Billy were on the sofa. Mother was in the wing chair across the room, next to the double windows. I lay across the hooked rug, close to the walnut-stained console that held our TV, radio, and record player.

The show's first act was a magician, a slight man wearing a tuxedo pressed so stiff it looked like cardboard. Accordion music, which I've always thought was the saddest music on earth, played in the background: "Ah, Sweet Mystery of Life," the song my father hummed every morning while he shaved at the bathroom sink. The magician placed his palms flat on a plain, square table. The table jiggled, then began to rise. Soon the table was moving around the stage, and the magician was practically galloping to keep up with it.

He looked like a woman trying to dance with a man who felt the music in strange ways. I knew there was a trick to what he was doing, but I could not, for the life of me, figure it out.

My brother was fourteen. Photography was not his only hobby; he was also fascinated with magic. He was always ordering books from a place in Newark, New Jersey, called Power Publishers—*How to Make Money with Hypnotism, How to Develop an Alarm-Clock Mind.* Billy said, "Oh, that's easy. What a fake! What a royal fake! There's a little thing in the back . . ."

"That's right," my father said. "You've got it." I think he even tousled my brother's hair.

The act ended; Ed Sullivan came out from behind the curtains, cracked a few jokes that weren't really jokes. Then, wringing his hands, he said, "Let's give a fine welcome to our next guest, Denise Darcel." And there she was, dramatic as ever, in black and white—in our den!

I watched my father watch her cross the stage: her long blond hair, strapless gown, the way she reached for the microphone stand with one heartless finger. My father put aside his newspaper, uncrossed his legs, slid over to get rid of the reflection of Mother's lamp on the TV screen. Then he actually gave a little whistle. That's the part that got me. The whistle. A grown man! My dignified father. Whistling at the television set!

I looked at Mother. She was cross-stitching a tablecloth that draped over her lap and fell in loose folds onto the rug. She stuck the needle—the size of a stripped tail feather—into the bleached linen, pulled it through, lengthening the thread, stuck the needle in, pulled it through. In. Through. In. Through. Was it my imagination or was she speeding up?

I can't be sure how much of my memory of that evening comes from what I actually remember and what merged over time with my family's account. In any case, the story goes that I got up, walked over to my father, patted his shoulder to quiet whatever had been awakened in him, and said with the innocent southern drawl I had then: "Don't think about Denise Darcel for one minute, Daddy. You've already got a pretty wife."

SIXTEEN

DURING THE NEXT FEW WEEKS, Peter and I had suppers together in the kitchen. With long, devouring silences expanding as the night went on. We went to a cocktail party at his law partner's house, where he talked with the men all evening and I talked with the wives. As usual, people sought him out, started long conversations with him, asked his opinion about this or that, told him funny stories. If he walked into the living room, where I was, I excused myself from the conversation to go into the study for a drink. If we were both in the dining room, we made sure he was on one side of the lace-covered table and I was on the other. Without looking directly at each other, we were acutely aware of where the other was.

The days dragged by. I previewed a confusing, incoherent action movie and wrote the most negative review I'd ever written; Peter went to the office. I emptied the dishwasher, he took out the trash. We discussed the Visa bill, why L.L. Bean charged us twice for the jacket I ordered, and did I buy anything for $29.90 from a store called B. Watson. (Yes, a purple sweatshirt with a black-and-white felt cat on the front.) I picked up his resoled loafers at the shoe-repair shop behind the drugstore. He had my windshield wipers replaced. While he sat in the chair across from the bed, peeling off his navy socks, slowly, tiredly, and I sat at the dressing table smoothing almond-scented moisturizing lotion on my face and neck, we complained to each other about the neighbor's yappy dog.

Peter pinched and pruned a new juniper for better balance. "Let 'em know who's boss," he liked to say about his bonsai trees.

He brought a new client home for dinner. A boring man with thick, prominent eyebrows who talked with his mouth full about a new kind of phone he was trying to patent. A phone that didn't have to be plugged in.

I gave a speech at a nursing home about the year's best films.

Peter and I slept in the same bed, an imaginary line drawn down the middle. Sunday mornings, we made up the bed together. I pulled the comforter too far over to my side; he pulled it too far over to his; both of us moved to the foot of the bed to try to figure out how to make it even.

I thought of the movie *The Reivers*. As the boy returns home—riding back into town—he can't understand how life there can continue to be so normal when such monumental things have happened to him while he was away.

I understood that boy's bewilderment as I took care of the ordinary tasks necessary to maintain a life, one step at a time, not covering much territory—all this after the scaffolding of my life had collapsed.

Why did Peter have to tell me? Why couldn't he have kept quiet? Why didn't he spare me his sad little secret and keep things the same between us?

I definitely didn't want anyone to know. Joy asked several times if something was wrong. I never liked telling her the details of what I was going through while I was going through it. That would feel like having strangers rummage in my underwear drawer. *Hmm, so this is the size bra Kathryne wears,* they'd say. *And these are her panties.* I did not like to tell her about a situation until after it was over, when I knew the outcome. Joy confided everything. It was easy for her. She said that talking about a problem while she was in the middle of it helped her understand what she thought. "How do I know what I mean until I see what I say?" she'd say, quoting E. M. Forster, her favorite author.

I wasn't ready to tell her about Peter.

We were on her patio. She was stretched out on a chaise—bare feet, tanned legs, Indian-cotton dark-print wraparound skirt, black halter top, beaded earrings, glistening forearms. I was in the rocking chair, and suddenly remembered the night she and I had met—at a film festival at the Visualite Art Theater. It was the summer after her husband had died. I introduced the film and afterward she came up to me to say that she enjoyed my reviews in *Charlotte Magazine.* She was not the type of person I was usually drawn to; in the first five minutes of our conversation, she told me about her husband's massive heart attack while they were hiking at Grandfather Mountain, how she was just now beginning to go out alone. Too much information too fast, I remember thinking. But something about her honesty and newly acquired self-confidence appealed to me. I also loved her looks, her style.

She'd just cleaned her patio with bleach. The mildew and moss were gone and the brick was bright and rust-colored. Large Italian terra-cotta pots were soft with oregano, basil so tall it was blooming, bronze fennel, sage, all kinds of thyme. One pot next to me overflowed with lemon thyme and I could smell it—such tiny leaves, such a huge scent. The sun was directly over us. I wanted to take from the afternoon everything it had to give.

"A lot has been going on," I started out. "Everything's great—"

"Kathryne, whenever you say everything's great, I know everything is not great. You know how you do that."

"Things are fine. Really."

"Is this true?"

"What do you mean, 'true'? Of course it's true. Life couldn't be better." Sometimes I was so afraid I'd say what I was thinking, I ended up going overboard the other way.

"Kathryne."

"Really." I buried my index finger in the soil around the lemon thyme, pulled my finger out, filled in the hole I'd made.

"Nothing's going on," she said. I knew what she was doing. She was letting me know she'd heard what I'd said and didn't believe a word of it. She leaned forward, toward me, her back away from the chaise.

"Really, nothing," I answered.

"Kathryne, dear Kathryne! Reality! This is not the movies."

"Well."

"Tell me." She pushed her face closer. Her neck was smooth.

I ended up telling the whole story. In spite of myself.

"I knew it," she said, flopping back. "I just knew it. In fact, I tried to tell you, didn't I? About Peter and Ann?"

"You did. You tried."

"But I'm so sorry you're having to go through this." She pointed to something leafy near the gate. "See the oak-leaf hydrangea I just put in? All the weeds coming up around it?"

"Well, yes."

"I just found out that weed seeds can remain in the ground, dormant for fifty years, or even more. Which is why you can plant something new in your garden, and all of a sudden weeds you've never seen before will start appearing everywhere. When you dig in the soil, you stir up those old, long-forgotten seeds and bring them to the surface. I have a feeling that's what's happening with Peter. He's been digging deep, and parts of his life from a long time ago have started cropping up."

I studied the hydrangea. Its leaves were the size of a woman's hand. The shrub was leggy, but weeds hid its bare stalks like a skirt.

"You know, Kathryne, for a difficult situation, it's as good as it could be. To admit you've made a mistake and say you regret it and it will never happen again—well, you can't ask a person for more than that. I have to admire Peter for how he's handled this. Not everyone can say I'm sorry."

Joy could always show me new ways of looking at a situation. As though she turned it over in her hand, and suddenly there were angles or curves I could not possibly have seen before. Who would have thought to marvel over Peter's apology?

I sat there nodding, my hands in my lap open.

"What's it like living with him now that you have this information?"

I stopped to think. I didn't know the answer. "The same. It's the same."

"The same?"

"Days pass, we keep pressing on. We don't talk about it. What else is there for us to say?"

"Well, did she move yet?"

"Did she—"

"Did Ann leave Charlotte?"

"I don't know."

"Aren't you curious? I mean, what if she's still around?"

"That's not really any of my business." I hated to think she might still be here.

"And you and Peter don't say a word about it? There was just that one conversation? If it were me, I'd be coming up with a million questions."

"Like what?"

"Oh, I don't know. I guess I'd want to keep talking about it until I had an understanding of what caused the problem in the first place."

"Well, what would you ask?"

"I'd want to know if he ever thought he was in love with Ann. Is he saying he won't see her again, even as a friend? What's he doing to get his life back on track? Is he seeing a therapist? Will he make any changes? And what about the things he said regarding Early? Is Peter going to have a talk with him? Try to explain to Early how he feels—about the two of them? You did say, Kathryne, that Peter was concerned about the kind of father he's been?"

That last question took me back to the day Neil Armstrong walked on the moon. Peter and I had been driving with two-month-old Early to Ft. Lauderdale. We'd gotten as far as St. Augustine when the moon walk was about to take place. Peter checked us into a Holiday Inn near the highway, and as soon as we were in the room, he clicked on the TV and held Early—his little chicken legs dangling—up to the screen. He said that years later he wanted to be able to tell Early they'd seen this together. I'd loved his being so excited about a closeness with his son. As excited as he'd been about the astronaut bouncing weightlessly in moon dust.

"Well, yes. I guess I could ask Peter." I'd almost forgotten what she'd asked. "But don't you think when he's ready to talk to me about those things, he will? Is it right for me to pressure him into discussing something he may not be ready to discuss?"

"Kathryne, dear Kathryne, you are so funny! Why do you give Peter such wide margins? Are you afraid of losing him?"

"He's just sorting things out. When he says he loves me and wants our marriage to work, I believe him." Joy was looking at me. An intense gaze. My eyes shifted to the brick wall over her shoulder. The mortar was thick and messy. Everywhere at Joy's there were wonderful textures. "Besides, you know Peter. Emotions aren't his strong suit."

"I think I know why you and Peter were attracted to each other! Neither of you is into examining your life too closely!" Joy laughed a soft laugh and came over to pick an eyelash off my cheek. She leaned in, blocking the sun, and the cool was a relief. Her olive skin is so flawless, I thought, she could model cosmetics. The stain of pink in her cheeks very natural. Everything about her was natural. Her looks. Her manner. Her wisdom.

"We need to be on nodding terms with our real selves," she said. "Otherwise, they keep turning up and asking us the really hard questions."

Later I was surprised and alarmed I'd told her anything at all. It was so *not* my way. Suddenly all those intimate details felt true and stark in a way they hadn't before. Telling something means that it's real. Worse than that, it can forever change the image others have of you. I wished I could take it all back.

SEVENTEEN

PETER HAD COVERED the ottoman with newspaper and was sitting in the leather chair, removing the dead leaves from an elm bonsai with tweezers, leaf by tiny leaf. I was at the game table, sipping ginger ale, beginning my review of the new Woody Allen movie, *The Purple Rose of Cairo*. I was writing about the scene where the actor steps right out of the movie screen. All of a sudden I felt a whiskery hair on my chin, which made me think of something Joy had once said. She refused to think of them as chin hairs. Stray eyebrows, she called them.

Peter lifted the tree from the newspaper for me to see.

"How do you know which side is the front?" I asked.

"Well, you're right. Sometimes the front *is* hard to identify," he said.

"Does a tree ever have two fronts?"

"That'd be like having two faces. Bonsai people say if you can't find the front, look for the back, then turn it around!"

I was glad to hear him joking. Glad to pretend things were okay between us. Part of me wondered if I'd made a mistake, not asking him the questions Joy had raised. Of course she hadn't asked me the big question: Did I love Peter? Certainly, he and I had more in common than just a son. Standing side by side in my parents' living room all those years ago, we'd recited the vows we'd written ourselves (I'd talked him into that) as though they could be a compass for love and would help us find our own world. We'd been alive with expectation. But what *had* we expected? That we'd satisfy all of the other's needs? That we'd forgive each other, once we realized total satisfaction was impossible? Is this what love comes down to? Two people trying to convince themselves that the newly discovered imperfections in the other mean nothing?

In the beginning, I'd loved Peter's strong principles, clear thinking, the cleanliness and orderliness of him. He was a good person. When had he become rigid, compulsive, cold? He'd fallen in love with my warmth, my beauty (yes, I'd loved his beauty, too). Maybe now he was wondering why I'd changed in certain ways.

When had resignation settled over our marriage? And when did we position our son between us?

I was barely conscious of how indulgent I was with Early. I was more conscious of his inability to keep his father interested in him, although maybe all Peter wanted was to teach his son to be independent, to function on his own. If only I'd allowed Peter in. If only he and I could have tempered each other by moving an inch or so closer in attitude, instead of pushing in opposite directions and forcing the other to take himself to the extreme. We parented like two kids trying to balance on a seesaw. One slides back, inch by inch, in hopes of offsetting the heavier one, until the lightweight eventually just drops off.

P ETER WAS STILL HOLDING THE TREE, turning it slowly for my benefit. I understood his fascination with bonsai, how those young trees could be made to look as though they'd withstood harsh winds and the passage of time. At one time, we'd pictured the same for ourselves, that we would float into the future, growing old together.

E ARLY WALKED IN from studying with Amy Whitley. He handed Peter his class schedule for next year, eleventh grade. I was surprised he didn't bring it to me. Well, he didn't actually *give* the form to Peter; he held it out for him to take. Peter glanced at it, slowly sliding the tree and newspaper down to the Oriental rug.

"Advanced English. Good." Peter's eyes moved down the form, which Early was still holding. Peter stood for a minute, straightened his pants, pressed his fists into his back, stretching, then sank back down into the cushion of the sprung chair. When he stood, I could have sworn I caught a whiff of lemon aftershave or cologne. Why would there be such a strong scent at nine at night when he'd splashed it on early that morning?

"Chemistry, American history. French. Looks fine. Clay Matters? What's Clay Matters?"

"It's a really cool elective I'm taking. Ceramics. An easy A-plus."

Early stood next to his father's chair, loose-limbed and malleable. Peter dug his heels into the ottoman to drag it closer, then stretched his strong, tight legs across. Why didn't Peter just take the form from him and tell him to sit down? Like in the article I'd read in the business section of the paper, how an employer, comfortably seated in his office, will keep an employee at a distance and in his place by not inviting him to sit.

"There are so many fine electives offered at Randolph Academy," Peter said. "I can't help but wonder why you'd choose pottery. Why not Shakespeare? Or art history? Or music appreciation? You don't want to take a class just because it's easy. You want to broaden your horizons, son, expand your intellect."

"Dad, they don't say pottery anymore. It's called ceramics. And Chip told me it's a great class. He's taking it, too." Early shifted his weight to the other foot and bit his cuticle.

He and his father stared at the paper between them.

"Another not-so-good reason for taking a class. Lord knows, you two spend enough time together without taking the same classes." Peter directed his comments to the paper.

"Not classes. *Class.* This would be our only one. In fact, the whole time we've been in high school, we've only taken one class together. That's why—"

"There's a pottery teacher at Randolph Academy?"

"A new teacher. Mr. Hamrick. Actually, he's an English teacher but since he knows a lot about ceramics—"

"He's an English teacher and he's not teaching English?"

Finally, Peter took the form. He held it by its upper corners, as if it had a bad smell.

This was making me squirm. Normally, Peter did not believe in picking a fight. He knew how to get what he wanted with diplomacy. His own gentle brand of persuasion. He was pushing hard now, though; Early was the only person who provoked this kind of behavior in him.

"No, I mean he's teaching this class along with his regular English classes," Early was saying.

Peter shot me a look. I started drawing in the margin of my paper. The same female faces I used to draw when I was little. They were always in profile. With their perfect noses, perfect lips, perfect chins, perfect hair.

When I sensed that Peter was no longer looking in my direction, I rolled my gaze to Early's face. He was still chewing his cuticles.

"Mr. Hamrick's supposed to be great, Dad," Early said. "Chip told me that Julie, his old girlfriend, had him for English this year and she said he's the best teacher she ever had. She signed up for ceramics next year, too. An A-plus will help my GPA a lot. I've got a three-point-five going into final exams. That's not bad. If I can raise my average a little, I'll be pretty high up in my class. Maybe even in the running for a Morehead Scholarship."

"High up? With your mind, you should be number one. Without having to take crip courses. Who in your class is brighter than you? I can't imagine your *not* winning a scholarship." He stopped, but I knew he was not finished with that thought. "I'll tell you why you're not first in your class. One word: Chip." He practically snorted when he said Chip's name. "Chip's going to have a tough time getting into *any* college with his grades, and he's deciding your schedule? That's quite an academic adviser you've chosen for yourself!"

"Peter," I said. It was obvious why Chip was taking ceramics. And it was disappointing to see Early following him. Still, shouldn't we allow Early to make his own decisions?

"Dad."

"Son, why did Chip all of a sudden quit playing tennis? And what about that hair? Does he actually think a ponytail looks good?"

"Dad! Chip was a great tennis player. He just got burned out. Don't you ever get tired of doing the same thing day after day? Who'd you hear that from anyway?" I couldn't stand hearing Early try so hard. And I couldn't believe Peter was repeating something I'd told him in confidence.

"His hair, you like it?"

"Peter!" I felt almost dizzy.

"Answer my question, Early. Do you like the way Chip wears his hair?"

"I don't know, it doesn't bother me. Anyway, it's his hair and he can wear it any way he wants. It's just his way of showing his individuality, which isn't easy to do at a school like Randolph, where everybody's trying to be like everybody else. It's a free country. He can do whatever he wants."

"You can do whatever you want," Peter said, "but you have to pay the bill when it comes due. Aren't there rules about how you can wear your hair at school?"

"Listen, Dad, you don't understand Chip. He's a creative person. All that time he spent playing tennis, well, what he really wants to do is play his music. Anyway, who told you he quit tennis?"

"What kind of music does he play?"

"He just started taking guitar."

"He already knows he wants to play his music, and he just started taking lessons?" Peter always said that lawyers never ask a question they don't already know the answer to.

"He's written a song every day for the past three months. He's got tons of 'em. And he's real good on the guitar. He can play by ear."

Peter made a sound like *ahem,* and said sharply, "You don't need to be hanging around him so much. You have plenty of other friends at school. Steven Todd. Eddie Jackson. Look what Eddie's done with his life. Against great odds. Didn't he just win the J. L. Beck Endowed Minority Scholarship?"

"He did."

"And also, Brian whatever-his-name-is."

"Coddington."

"Coddington? Who's Coddington?"

"Brian Coddington. That's who you were talking about."

"Well, anyway, those boys work hard in school and they're involved in extracurricular activities. I don't want to see Chip in this house every other day." He scraped a piece of lint from the arm of the chair, rolled it between his fingers, and flicked it to the floor. "Another thing, I think it would be good experience for you to get a job this summer."

Get a job? A job was the last thing he needed. Summer vacations were for relaxing. The year before, Peter had said that Early should get a job, but I'd told him not to worry about it.

"I saw a sign at Häagen-Dazs," Peter was saying. "They're hiring."

"Dad! Why are you so against Chip? We've been best friends since my first day at Randolph. Maybe he's got a few problems. But who doesn't? He's real well liked. Everybody thinks he's cool. He's funny. And he's supertalented. He's my oldest friend."

Here's what went through my mind: Yes, Peter can be very convincing. And yes, I had many of the same concerns he had about Chip's influence. But it was comfortable for me to settle in to Early's side. Seeing things through his eyes felt *right* to me, like being home. Listening to the two of them go back and forth, hearing the strain in Early's voice, was more than I could take. How would I like it if someone told me I couldn't be friends with Joy? Would Peter want to be told whom he could play golf with? What right did he have to choose Early's friends? Chip had been floundering, but he'd pull himself together. All adolescents have problems. Do we drop him just because he's going through a tough time?

And whatever happened to Peter's promise to go easy on Early? I was glad I hadn't told Peter anything other than the fact that Chip was quitting tennis. He didn't need extra ammunition. (Of course I hadn't told him *how* I happened to know that.) Beneath it all, I had a basic trust in our son and in his ability to make good decisions; I did not believe he would allow himself to be influenced too negatively by Chip.

I anchored my chin with my thumb and suddenly saw myself standing beside my father, not getting what I wanted. Like in a dream, when one person dissolves into somebody else—Peter and Early were now my father and me.

My first year in high school, I'd brought home a report card with all A's and glowing teachers' comments. My father was reading, surrounded by his solemn monuments of books, tall stacks of biographies and history that flanked his chair and never seemed to recede because he just kept replacing the ones he'd read. He raised his eyes, glanced at the report card still in my hand, and said, "Good, Kathryne." Then he went back to his reading. I wanted to pull his arms around me.

All those years, not getting what I wanted from my father.

When Early bit his cuticles, my fingers stung.

NOW EARLY WAS UP IN HIS ROOM, getting ready for bed. Peter moved the newspaper and bonsai tree back onto the ottoman and was just sitting there, staring at the dwarf he'd created. I thought of something he'd said many times, that if you remove a bonsai tree from its shallow pot and plant it in a deep pot so its roots are no longer confined, the tree will revert to normal growth.

If Peter would just stop directing Early, I thought, and treat him the way he treats his business and golfing pals—with that same good-natured chumminess—Early would grow up fine.

I decided to finish my movie review. No need to say anything to Peter. It seemed hopeless to try to change him. I would simply do what *I* thought was best for our son. I picked up my ginger ale and took a swallow. The curved glass was cold and wet and left a blurry *O* in the mahogany. I rubbed it away with my sleeve.

THE NEXT WEEK Peter was busy at work with a new client, a company trying to get a patent to use the methane gas emitted by turkey manure to fuel the heat in turkey houses. Peter was gone before Early left for school, stayed late in the office, and brought home papers that kept him at the table in the den until long after Early—and I—went to bed. When Peter had free time, he was on the golf course or working with some committee at the Y. I didn't bother enforcing the rules he'd laid out the evening Early had brought home the form. Early and I just worked around his father. Early's schedule for the following year was set: English, French, American history, chemistry, Clay Matters. Chip was coming around as often as ever. And Early was not going to look for a job that summer.

EIGHTEEN

I suppose I knew, on some level, there were truths that were unavailable to me at the time. I didn't set out to ignore them. I just couldn't quite grasp them. I never imagined those truths would one day come for me with such a vengeance. There was no way I could see how polarized Peter and I were becoming, how we were working against and undermining each other. The tighter I held on to Early in my way, the tighter Peter held on to Early in his way. Looking back, I wonder if there was an unconscious impulse in Early to flee.

Occasionally, I thought I heard a terrible sigh, a tapping on the wall—signs that should have brought me to my senses. But I couldn't be sure of what I was hearing. And anyway, I was busy raising a son, being a wife, going through the simple acts of daily life I happily, almost hypnotically, concerned myself with.

TWO WEEKS LATER, Peter and I flew to New Orleans. I hadn't been since my tenth-grade class trip, when I made out with my boyfriend on the train all the way there and back. I didn't learn one thing about New Orleans history or culture. Teachers, school, parents matter so little to adolescents; it's all about peers.

Peter's conference was at the Hilton. He had meetings all day our first day, so I slept late, took my time showering and getting dressed, called Barbara Dunham to find out how Early was. (He was staying with them.) Barbara was almost out the door for a facial, said he was fine. She didn't take the time to give even a sketchy report. I'd already thought about calling again that night so I could talk to Early, just to hear his voice. Now I decided I'd definitely call, since Barbara reported so little.

I took a cab to Café du Monde for breakfast. It was after ten and the café was full.

I found a table over on the side, next to the railing. An Asian girl took my order. She held the pen in that awkward way young people today seem to favor, four fingers and thumb all pinching the pen. Made me wonder if her mother had tried to teach her to hold it correctly when she was learning to write.

Less than two feet from my table, out on the sidewalk, a tall, slender mime dressed like Uncle Sam stood dead still, one eyebrow cocked, right arm and left leg pointed straight out, his body an arrow. The whole time I sat there, eating my beignets, drinking my thick, sweet, creamy coffee, the man did not move. I couldn't even catch him in a blink.

After breakfast I walked around Jackson Square, past the artists setting up their rickety easels, past horse-drawn carriages waiting for customers with too many blisters to walk another block. One tour guide looked like Sylvester Stallone. I glanced back over my shoulder at Uncle Sam; he still hadn't moved. A saxophonist was playing "On the Sunny Side of the Street." The day was hot, not sunny. The sky was the color of smoke. Thick humidity. The air smelled musky and greasy at the same time, like flounder frying. I was wearing beige linen pants and a matching blouse. My hair, lighter now and longer—the gray actually making it appear blonder—was tucked behind my ears. I was going for a Diane Sawyer look rather than my old Jane Pauley look.

All of a sudden I saw Hubba Bubba, whom I'd read about in my New Orleans guidebook. Taped to the front of his card table was a *New York Times* article, blown up to the size of a poster. The headline: ENTREPRENEUR OF HUNCH. A framed autographed picture of him shaking hands with Johnny Carson (Carson's famous desk and starry view of Manhattan in the background) sat on the table. In person, Hubba Bubba was large, very large, and wore a red turban with a rhinestone pin fastened to the front. Fleshy is what he was. And flashy. He sat on a gray metal folding chair and he enveloped the table. His body's heft and authority seemed to fill the entire park.

"Hubba Bubba," I said. "I've read about you."

"Oh yeah," he said. Cigarette voice. "Everybody knows Hubba Bubba!"

Ten dollars for a palm reading, fifteen if he used tarot cards. I chose the palm reading, sat down across from him, let him take my hand in his two giant, hammy ones. Lots of silver rings: cheap turquoise, more than one skull and crossbones. His fingernails were outlined in black. When I looked closer, I saw that it was dirt.

"Oh yeah," he murmured, jowls vibrating. "You got a long lifeline." His chunky finger followed the scattered lines in my palm. A nice tickle.

"How long?" I asked. If Peter were here, he'd think this was really hokey. He would no more let this man hold his hand than fly to the moon.

"You going to live to be eighty-five." He let that sink in and then said, "Now." As though he'd gotten the how-long-will-I-live info out of the way and could finally get to the juicy part. "People are drawn to you. You got magnetism. You always been popular. Not to mention real pretty." He winked and grinned a wide grin. I saw a space where a tooth should be.

"Well, thank you!" I sounded like I was purring.

"You never like to upset the applecart. Peace at any cost. Oh yeah, and here I see . . . I see a long line of successes in your life. Success in school, success in love . . ." He stopped to study my hand, drawing his full mouth in, pink and tight. "Your life has taken an unexpected turn. Am I right?"

A Dixieland jazz band started playing nearby. I heard a saxophone, so sweet and tender it could make you cry.

"Keep going," I said vaguely.

"I'm thinking this involves your husband, yeah?" I hid my left hand in my lap, under the table, not wanting to influence what he might tell me. "Not paying enough attention, maybe?" There was sweat on his forehead. His face was red, eyes watery, not from tears, just watery. "Don't worry. You and your husband will have a long and happy marriage, beginning now."

"Beginning now? What does that mean?" I pressed my shoulder blades together, lengthened my neck. Relax.

"Today is the first day of the rest of your life." I wished he hadn't said that. I kept hearing his remarks through Peter's ears, which was making me wonder just how telepathic this guy really was. It reminded me of the time I'd talked Peter into attending a séance at Joy's house. Joy had invited four friends she'd met at various self-help workshops and Peter and me. The psychic, from Mobile, was in town for some kind of national psychic convention. Peter was the only one at Joy's dining room table who didn't believe it was possible to contact the dead, so, of course, he was the only one who wasn't able to do it. We joined hands and closed our eyes. We were then instructed to announce whom we wanted to summon, and the psychic, named Virginia, would describe the "presence" as he or she "entered the space." We could ask the dead person—through Virginia—one question. I contacted my mother, and Virginia's description of her was totally accurate. "She's here. I see her. Very attractive woman," Virginia said, "blond hair turned gray, like yours, Kathryne. She's about your height. Slender. Delicate features. In fact, you look just like her." I could feel the positive and protective power of my mother. Before I had a chance to ask my question, Peter mistakenly thought it was his turn and called forth his father. Virginia said that he, too, had entered the room and that he was tall and bald. "No," Peter said with great irritation, "my father was most certainly not tall. And he was not bald. He was short and had a full head of hair." I remember thinking, *Come on, Peter, try. You can do it. Concentrate.*

"You have children?" asked Hubba Bubba.

"Mm," I said.

"Like I tell all the ladies, you gotta give 'em up in order to have 'em. Unh-huh." His oversize chest and stomach rose and fell with that. Was he talking about my son? Or my husband?

The music was circling me. "When the Saints Go Marching In." Loud. Pressing in. If Hubba Bubba was talking, I couldn't hear him. All I could do was open my face to whatever came next.

OUR LAST NIGHT in New Orleans, Peter and I ate dinner in a shadowy, oil-lit restaurant in a historic house at the edge of the French Quarter. The food was perfect, the setting perfect, service perfect. We found ourselves blushing after a bottle of red wine, laughing together for the first time in weeks. Later, we walked the streets. On Bourbon Street, young people were staggering in and out of jazz clubs, roaring down the middle of the street, couples holding hands, happy throngs of people holding paper cups, yelling to one another. It was so hectic we didn't have to make conversation. I saw a boy on a second-floor balcony, the leafy iron fretwork framing his young face. Probably Early's age, and he looked as if he were calling to me. When I glanced to my right, I saw that he was talking to a boy next to me on the sidewalk. All of a sudden the boy on the street pulled down his pants and mooned his friend on the balcony. I looked away, then back at the boy beside me, but in that instant, he was gone. I looked both ways. He'd disappeared into the crowd. Walking toward us—down the middle of the street—was a girl, sixteen at the most, who'd pulled up her blouse and was displaying her small, pearly breasts. The evening had turned into a bluesy, pulsating howl.

When Peter and I couldn't walk anymore, we went back to our room.

Everything funneled down to this: We made love. I didn't bother turning off the overhead light. In fact, I rolled over and turned on the wobbly lamp on my side of the bed. Because this was the last remnant of our vacation and we both seemed to sense the minutes dwindling, time took on a luxury and our every move turned slow and deliberate—the long kiss that started it, undressing, piece by piece, one sandal, my other sandal, candy red sundress unbuttoned down the front all the way to the hem, my bra, panties. His loafers, socks, knit shirt, khaki pants, belt still dangling from the loops. Jockey underwear, elastic pulled wide, stepping out of. Lying across the tufted bedspread. Colors quilting together—beige, brown, yellow, aqua. No limits, just the two of us and our powdery bodies rubbing smooth together. Not a sound to break the surface of peace. The scalloping of fingertips. We could've been sliding sideways off a raft, the way everything was turning liquid. That old familiar gathering deep in my body. Warm, hard pressure accumulating, like the thickness of gravity. Until the air conditioner in the room shuddered, as if in shock, and cracked from strain—the quick rise of heat in the room—and we gave up, gave in, worked ourselves loose together.

NINETEEN

MINUTES AFTER we'd walked into the house from New Orleans, Early came in from the Dunhams. He seemed to be limping. His front tooth was chipped—half gone!—and his top lip was as swollen as a Parker House roll.

"Early! What happened?" I said, dropping my carry-on bag on the hardwood floor, as though it was no heavier than a summer purse.

"Hey, Mom! Hey, Dad! Wait, before you start worrying, Mom, it's not so bad." The cracked tooth made him look like one of the backwoods people in *Deliverance*.

"If this 'isn't so bad,' I'd hate to see what the other guy looks like," Peter said in a jokey voice, as if there could be anything funny about our son getting hurt. Sometimes I wondered if I were totally clueless about the strange rituals fathers considered absolutely normal for sons.

"Dad, that's exactly what happened!"

"You were in a fight? Did you see a doctor?" I sputtered.

"I didn't need a doctor. But wait, let me tell you. You're not going to believe this!" *I* couldn't believe how his face, aside from the bruises, was—glowing. The way a bride is transformed on the day of her wedding. That's how sunshiny—illuminated from within—his face appeared. I also couldn't believe that my own flesh and blood— Peter's and my flesh and blood—had actually gotten into a fight.

"Friday, after school, Mrs. Dunham dropped Chip and me off at the Cherry Neighborhood Center to play basketball. We heard they had some good pickup games there and for a long time we've been wanting to check it out. Eddie Jackson and Steven Todd met us there. The center's right behind Eddie's house."

I was relieved Eddie had been there, since he was from that neighborhood.

Peter plopped our suitcase on the bed—we were all in the bedroom now—and started unpacking shoes, belts, dop kit, travel alarm, electric razor. Peter was such a minimalist. He never packed one extra shirt, one extra tie, one extra anything. He could always envision exactly what he needed for a trip.

After putting away his things in the closet and bathroom, he went back to the suitcase and carefully stacked my clean, unworn clothes on the bed. Then he dropped our dirty clothes in a neat pile on the floor. I stood beside the doorway, close to Early. He was pacing back and forth.

"So, Dad. It was really cool. Chip, Steven, and I were the only white boys in the whole place. There were some great players. You should've seen some of those guys. God, could they play! See, the way they do in pickup games, Mom, there are all these different teams, and if your team wins, you stay on the floor. The minute your team loses, you have to sign up to play again."

"Was everybody there your age?"

"Yeah, probably. They looked like they were fifteen. Maybe some of them were sixteen. Or seventeen."

"Who was in charge?" I asked. "I mean—"

"Nobody was in charge. There was an old man, a custodian, I guess, but he was back in the supply room. Anyway, Chip, Steven, and Eddie were on the same team and I was on a different team. It was fun—man, it was fun!"

"How'd you do against that level of competition, son?"

"Not too bad. You would've been proud of me, Dad. I hung in there. It's absolutely probably the best I ever played."

"Absolutely probably, huh?" Peter was rerolling all the socks in his sock drawer and lining them up. Brown together, black together, navy, gray. White golf socks off to the side.

"But what about the bruises?" I asked. Let's not get too caught up in the wonderfulness of the whole thing. It was obvious he'd been hurt. Badly.

"Well, Mrs. Dunham picked up Chip and Steven around four-thirty. She had a hair appointment and Steven had to be home early, I forget why. Anyway, I was having so much fun I didn't want to leave. They asked if it was all right if they left me there and I said, sure."

"Mrs. Dunham left you?" I said. Typical, I thought. What other mother would do that?

"Eddie was still there."

"So it was just you and Eddie and those other boys?" I said.

"And that was awesome! I was the only white person in the whole place. I mean, Mom, Dad, have you ever had that experience in your life? It was incredible! Eddie and I—we *all*—were having an amazing time. We were on fire! There was this guy—I can only re-member his last name, Campbell—he was about my height, but he was really built—you wouldn't believe the size of his arms—he was wearing a West Charlotte T-shirt. Anyway, he's Eddie's cousin. Well, toward the end, he started giving me a hard time, really picking on me. Talking trash."

"Talking trash? That doesn't sound so good," I said.

"It's what athletes do, Kathryne," Peter said. "You're trying to distract them, make them lose concentration, force them to focus on what you're saying rather than on the game."

"So I've got the ball and this guy Campbell starts guarding me pretty close, throwing a few elbows—that's how I got *some* of these bruises—"

"I've seen enough school games to know that nobody ends up looking the way you do after a normal, everyday basketball game," I said. I picked up one of the dress shirts Peter had worn on the trip and stretched it out on the floor, like a chalk outline on asphalt. I bunched the dirty clothes in the middle of the shirt, tied the arms together, tossed the bundle in the doorway to take to the laundry room later.

"Well, this guy Campbell was saying, 'Come on, white boy, come on! Show me what you got! I bet you ain't got much!' And he was saying some things I can't say in front of you, Mom. Pretty rough stuff. Right then, I put a move on him and scored."

"All right!" Peter's fist was actually in the air! I couldn't believe this whole scene. It was as though we were back in the time of the gladiators and the smell of torn flesh had made Peter and Early drunk.

"The next time I got the ball, I was on fire, Dad! I couldn't miss! They kept passing me the ball. This Campbell guy was really pissed and was doing some big-time pushing and shoving."

"What about Eddie? What was he doing?" I asked.

"Oh, Eddie wasn't there."

"I thought you said he stayed," I said. Peter stopped sorting socks and sat down on the corner of the bed across from Early, who was now standing still, facing the bed. I leaned against the wall, beside him.

"He did, but then he had to go home."

"He left you there?"

"He offered to have his mother drive me home, but I told him I wanted to stay. How could I leave? My team was winning."

"But how were you going to get home? I mean, to the Dunhams?" It was definitely not walking distance from Cherry to Ridge Avenue.

"I figured I'd just call Mrs. Dunham when we got through. She'd be back from the beauty parlor by then. I wasn't worried."

"Keep going, son."

"Well, this guy Campbell was a point guard basically, and he was bringing the ball up the court and I picked his pocket."

"You what?" I seemed to be the only one in the dark about most of what was being said.

"I stole the ball from him. Anyway, I was going up for a layup and he took me out. He hit me right on my hips. I got crushed. Landed hard. See, Mom, even in pickup games, you don't do that. You're really vulnerable when you're up in the air like that. So when I finally stood up, I pushed him and said, 'What the hell is your problem?'"

Standing behind Early, I could watch him without his being aware. He was granitelike and, at the same time, trembling. Not the kind of trembling from being frightened, though. More like a surge, an aggressive surge.

"The guy reared back and slugged me in the mouth. It threw my head backward. I was crouched down, holding my face. I knew he'd broken my tooth because there was so much blood. I had no idea whether he was still standing over me or whether he'd walked away, but I just came up swinging, with a wild windmill motion. He was right there, and I cracked his face with a full punch!"

"Oh, my God, Early!" I said. I put my hand on his shoulder and it felt hard. I'd touched a muscle that was tight as a fist.

"No, no, I wasn't scared. I felt like a, I felt like I, like it wasn't even me. I was fearless. I didn't even feel his punch. He could've punched me till my eyes flew out the back of my head and I wouldn't have felt it!"

"And then?" Peter.

"And then everybody, I mean the guys who weren't playing, ran onto the court. They were all trying to pull us apart. The guys on my team were holding me back or else I would've hit him again. I could've thrown punches till both my hands were broken. I wanted to beat the living daylights out of him. I know I could've done some real damage!" What he was saying took me back to the temper tantrums he used to have. The sudden flash of anger. The overreaction. Going further than the situation warranted.

"What was the other guy doing?" Peter asked.

"He wanted to kill me. The guys on his team were holding him back, but they looked like they wanted to kill me, too. Since I was the only white boy there, I was not the popular choice."

I looked at Peter's face. He was beaming. This man who, his entire adult life, had believed in resolving disputes without violence, who was a master of diplomacy no matter how intricate the circumstances, was downright grinny.

"That guy, Campbell, started yelling, 'I'm gonna kick your fucking ass, you honky! I'm gonna get you for this, you chickenshit!' Somebody went to find the custodian and he got me out of the gym and into the parking lot." Early looked over his shoulder at me. "Sorry, Mom. For the bad language."

"How'd you get home?"

"The custodian gave me a ride. I kept looking back to see if anybody was following us."

"Do you think that boy meant he's going to come get you? Are you in any danger?"

"Naah, that's just the kind of thing somebody like that says."

"Why didn't you tell me about this when I called? You didn't say a word."

He turned all the way around, faced me, put his hand on my arm. I was struck with how very different he looked—but if I were asked what the difference was, I wouldn't have been able to put it into words.

"Why didn't you tell me?" I asked again.

"It felt good to keep it to myself for a while."

This was the first vacation Peter and I had taken since my mother died. I hadn't felt comfortable leaving Early with anyone but her. I remember thinking: We won't leave him again.

TWENTY

IT HAD BEEN a little over a week since we'd gotten home from New Orleans. Early's bruises were healing, and I was growing accustomed to the broken tooth; in a way, it gave him character. Peter had talked me into believing these were the kinds of things boys needed to experience. He told me about a time at Valdosta High when he'd gotten into a fight with a boy who'd called him a "dirty bastard." He made it sound as if a punch in the mouth was merely a step along the way to manhood, right ahead of a kick in the shin and just behind a bloody nose.

I was squatting on the cold tile of the bathroom floor, leaning into the cabinet under the sink, looking for soap. I knew I'd just bought eight bars of Dove and I wanted to take out a fresh one for the shower. For some reason, there were none left.

"Peter, did you move the soap?" I called out. He was in his closet, getting ready for work. I could hear him shifting the ties forward on his tie rack, then taking the wooden shoe trees out of his loafers. Even after that last night in New Orleans, we were not what you'd call normal. But at least we weren't avoiding each other. It was as though we were suspended in air, occasionally coming together, mostly just floating close.

"I'm not sure what you're talking about," he called back. "I haven't touched the soap."

I thought of Phyllis. She'd been here the day before, cleaning the house. She came every Tuesday. Phyllis and her stylish clothes and hairdos, her light brown skin and flute voice. She worked hard, and she worked fast. Cleaned the entire house in five hours. The year before, her husband had gotten into a fight with a coworker and been fired. He'd also slapped Phyllis around and been under a court order not to come near her. *She* told me she'd gotten her black eye at the beauty parlor. The beautician, she said, had accidentally scraped her face with a comb. (Joy's cleaning woman, who rode to work with Phyllis, told Joy the real story and Joy told me.) Now Phyllis and her husband were living together again. I couldn't believe she'd taken him back. How many times would he hurt her and she forgive him?

They had two sons, in their early twenties, both in prison for burglary, though she truly believed they were innocent. All I remember about the circumstances is that she told me her boys had been with people who were a bad influence and they'd been in the wrong place at the wrong time and then they were *incarcerated.* That's the word she used. She visited them on Sundays, whenever they were transferred to a prison within driving distance. I don't know why those boys were moved around so much. Sometimes it was such a long drive, visiting hours were over by the time she got there and she'd return home without even a glimpse of them. Sometimes they were in different prisons and she had to choose between them. More often than not, her car broke down before she even got to the prison. It didn't matter to her that her driver's license had been taken away (too many speeding tickets). I kept telling her how risky it was to drive without a license. She assured me that she was a slow driver and wouldn't get caught, and as soon as she had time, she'd apply for a new license. She drove her no-color Ford to Georgia, Tennessee, Virginia, wherever her boys were, to spend an hour with one or both, a few hours at the most.

The day after I'd noticed the soap missing, I bought four new bars and stacked them in the cabinet under the sink.

The next Monday—the night before Phyllis was to come again—I checked. The four new bars were there. I couldn't believe I was counting soap. What else could she be taking that I hadn't noticed? The part that bothered me was that she'd feel entitled to take anything without asking. Whatever she might want, I'd be happy to give her. Sometimes she'd call from one of the other houses she cleaned, asking for an advance. She'd give me directions and I'd drive over with the cash. I never made her work it off. Forget it, I'd say. I couldn't stand the thought of her spending a long day at my house and all she'd done was work off a loan.

On the other hand, so what if she took a few bars of soap? I had so much. Imagine how our life must appear to her. How easy. How full.

Tuesday, after she cleaned my house, I looked in the cabinet.

All the soap was gone.

When Peter came home, I told him.

"Well," he said. I could see the scales of justice in his eyes. "You know it's probably pretty tempting, working in a house where there's so much, then going home to so little. Does it really matter? Phyllis is a good person and a hard worker. I'm sure soap is all she's taking." He was sitting at the kitchen table, glancing sideways at the paper, trying to appear involved in our conversation when what he really wanted was to read the front page.

"But stealing is wrong." I was at the stove, sautéing boneless chicken breasts. When I turned them over, the oil popped and stung my wrist. Like sparklers on the Fourth of July. When I was young, I loved fireworks. But never sparklers. Their fire was too close.

Early was having dinner at Chip's house, so it was just Peter and me. I made a conscious effort to relax my face, which I always tried to do while I was cooking, to smooth away those vertical lines between the eyebrows. "If she stole from me twice, she'll do it again," I said. "I don't want to check behind her every time she comes."

"Then you'll have to let her go."

"But she's really sweet, and I feel sorry for her and the life she has to live. Two sons in prison. A violent husband." I realized I was taking the opposite view of whatever he said. "Oh, I hate this. Hate that she's put me in this position. Hate that taking soap matters."

The stovetop was a mess, but the chicken smelled good. I scooped it up, along with the scabs of crust left in the pan, buried it all in brown rice, and brought the platter to the table. Then our salads. No silverware or napkins. I jumped up to get what we needed, back to the table. The chicken had a nice flavor, simple, cooked with garlic, red pepper flakes, and the fresh Mexican oregano I'd brought home from Joy's.

"This makes me feel like a racist," I said.

"I don't know, it doesn't seem to have anything to do with race. Phyllis is just someone who's had a hard life." He wiped his mouth with his napkin.

"Well, I've always thought of myself as a person who's concerned about people who've had hard lives."

"You are."

"This makes me think of Emmalee."

"Emmalee?"

"When I was little, my parents went to Myrtle Beach and left Billy and me with this elderly black lady who baby-sat for a lot of children in the neighborhood. I was crazy about her. Everybody was."

"Kathryne—"

"Wait. Listen. One afternoon Emmalee and I walked up to the school playground, and I started showing off for her, climbing to the top of the jungle gym, hanging by one hand. All of a sudden I fell. Ripped open my underarm on one of those steel bolts. I was bleeding like crazy. Emmalee picked me up and ran all the way back to the house. She wrapped my underarm in a dish towel and called a taxi to take us to the hospital. You know what I heard her say? I heard her ask for a *colored* cab. That made me sick. I'd never imagined there were separate cabs."

"Kathryne, I don't think this is about race—"

"That's not the worst part. At the hospital, they took me to the white waiting room, which looked like some kind of parlor with so-fas and carpeting and all that. And they made her go to the colored waiting room. I remember I went to find her and she was sitting on a hard-back chair in this dark little room with a linoleum floor that probably wasn't even that clean. I thought she'd pull me onto her lap and I could stay there with her. That's what I wanted. But here's what she said: 'Go back, child. You go on back where you belong.'"

"It's an interesting story, Kathryne," Peter said, "but—"

"I've always thought of myself as so liberal."

"Well, the reality is, we may not be as liberal or as righteous as we think we are. Sure, we want to do the right thing but sometimes our own self-interest takes over. Our attitudes toward race can be pretty complicated—"

"What's that supposed to mean?" At the time, I thought he was going global. Turning a small difference of opinion into a sign of some far-reaching character flaw. In me. Now I wonder if he was simply doing what I'd admired in him when I first met him: appreci-ating ambiguity, seeing opposing sides of an issue. The "on the other hand" part of his personality. Which made him the skilled lawyer that he was.

"Look, you're going to have to be the one to make the decision," he said. He was finished with his chicken and rice and was patting the last chunk of tomato in a pool of dressing on his salad plate. "It's not going to be easy. Why don't you take some time? This situation may have been going on for a long time, so if you wait awhile to decide, it won't matter."

"Maybe so." I was glad for the conversation to end. I needed to think about this. He could go in and catch the last of the news.

When Early got home from Chip's, around nine, Peter was watching television and I was at the desk in the kitchen, making a grocery list for the next day. I told Early about Phyllis. He begged me not to let her go.

"I know," I said, "but stealing is wrong."

"It's only a few bars of soap," he said. "Besides, I think it's sad somebody as nice as Phyllis has to have such bad luck. It's not fair."

FOUR WEEKS PASSED. I went back and forth in my mind. More things disappeared. Toothpaste. Two cans of baked beans. Kitchen scissors. Nothing important. Still. They were there before she came and missing after she left.

Finally, I knew what I was going to do. I called Peter at the office.

"Hey," I said after his secretary put me through.

"Hey," he said back.

"Is this an okay time to talk?"

"I can talk, yes."

"I know what I'm going to do." I tugged at the telephone wire, coiled it around my wrist like a bracelet.

"Oh?" he said.

"About Phyllis."

"Oh." Relief in his voice. Maybe he'd thought I was calling to talk about us.

"I'm going to let her go."

"Uh-huh. And what do you plan to say to her?"

"I'm not going to give her an explanation. I'm just going to tell her it has nothing to do with the quality of her work but I can't continue to have her work for me. She'll either make the connection, or not."

"Well, I don't know about not giving her a reason. There are some pretty basic rules of honesty—"

"I don't think I'm being dishonest. I'm just not telling her everything. When she made the decision to steal, didn't she give up certain rights? And you know how she has a hard time assuming responsibility. She has yet to acknowledge her sons did anything wrong. If I confront her, there's a good chance she'll deny it. Accusing her of stealing is the last thing I want to do, especially now that she's back with her husband. Who knows what his reaction will be? He could get mad at her for jeopardizing her job. Or get mad at me for accusing her. You know his temper."

"Well, I think she deserves—" He stopped in the middle of his sentence. Good. I didn't want to hear another way of looking at this.

I didn't say anything.

"Kathryne?" he said. I still didn't say anything. "You there?"

"Look," I finally said, "I've worked hard to arrive at this. Letting her go is so *not* what I want to do. It goes against everything I've ever stood for. She steals—and I feel guilty."

"Okay, okay. You've made your decision. It's fine."

Since the night he'd told me about Ann, he'd been careful to be agreeable, or at least careful not to upset me. I found myself wishing we could have an all-out argument. Maybe I just wanted to throw a tantrum. Of course, getting all-out, knock-'em-dead angry with each other had never been our style.

Here's how we operated: first, a neutral time, a withdrawal from the other, when we were no longer *part* of each other. Unattached. Careful. Conversations kept to the strictly functional. Then a period of politeness. Thank you, he'd say when I put dinner on the table. Good morning, I'd say when he came into the kitchen. You're welcome. Please. Of course.

Finally, after all this, there was normalcy. As though nothing had ever happened.

We were now in politeness.

WE HAD NOT HAD SEX since New Orleans. Twice, he'd reached over while we were in bed reading, just before we turned out the light, to rub my shoulder. Both times I smelled something chemical, vaguely metallic. The nasal spray he used to help him breathe at night. I continued reading. Once, after we'd finished supper, he said, "Any chance we could have some time together later tonight?" I never realized how much energy *not* responding takes, like trying to pass through solid objects.

WHEN I TOLD PHYLLIS I had to let her go and that it had nothing to do with the quality of her work, she said, "Am I charging too much? Is that it? I can go down on my price."

I answered no, there was nothing wrong with what I'd been paying her.

"You're worth every penny," I said next.

"Is it my cleaning, then? I could do better. You just tell me." She was looking me over, as though the answer might be written in my skin, and if she looked hard enough, she'd find it.

I repeated that this had nothing to do with the quality of her work, but I could not continue having her work for me. As if that explained everything. I hated myself for this. My eyes filled. I twisted my neck so she couldn't see my face. Of course she didn't understand what I was saying. How could she?

She had just finished cleaning my house—all four bathrooms scrubbed, hardwood floors mopped, rugs and drapes vacuumed, chandeliers and lamps and mahogany tabletops and collections of antique biscuit jars and paperweights and Royal Doulton mugs dusted, quilts and down comforters and pillows fluffed, wood moldings and chair rails wiped clean, kitchen, den, living room, dining room, bedrooms, every room in my house spotless. She'd done the best she could and we both knew it. I turned to face her. I reached my arms around her back and she allowed me to hug her in the doorway before she left to crank up a car she could never depend on.

TWENTY-ONE

A FEW DAYS AFTER I let Phyllis go, Joy called to tell me what her cleaning woman had told her: Phyllis's husband had gotten drunk and beaten her up, stolen the little bit of cash she'd saved, and run off with another woman.

"How bad was she hurt?" I asked Joy.

"He broke her wrist when she wouldn't tell him where she'd hidden her money. She has a good many bruises, but she'll be all right. She's a strong woman."

Early was at the kitchen table, eating a ham sandwich. It was Saturday and he'd gotten up before eight, gone to school to work on the yearbook, had just come home for lunch. He and the other boys were going over to Chip's that afternoon to watch the game on TV. I loved the way boys always knew which sport—which specific teams—they meant when they referred vaguely to "the game."

"What happened to Phyllis?" he asked.

"Well, it's not good," I said. "She's been hurt. Her husband beat her up and now he's gone. Out of her life."

"That's so awful," he said. "I can't stand hearing it. The part about him beating her up, I mean. Maybe it's not so awful that he's gone."

"I know. He's been nothing but trouble. I'm going over there to see what I can do."

"Will she come back to work for us?"

"I don't know. That might be a little awkward. Maybe I can do something better than that."

I explained what I was thinking, which he seemed to think was a good idea; he finished his sandwich and left.

It was already past two and I was eager to get to Phyllis's, so I finished writing my review of the new Robert Redford movie (in my opinion, his creased face always steals the show), took a quick shower—what I call a "three-point landing," where you just hit the high spots, under both arms and down below. Then, because I didn't stop to eat lunch, I grabbed an apple on my way out. I finished it as I started up the steep hill on Providence Road, just past the "Limited Sight Distance" sign. To the left was the turn for Partridge Circle. Ann's street. Partridge Circle was curvy so you couldn't see beyond the first few houses. Why did it have to be such a secretive street? I pictured Peter turning here to go see her. What would he have been thinking right about here? Did he leave the office in the middle of the day to meet her when she came home from school? How many times?

In the middle of the engine-room hum of my thoughts, I pulled my right arm back and threw the apple core, slinging as hard as I could to land it deep in the woods across the street. A huge *splat!* Apple bits everywhere! All over the glass, the upholstery, me. I'd forgotten to roll down my window! Now I was not only glancing in my sideview mirror at Partridge Circle, I was also picking damp shreds of apple off my clothes.

Why did I come all the way out here? I meant to drive in the opposite direction on Providence Road. A left instead of a right.

I pulled into a gas station and brushed myself off with the towel I kept under the front seat. It was adding white lint to my shirt and pants. I tried a Kleenex wet with spit. That helped. If only I hadn't worn black. But how on earth would I have known to wear an apple-colored outfit?

As I rounded the pumps heading toward the street, I noticed a sign posted in the front window of the gas station: MONKEY ORDERS HERE. Could there be that great a demand in Charlotte for monkeys? I looked again and it turned into MONEY ORDERS HERE.

What was wrong with my brain?

New development after new development out here, except for one leftover, bunched-up shack on the right with peeling paint and a falling-down, plank front porch. I always wonder about people who live in a house like that, surrounded by new construction. Are they holding out for more money? Or just trying to hold on to what they have?

Up ahead, one of those new gated communities with a guard booth at the brick and stone entrance. The man in the booth was waving a Cadillac through. The driver was waving back, as though she and the man in the booth knew each other really well. They were acting so friendly you'd think she spent long afternoons with him in his little booth, playing cards and sipping iced tea.

I know gated communities are supposed to look like small towns from the 1950s, but I don't believe small towns ever looked like this. Rock Hill was pretty and pristine, but not *planned*. Developments are being built farther and farther out from the center of towns, trying to be what the builders believe we've lost, although no one knows exactly what it is we've lost. Have we lost brick walls girdling our neighborhoods? Iron gates? Have we lost guard booths?

Partridge Circle put me in a foul mood.

Now where?

Fairview Road to Tyvola Road.

Down the ramp onto the expressway. Five miles. To Griffin Road exit.

Just after the convenience store, left into Phyllis's neighborhood. Past the housing projects, called Griffin Court. I remembered from the few times I'd driven her home that you can't turn onto her street because some white man (Phyllis told me this) who owns all this property, including the street itself (how in the world can somebody own a street?), deposited a jumbo Dumpster in the middle of Griffin Road, so there's no through traffic. You have to drive one street past her street, then circle back.

There, on the right, her small brick house.

I walked up the concrete walk to the front porch and rang the bell. On the door was the handcrafted wooden sign I'd given her as part of her Christmas present the last year she'd worked for us. It had bright blue and green letters spelling WELCOME.

"Who is it?" Phyllis's voice, which didn't sound quite right, from behind the closed door.

"It's me. Kathryne. Kathryne Smallwood."

"Mrs. Smallwood?" Phyllis opened the door wide. I could tell she was surprised to see me. *I* was surprised at how bruised her face was. Instead of her smooth skin, there were dark, angry patches on her cheeks—not enough time for scabs to form—and her left eye was swollen shut. One large Band-Aid covered most of her chin, which is why her speech was slurred. Her lower arm and hand were in a cast, her fingers curled up like little crab legs. She just smiled, a sad and nervous smile.

"Phyllis. Oh, Phyllis." I could've cried. "I'm so sorry. I'm sorry for everything." Was I referring to what her husband had done—or to what I'd done?

"Can you come in? Do you want me to come out there?" This made me feel even worse, that she'd think I wouldn't want to come inside her house, that she would have to come outside to talk with me.

"Oh, I can come in. I mean, if this is a good time."

"Sure, it's a good time."

I followed her into her small living room, filled with furniture. A love seat covered with a tan, peach, and blue afghan she'd probably made. Coffee table. Wing chair with brown fabric worn to a shine. End tables. Two wooden kitchen-type chairs. It suddenly occurred to me that during all the years she'd worked for me, I had never been inside her house. She pushed aside the baby blue curtains, but one of the hooks that moved along the curtain rod got stuck. With one hand she tugged, then tugged harder, until the hook gave way, snapped, fell to the rug. She finished pushing the curtains aside. Now light streamed through the double windows across the front of the house. From the wing chair, I could see a taxi speeding down the street. Phyllis was still standing. She wore a milky beige dress and a necklace made of glass stones.

"Would you like some coffee?" she said. "I just made some."

"No, thanks. Here, sit down. Sit here . . ."

She pulled one of the wooden chairs close and I asked about her boys. She said she'd been to see them Sunday, the day before the "accident," as she called it. They were both in Huntersville Prison, not far from Charlotte. "A true blessing to have them so close to home," she said. "And seeing the two of them together made me feel good. Unh-unh, are they sweet! They don't deserve what they got."

"Phyllis," I said. "I had to come when I heard what happened to you."

"Well, no need to go over all that. It was a blessing. I believe the Lord was looking out for me. It could've been a lot worse."

She eased one shoe off. Her baby toe was dark and puffy, like an acorn. The nail was torn.

"Your toe—"

"It's just sore. I don't think it's broken. When I fell backward, I twisted it."

"Phyllis," I blurted, "I want to do something for you."

"Oh, Mrs. Smallwood, you don't need to do anything. You've done enough nice things for me."

"Kathryne. Call me Kathryne. Here's what I want to do. I'm going to set it up so every month there'll be an automatic deposit into your checking acount of fifty dollars. You'll know you have that, no matter what. Do you have a checking account?"

"Oh sure. At the bank up there on Griffin Road. I can't believe you'd do that, Mrs. Smallwood."

"It's the least I can do. I know I didn't treat you very well before. When you had to stop working for me. And I want to make up for that. I hope this will bring you some measure of security."

She didn't pick up on the part about my letting her go—she just thanked me for the money—and I was glad about that. I didn't try to talk about the incident with her husband, and she seemed glad about that.

She would never admit to a life coming apart at the seams. And she would never see any bad in her sons. Was I aware of the resemblance between us? Could I have imagined how my life would follow hers? Sons. Husbands. When I look back, all I see is how oblivious I was.

I stood to leave. She put her arms around me and I hugged her, gently. I didn't want to hurt her; she had to be sore.

As I walked to my car, an elderly woman was crossing the street toward Phyllis's house. She stopped to look at the rosebush in the corner of Phyllis's yard, each cupped rose as big as the woman's face. When she saw Phyllis on the porch, she smiled a toothy smile and asked how Phyllis was feeling. The woman had to be in her eighties: she leaned on her cane and walked in a fragile, uncertain way, each foot trying out the ground before it actually committed to it.

At that time, I had no idea my family's attitudes toward race would ever be questioned. I felt confident, in that way those of us who've always been liberal assume we'll come down on the right side of most issues. Surely, I'd proven myself over the years, shown how much I cared for people different from and less privileged than myself, how much I cared about injustice. Maybe Peter was right, though, trying to show my better side to the world had its own smugness. Do we organize our lives only for effect? Nothing is simple. My first year of teaching—after graduating from college—had been the first year of integration in the state of Georgia, and the school where I'd taught, Roosevelt High, in the poorest neighborhood of Atlanta, was the largest in the state and the first white school to admit black students. The school system had been desperate for teachers; white teachers wanted to teach in all-white schools. Black and white students got into fights every day that first year I taught; police were stationed on all three floors of the school; newsmen broadcast from the parking lot, their mobile units lining the street; photographers crawled through the bushes, cameras on their shoulders. Young and virtuous, full of conviction, I'd jumped at what I'd believed was an opportunity to make the world a better place.

When I got in my car, I looked back. Phyllis had come down from her porch and was standing in the grass, talking with the woman. The way Phyllis was chatting and gesturing, her head thrown back in laughter, you'd never know anything bad had ever happened to her.

TWENTY-TWO

I TRIED TO KEEP BUSY, knowing how the mind can bring too much into focus, put you under. I didn't want to think about Phyllis. Didn't want to think about Peter and me, or our marriage.

The last Parents' Council meeting of the year. End of my first term as president, 1985, May of Early's sophomore year. Polly Murdaugh, the mother of a freshman girl, brought up the question, How involved should the school be in the private lives of its students? Polly wore a beige brocade suit that made her look like she was wearing her sofa. Her ivory earrings kept twisting. She said she believed the school should be very involved, that what goes on outside of school can have an impact on what goes on in school, and what one child does can affect others. I wasn't crazy about Polly. She's one of those people who adores you when she first meets you, idealizes you; then, as she gets to know you, when she discovers your first flaw, she writes you off. Everyone eventually loses her sheen with Polly.

Amy Whitley's mother, Janet, expressed concern that the school might be venturing into questionable territory, that it sounded as though we wanted the administration to take over our job. The school's job—she said in her soft, charitable voice—is to teach, and the parents' job is to parent. Janet Whitley had that perfect hairline wealthy women have, and the clear, luminous skin. It was hard not to pay attention to her because she'd done such a good job raising Amy. I'd known Amy since kindergarten—that long ponytail in elementary school, the awkward middle-school stage when everyone's arms and legs are too long, and now—poised, popular, smart, almost-grown Amy.

Of course I could tell the twelve women sitting around that table wanted to hear from me, too. Like Amy, Early was an excellent student, active in clubs and sports. There were certain mothers the others looked up to. Parents' Council was a hierarchy similar to what our children experienced. When a child was popular and a high achiever, that child's mother was popular with the other mothers. Cliques among parents were similar to the cliques of their children. You could even see it at sports events, where fathers jockeyed with one another, high in the bleachers, to sit next to the star athlete's father.

Polly was saying, "There's a freshman girl right here in this school—not my daughter, someone else, and she will remain nameless—but she is being driven crazy by a certain tenth-grade boy who will not leave her alone." Polly's daughter was good friends with Julie Cauthen, Chip's old girlfriend. I could feel the color change in my face and neck, blood rushing there. I couldn't believe this was being brought up in Parents' Council. "This boy calls, and when she answers, he hangs up. All hours of the day and night. And he won't leave her alone at school." With that, Polly practically rose up out of her chair. "He has even threatened to commit suicide if she doesn't pay attention to him." She stopped to let what she'd said sink in. I touched my hands to my neck—fiery hot—and looked around the table. Polly had everyone's attention. "Oh yes, he's already tried once. He didn't tell anybody about it, except the girl. The boy slit his wrist. Slit his wrist! Not so bad that he was actually in danger. I think it was only a cry for help. I heard he has a gun—a gun!—but I don't believe he's the type to actually do anything. And maybe that last part about the gun is not true. I'm not really sure. Anyway, I'm not naming names here. The girl feels sorry for him, but at the same time she wants him to leave her alone. Don't y'all think the school ought to help?"

Chip had a gun?

The room was heavy with whispering. We mothers love for someone else's child to have a problem. A few of the women raised their hands and spoke with a lot of emotion—"Yes, we ought to help" is what they were saying; others were more tentative, almost afraid to get too close to the subject or to the people involved. As though it—whatever *it* was—could attach itself to them and their children. I wondered if the women knew it was Chip. And did they know Chip was Early's best friend? Surely, they did. Mothers at this school knew everything about their kids' friends. Did they know about Chip's family's history? The attempted suicide. Five-year-old Chip's phone call to his father at work: *Come home. Something's wrong with Mommy.*

Polly's dramatic delivery had made an impression. On the other hand, so had Janet Whitley's quiet "hands off" comments earlier.

Finally, I spoke. In an even, measured voice, like some secretary of state. "What you've opened up, Polly, is very important, very serious, and certainly something many of us have strong feelings about. But it seems to me, there are two issues here. One is the particular problem involving this boy and girl. I think we need to turn that over to the school counselor as soon as possible. Would you be willing to talk with Mrs. Cohen—confidentially, of course—about this?"

Nancy Jan Todd raised her hand. Was her face really that pale or did she just use too much powder? "Good idea, Kathryne," she said. "As usual, you're leading us in the right direction."

Others were mouthing yes.

I waved Nancy Jan away and started a sentence I didn't finish: "Oh, sometimes I do and sometimes . . ."

Polly pressed her thin lips together in something that passed for a smile.

Yes, Chip needed professional help. I wasn't going to respond to what Polly had said about the gun—she was pulling out all the stops—but he did need help. This was his best chance for getting it. I felt relieved over this turn of events. Actually, I couldn't ask for anything better, for Chip or for Early, than for Chip to get counseling. These nodding women were agreeing with me.

"Now, there's also the broader subject," I said. "How far we want the school to go in managing our children's lives. Do we want the school to set their curfews? Discipline them for problems outside of school? For drugs? Alcohol? I think the best thing is to appoint a committee to look into these questions and have them report back to us in the fall."

I turned to Janet Whitley at the end of the table. She was not meeting my eye. Did she know this concerned Chip, Early's best friend, and feel embarrassed for me? Or did she just not want to be in charge of another committee? Goodness knows, she was chairman of everything at this school. She wiped her glasses with the corner of her gold silk scarf. The scarf was monogrammed.

"Janet, would you head this committee?"

She nodded her head yes and continued wiping. Maybe it was just that she didn't want to draw attention to herself.

"Any of you who'd like to serve on this committee, please let Janet know after the meeting," I said, trying to sound calm and not so connected to the kids we were discussing. "Janet, you might want to ask members of the administration to join your committee." Janet nodded. She'd probably already thought of that.

"Also." Polly again. "We need to discuss another matter."

"Okay, Polly. Go ahead." Actually, I'd had enough of Polly.

"What about this business of the prom?"

"What business of the prom?" I said.

"Well, you know. Eddie Jackson." She breathed into the name as if it were a handkerchief.

"Eddie Jackson?" Early's friend. On academic scholarship. Good-looking boy, popular, bright as could be, a genius when it came to math. He'd led the math team to first place in the state contests that fall.

"Y'all know, that black boy. The math student. But the main problem with him going to the prom, he's only a sophomore. Isn't it a *junior-senior* prom?" Polly stretched her neck with a sense of purpose.

"Juniors are free to invite sophomores." I knew what she was upset about and I was not going to give an inch. In fact, I now understood her original question—How involved should the school be in the lives of its students?—which had led to the discussion of Chip and Julie. Polly really wasn't that concerned about Julie's problem. All that was merely leading to this.

"My daughter is a freshman," she was saying, "and I certainly wouldn't let her go if a junior or senior invited her."

"But a junior has the right to invite anybody to the prom he or she chooses, even a freshman." I ran my fingers over my mouth.

"Well, I'm just wondering if this is what we want for our school. I enrolled my daughter in Randolph Academy when all that busing business started. For a reason." Polly leaned forward, her chin resting on the knuckles of both hands, elbows planted firmly on the table. The position created a million unflattering wrinkles in her face.

I glanced over at Janet. She smiled. I knew what I would say.

"Juniors inviting sophomores to the prom, juniors inviting juniors, seniors inviting freshmen—whatever configuration we can think of—is exactly what we want for our school. Students attending the prom is what we want. As many students as possible socializing in a safe, protected environment. And . . ." I moved my hand away from my face. I wanted Polly to hear what I had to say, loud and clear. ". . . if a white girl inviting a black boy to a school prom is a problem for you, perhaps you ought to consider a different school." Or a different century.

Before anybody could react—before Polly could bring her lips together after her mouth had dropped open—I went right into the subject of planting the entrance of the school. Time to replace the pansies with summer flowers. Foxgloves, hollyhocks, geraniums, I suggested, adding that I wouldn't mind buying the flowers and planting them myself. Large, showy flowers, I thought we should have. Flowers that made an impact. A good first impression was what we were after.

Everyone seemed satisfied with my flower suggestions. Or maybe they were too stunned to speak. Anyway, I decided to take their silence as approval. Meeting adjourned. Have a good summer.

As I walked to the car, my legs felt wobbly. I'd never dreamed that being president of Parents' Council would mean I'd have to deal with such complicated issues. I'd accepted the position because I thought it would be a good way to get to know the other parents, make a contribution to the school, have a voice in the way the school was run, make sure Early was getting the best education possible. I had not bargained for controversy.

TWENTY-THREE

A PALE JANUARY MORNING, the sky low. Snow falling in downy pools. Early's junior year: 1986. On the radio in my bedroom, long lists of school closings. Charlotte-Mecklenburg public schools would let out at eleven. The four private schools had just closed for the day. *Charlotte Magazine* offices would close at noon, which meant I'd have an extra day to write my review. I thought about how snow days feel the same whether you're a child or a grown-up. Suddenly you're free. All responsibilities canceled. The day seems twice as long as normal—and the world gets very quiet.

More cancellations—day-care centers, the library, Job Fair that evening, Little Theater auditions—and the back door opened. Early and Chip. I could hear them in the kitchen: the back and forth of their good-natured teasing. The thick wetness of jackets dropped over the backs of kitchen chairs. Refrigerator door opening, closing.

The rumbling grind of its motor. Coke caps twisted off, hissing. Bags of potato chips.

"Come on," Chip was saying, his mouth full, "let's go. Get your coat."

I pictured Chip in his work boots, baggy jeans, stretched-out T-shirt, his ratty oversize jacket from the army-navy store. In a short time, he'd gone from letting his hair grow, to pulling it back in a ponytail, to a grumpy disregard for appearances in general.

"In a minute," Early said. "I want to say hi to my mom first."

"She'll want us to stay and talk to her. I mean she's great and all, but you can see her later. Let's go, man."

"I'm not even sure we should be doing this."

"What could happen? You're too hung up on rules. Anyway, we're not breaking any rules. It's a free country. Just get your coat on."

"Chip, this is not smart. You could end up looking pretty bad."

Chip said something I couldn't hear. Then, as abruptly as they'd burst in, they were gone.

I hurried into the kitchen. Through the frosty window over the sink, I could see them backing out of the driveway. I moved the little wooden "Mother of the Year" plaque Early had given me years before, which I kept on the windowsill, and I moved the things he'd made out of clay when he was in grammar school: the lumpy green turtle, Indian moccasin, lopsided vase. I leaned over the sink, as far to the right as I could, and watched them drive down Ridge Avenue to Providence Road. What unsmart thing were they getting ready to do? I grabbed my warmest coat—my L.L. Bean jacket with the wool plaid lining—and my keys and opened the door to the wintry light.

The snow had not been falling long enough for me to have to scrape the car windows. My wipers would do the job.

And, there they were, in Early's '82 beige Honda, in the right-hand lane on Providence going away from town. With traffic moving so slow, it was easy to follow them. Everyone in Charlotte was leaving work or school, going home. I pictured the grocery store. It would be running out of milk and bread right about now.

Chip and Early stayed on Providence Road. Past the gas station at the corner of Providence and Old Providence. Left. Then right. I kept my distance so they wouldn't see me. A school bus snorted and chugged between us. It stopped; the doors cranked open; children spilled out. They tossed a few snowballs. The snow was too dry to stick together and it looked like they were throwing ashes. The bus pulsed off.

Now Early was slowing down, turn signal on, pulling over in front of a new, two-story fake Tudor with gangly young river birches in the front yard. People are fooled into buying the tallest tree they can afford. Peter always says it's smarter to buy a small tree with a good shape. I would never buy a river birch anyway. They start losing their leaves in July, so you have five months of autumn; they drop twigs and branches all year; in the spring, they produce the worst pollen of any tree.

Through the large, loose snowflakes, I could see the Italianate ceramic numbers over the front door: 2113. Chip and Early were sitting still, both of them, staring at the house. They didn't appear to be talking. They were just sitting there, leaning in. I turned into a driveway, three houses before 2113, and headed in the opposite direction up the street. Then I slowed down and watched in my rearview mirror. They pulled away from the curb, came to a stop again, a few feet away, and remained in that spot, staring at the same house as before. Then Chip got out, walked against the wind, opened the mailbox, and seemed to be leaving a letter.

When I got home, I took out the phone book. *Caudle. Caulfield.* The pages stuck together and I had to peel them apart. *Causey. Cauthen. Brandon L. Cauthen. Frank D. Cauthen.* Move down the page quicker. *Roger.* That's it. I dragged my nail beneath the listing, leaving a faint dent in the paper. *Roger Cauthen*. I remembered the name from a Randolph Academy newsletter. Roger Cauthen. Julie's father. *2113 Chatham Road*. Chip and Early had been sitting in front of Julie's house.

What was wrong with Chip? Why wouldn't he leave Julie alone? Why was he so unhinged? Had he ever seen Mrs. Cohen, the school counselor? Polly probably never even contacted her.

Early was such an innocent. Trying to be a good friend. I could hear him defending Chip. *But, Mom, Chip just wanted to go by Julie's house. Since it was snowing and we were out of school, he figured she'd be home. All he did was leave her a note. No big deal.*

I understood Early from the inside out. I could *feel* his thinking. I knew how he liked to help people. Years before, his second-grade teacher had told me that on school trips she always paired Early with the child nobody wanted to sit beside—for two reasons: (1) Early didn't seem to mind; and (2) the other children liked Early so much, they were nicer to the child when they saw him with Early.

Chip was using Early as a repository for all his problems, talking, talking to him—those aimless, endless phone calls—as though my young, inexperienced son could actually give him guidance. The worst part was that Early wanted that friendship more than anything in the world. Chip was making sure Early stayed in his clutches. Once Chip fastened on, he would not let go. It was as though he had my son in his teeth, shaking his head from side to side, like a stubborn dog.

I sat at the desk in the kitchen with the phone book open, snow filling the window, the yeasty drift preventing me from seeing into the distance. My first impulse was to pick Early up, as I'd done countless times when he was little, remove him from the situation, put him into a safer one. Take him away from that friendship. I just didn't know how—or if I had the right—to do it.

B Y EARLY SPRING, New Beginnings, an evangelical Christian youth organization, was becoming *the* organization to join at Randolph Academy. Friendly, appealing, well-dressed adult advisers came to campus during lunch to recruit students. They invited them to parties at Godfather's Pizza, took them to Blowing Rock for the weekend, to Myrtle Beach. Julie Cauthen helped organize the group, became its first president—which meant Chip joined. Soon he was recruiting for them, handing out flyers at school, manning an information table on Saturday mornings in front of the fountain in SouthPark Mall. Chip's hair was clipped close now—no more pony-tail—and he dressed conservatively. Coat and tie, even to school. I was glad to see him *looking* normal, at least. Doing something more meaningful than driving through neighborhoods staring at half-timbered houses.

Early went to a few New Beginnings meetings and dropped out. He went on one of their weekend retreats, to Charleston, dropped out again. I felt sure Chip was putting pressure on him to belong. Early had not had any experience with Sunday school or church, so I'm sure the religion part felt strange to him. I found it interesting that Chip was so involved. His parents weren't the least bit religious. Their religion seemed to be all about wanting. The things you buy.

"You don't have to join," I told Early, after hearing him explain to Chip on the phone why he'd missed a meeting. I was reading a magazine, sitting across from him in the den; he'd just hung up the phone.

"I know I don't have to," he said, dialing again and, I could hear, getting a busy signal, "but it's important to Chip. And some of the things are fun. I can be a member without going to everything. No big deal, Mom. I'll work it out."

As much of a problem as New Beginnings must have been for

Early, I could see it was perfect for Chip. New Beginnings allowed him to be obsessed in an acceptable way. Now it was not just with Julie, it was with God. This boy's mother had almost left him for good. His girlfriend was gone. *Surely,* I sadly imagined him thinking as he sank down to his knees at night, *God will not drop me.*

TWENTY-FOUR

LATER THAT SEMESTER, Early's junior year. Late spring. Delicate, sweet-smelling spring. We'd had spring, had winter again, now it was spring for good. I was at the kitchen table, working on my agenda for a Parents' Council meeting. Near the end of my second term as president.

I felt happy just being home. I said to myself, There ought to be a word for a person like me, a person who loves her house. "Agoraphobic" is not it; that's when it's not really a choice to stay home. "Nester" is not right either. A little too domestic.

Early and Chip were on the screen porch. They'd closed the French doors into the den. I could hear faint murmurings over the thump of music from the speakers on the porch, but I wasn't really listening. I was concentrating on organizing my notes, whistling under my breath, a loose tune from some movie.

"The banana peels were a bust," I heard Early say. Then he said something I couldn't make out.

"The banana peels didn't do shit!" This was Chip. Then *he* said something I couldn't entirely hear. A long involved something about cough syrup and how that wasn't any good.

"I'm not kidding." Early again. Something else inaudible. Then: ". . . the scariest night I ever had. I feel awful today. I've never had a hangover like this."

Chip laughed and I could picture him punching Early lightly on the shoulder.

"Amazing how long it took!" Chip's voice, loud and distinct now. I'd slipped through the dining room (the Oriental rug muffled my steps), through the living room, across the front of the house so they couldn't see me, into my bedroom, where a window was open to the porch, but hidden by the painted silk curtain. "I bet it was three hours before the nutmeg kicked in. I didn't think it was going to work."

"Which is why we ended up at Lupie's." Early. "Remember you said let's just go get something to eat? Since we weren't feeling anything?"

"And you're in the middle of Lupie's scaring that poor waitress to death! You kept telling her to turn out the light!"

"Oh man, I couldn't tell the difference between good and bad. No, no, no, that's wrong—actually, everything seemed bad. Like, for example, the light was on—and all of a sudden the light was *on!* And I'm going, 'Oh, my God, somebody turn out the light!'"

"That was awesome!" Chip, laughing.

"I wouldn't call it awesome. It scared the hell out of me."

"You always get scared. Like when we were little and we were playing with matches in my garage and that puddle of oil caught on fire and I was going to stamp it out before it got going, but then you had to go and sit on it. You could've burned your butt!"

"You don't remember what happened, Chip. You tried to put it out and couldn't. If I hadn't sat on it, your house would've burned down."

"Well, anyway, last night I'm in the bathroom puking up my guts and you're screaming about the light and the waitress is freaking out!"

"Oh man, I forgot you were sick."

"Shit yeah, I threw up like five times. That's how I knew it had kicked in."

"I remember looking at things that were square and seeing them turn into rhombuses—"

"Rhombuses? You *are* a brain!"

"Anyway, I guess that's what a bad trip is."

"Fucking cool!"

"I never want to go through that again." Early, sounding very serious.

What were they talking about? Pot? Was nutmeg some sort of slang for marijuana? Surely it wasn't LSD, I thought. Early *did* say something about a hangover. Didn't that mean alcohol? Maybe they were talking about some kind of mixed drink. Vodka and fruit juice and nutmeg? Of course, I knew that teenagers experimented with drinking. It was unrealistic to think they would never take a drink. If that's what they were talking about, then maybe, just maybe, it wasn't so bad. Anyway, Early didn't seem to think whatever they'd done was so great; at least he still had his good judgment.

"Mom! What are you doing in here? I thought you were in the kitchen." Early's voice was a jolt, deep in my stomach. He was standing in the doorway to the bedroom. The sun coming through the window across the room was too sharp, too bright. It was making everything in the room go white. I rearranged my face to hide my shock and concentrated on his blue T-shirt, washed so many times it was not really blue. My eyes moved to his tattered jeans, to his right knee poking through like a hairy face.

"I was just coming in here to get my stapler," I stammered. *Collect yourself. This is your house and this is your room. You have a right to be here.* I shook my head like somebody waking from a dream and went to the oak rolltop desk, the last gift my mother gave me before she died. I made a point of sliding the stapler out of the cubbyhole, then making a wide detour around Early to head into the den. I was a person with work to do.

I stopped to wave at Chip through the doors. He was wearing khaki shorts and a blue Polo knit shirt; he'd installed himself on the antique glider in the corner of the porch, his legs—meaty as drumsticks—hanging over the arm. He smiled a big smile, scratched at his bare calf, waved back.

Early followed me.

"Are you sure you weren't listening to our conversation?" he blurted, his voice deep and—was it angry?

"Why are you so worried about my listening to your conversation? Were you saying something you didn't want me to hear?"

"That's not the point. I ought to be able to have a private conversation with a friend without you being a part of it." He took a step forward. He was standing close. Too close. "*Were* you listening? *Were you?* For once, tell the fucking truth!"

He'd backed me against the wall between the den and the kitchen. I felt hot and tearful. My hands tightened as if I were holding on to something.

"First of all, watch your mouth. And let me tell you something," I said, stepping sideways. "You need to know that whatever you do, no matter where you are or who you're with, I'm going to find out. That's just the way it is. It's what mothers do. So make sure you're never doing anything you don't want me to know about. I love you. Which means I'll do whatever it takes to keep you safe."

"What's that supposed to mean?" Angry, angry.

I swallowed hard several times and made my voice very calm. "I'm not worried. I know you'll do the right thing."

"You *don't* know that! You don't know *me*! You only see what I want you to see. Maybe I won't do the right thing. Maybe I'll do what

I want to do. You can only control me some of the time. When I'm in the house. You can't control me every second of my life!"

His breathing was irregular and heavy. His gaze was hard, something I'd never seen before.

"Early, calm down. And lower your voice. Go back to your company. I'm going into the kitchen to finish my notes for the Parents' Council meeting. This is not worth fighting over."

There. At least I'd gotten him off the subject of whether I was listening or not. Still, his outburst dazed me. The brittle language. The way he hunkered in his shell, closing me out.

I watched him open the door to the porch and slam it shut, then slouch down in the cushioned wrought-iron love seat. He picked a tender young leaf from the peace lily on the glass-top table, rolled it between his finger and thumb, stuck it in his mouth, and began to chew.

I tried to think of something, anything, to get my mind off the way he'd spoken to me. I remembered an article I'd read in a magazine that said it was "age appropriate" for teenagers to keep secrets from their parents. It also said that it's normal for teens to react with stronger anger than a situation might warrant; otherwise, those feelings would be left unresolved and might reappear later. The fact that Early sounded upset over whatever it was he and Chip had done made me think I was right not to make a big fuss and ground him or take away some privilege. I would just let him teach himself this lesson by allowing "natural consequences" to take over. The incident frightened him, so, of course, he wouldn't want to repeat it. Wasn't that better than my stepping in and *creating* consequences by punishing him?

In the kitchen, I decided to concentrate on coming up with the right word for myself. "Homebody" was close, but not quite it, though I loved being home, loved checking things off my to-do list. Loved being a mother. Even when it rocked my heart.

I found myself opening the door to the spice cabinet and spinning the lazy Susan. Everything in alphabetical order. Next to Mint Flakes was Ground Double Superfine Mustard. Next to that, Oregano Leaves. There was an empty space where Nutmeg was supposed to be.

TWENTY-FIVE

PETER WAS IN HILTON HEAD with his golfing buddies the night of Early's prom, May of his junior year. Thirteen months after Peter's affair. Life was pretty much back to normal. Each day the same, each day different. The familiar blurry pattern we get used to and count on.

Chip was spending the night at our house. The boys had gotten dressed upstairs in Early's room, then came down to show off their shiny black tuxedos. All of a sudden, it seemed, they both were so tall. Rangy. Chip must've been six feet. Early was at least as tall as Peter, five-ten. Chip wore a black cummerbund and tie. Early wore the matching red paisley cummerbund and tie we'd bought together at SouthPark. The whole time we'd been shopping, I was close to tears, nostalgic about all the times he and I had strolled from Belk's to Dillard's, in and out of the stores, weaving around shoppers in shorts and sandals or puffy winter coats, people walking too slow, their

arms loaded with packages or babies. Remembering how we'd always stopped at the food court for cardboardy slices of pepperoni
pizza that soaked the paper plates with grease. How we'd bought
soccer cleats, basketball sneakers, back-to-school jeans, Christmas
presents for teachers (those coffee mugs with funny sayings), birthday presents for friends (stuffed animals or diaries for the girls,
board games for boys). Wherever I looked, I saw our history together, the way a mall's tinny, piped-in music can rise around you
and bring with it every year you've ever known. When Early was little, he'd touch my hand absentmindedly as we walked. We were a
mother and son who could talk easily, laugh together. We would
never have to send each other those guilty Hallmark birthday cards
that confess, *Though I don't often show it . . .*

Prom night, I was aware of my warm feelings toward Chip, too.
After all, he'd practically grown up in our house. I took pictures with
Peter's Instamatic before the boys left to pick up their dates (Early
showed me how—"press this button, Mom; don't jiggle it; remember to wind the film"): Early, standing in front of the mantel, looking so much like me at that age. The chin. The smile. And always, his
familiar pose, right hand cupping the elbow of his left arm, left hand
flat against his cheek, covering the scar. Chip, half sitting, half
standing, propped on the arm of the sofa, looking as if he were
passing through for only a second.

Their dates were best friends: Amy Whitley and Ellen Booth. A
month before the prom, when Ellen had joined New Beginnings,
Chip dropped his obsession with Julie Cauthen—just like that!—
and started dating Ellen. Ellen used to be slightly antiestablishment,
with pierced earrings all the way up one ear and curly red hair worn
full and wild. Since joining New Beginnings, she was preppy, one
conservative earring per lobe, hair pixieish. Early and Amy had been
good friends for so long, I wondered if they were boyfriend and girl-

friend. They'd gone out on dates—I knew that. But whether it was serious, I couldn't tell, and Early wouldn't say. If they were serious, though, wouldn't I know?

The boys left to pick up Amy and Ellen, and the four of them came back to the house for more pictures. First, the girls posed, pert and hopeful in their carnation corsages and evening gowns—Amy in green, Ellen in tea-colored satin. I snapped them the second they caught each other's eye. Then the two couples posed—the awkwardness of where to put arms, how close to stand. Then Chip and Early, side by side on the sofa—Chip making horns behind Early's head. I loved every minute; Early understood and good-naturedly let me take the whole roll.

Because I was head of Parents' Council, I was in charge of the breakfast after the "after-party," the mothers' strategy for discouraging drinking and keeping the kids safe. I'd decided not to have the breakfast at our house, since Peter would be in Hilton Head. Janet Whitley offered, so I volunteered to cook the main dish and take care of the gifts for the seniors, engraved alarm clocks for college, which I'd ordered and wrapped—I liked for things to be gift-wrapped a certain way, with two-sided tape and double bows. I also said I'd help chaperone.

I made "Basic Breakfast Strata" from *Joy of Cooking*—eight three-quart Pyrex casseroles! Twelve pounds of sausage, sixteen cups of sliced mushrooms, four cups of chopped onions, thirty-two eggs, four quarts milk, eight loaves of bread, and a lot of grated cheese. The good thing was, I could make the stratas ahead of time and leave them in the refrigerator overnight. They needed one hour of baking. That was the tricky part—how would I bake eight big casseroles so they'd all be hot at the same time? *Where* would I bake eight big casseroles so they'd all be hot at the same time?

I assembled the casseroles Thursday (it took all day!) and Friday afternoon, delivered two casseroles each to three different mothers—Nancy Jan Todd, Dora Jackson, and Peeps Coddington. All I had to bake were two casseroles, just before I left for the Whitleys' early Saturday morning. Nancy Jan, Dora, and Peeps would do the others. I'd asked Barbara Dunham, but she'd said no.

Prom night, I turned out my light around midnight, after Early had called to let me know they'd gotten to the after-party. I always insisted Early call home when he was out with his friends or on a date with Amy and they changed locations. He'd never objected. Well, he did once. When I explained that I knew it was inconvenient but I just needed to know he was safe, he'd said okay.

I set my alarm for 3:30 A.M., sprang up, went into the kitchen to take the casseroles out of the refrigerator so they could come to room temperature while I showered and dressed. At four, the casseroles went in the oven. By five, they were done, and I loaded up the car to drive to the Whitleys, down Providence Road, five minutes away.

Charlotte, North Carolina, was fast asleep. My headlights made a bright path in the half dark.

A little after five-thirty, the kids straggled in to the Whitleys'. They were very polite, stopping to say hello to each mother and shake hands with each father. These were children from homes where manners were not only taught but relied upon to preserve a certain sense of order. I thought of Joy and how she used to say that a person's best trait could be flipped to show a negative side. Southern politeness makes for very civilized interaction between people, and because of that, it creates calm. Some people think the emphasis on appearance—image, above all else—and the effort required to maintain appearances is not so good. I would have chosen civility and calm any day.

The kids looked like hand-tinted photographs in their prom clothes. Pastel and sweet. I was glad to see Eddie Jackson there, with a senior, a white girl named Nancy Willis. Early walked in and gave me a kiss on the cheek. I knew the other mothers, whose sons wouldn't be caught dead kissing them, were watching. Watching with envy.

I went over to Barbara Dunham and said something about how our boys had gotten to be so old. She was wearing black jeans—this was back when jeans meant *blue* jeans to most people—and a camel-colored knit top with thin black stripes woven into the neck and cuffs. She always wore the right outfit, the right jewelry, had the right haircut. It was as if someone had told her, *I wish you the best of everything,* and she'd taken that on as an assignment. Chip came in and gave an indifferent half wave from the other side of the sunporch. I figured he was caught up with his friends and the fun of the evening. I'd seen him ignore his parents before. Barbara didn't seem to notice. She went right on talking, telling me where she got her hair colored, a different beauty salon from where she had it cut. Chip looked cute, even with his tux jacket off, shirttail out, tie and cummerbund hanging out of his pocket.

I left the breakfast around 6:30 A.M., drove home under a pink sky, fell asleep the minute my head hit the pillow. When Early and Chip came in, they were trying to be quiet, but I could hear them tiptoe upstairs and close the door to the landing. It was almost seven o'clock.

I slept till ten. When I buttoned my robe and walked out into the early-May chill to get the paper, I noticed Chip's car was not in the driveway.

It was two in the afternoon when Early finally came down. I was at the kitchen table, adding up my expenses for the breakfast to turn in to Janet Whitley, Parents' Council treasurer. He flip-flopped into the kitchen, wearing a white T-shirt and cotton boxers with a Mexican-pepper print. He was hunched over, pressing the heels of his hands into his eyes. His hair had that wonderful slept-on-wrong, cowlick look.

"Hi there," I said gaily.

"Hm," he said, short for "hi there."

"Where's Chip?"

"Home." He opened the door to the refrigerator and stared at the orange juice carton.

"Home? When did he go home?"

"This morning."

"This morning? You guys didn't come in till seven. I looked at my clock."

"He left around nine. I think."

"You mean he slept from seven to nine and then left? That doesn't make sense. Why didn't he just sleep at home?"

"I don't know."

This was beginning to feel like a "where did you go?"—"out"—"what did you do?"—"nothing" conversation.

By this time, he'd poured orange juice to the rim of a tall glass and was gingerly crossing the kitchen, taking sips. His flip-flops made quarreling sounds on the hardwood floor. When he got to the table, he turned to the comics, spread them out, and began reading. His face was two inches from the paper, his way of saying the conversation was over.

"All right, honey, you can read the paper in peace. I'm going upstairs to change the beds in your room."

He jumped up, grabbed my arm. "That's all right, I'll do it. I'll take care of it. Right after breakfast. Don't worry."

"I don't mind. I just want to get the wash going."

He'd maneuvered himself between me and the doorway and was suddenly very broad. He could've been blocking a field goal.

"Early."

"It's nothing, Mom. Really. Just relax."

"I *am* relaxed."

"Okay," he said. "Chip wasn't feeling so hot when we got home last night."

"Why didn't you wake me up? If he needed me. Is he okay?"

"Well, he drank a little too much and that's why he wasn't feeling good."

"Oh . . . And?"

"And. He must've gotten up after we went to bed, and he didn't make it to the bathroom. I guess he went home after that. I was sleeping. I didn't hear him. No big deal. I'll clean it up. You don't have to go up there."

"Did *you* drink?"

"No, I didn't. I promise." The way he said it, the look on his face, I knew he was telling the truth.

And then, I don't know what got into me—maybe it was because Peter wasn't home and I decided to take on his role—but I pushed past Early and marched upstairs. He was right behind me.

I couldn't believe what I saw. Chip had thrown up in the bed, all over the sheets, the pillow, quilt, down the side of the mattress, on the bed frame itself. He'd thrown up on the carpet in small violent splashes. Some was on the baseboard near the bed, even splattered on the wall. On the tile floor of the bathroom. The side of the tub, cabinet doors under the sink, the toilet. The smell was making me gag.

Chip had made this gigantic mess and left it for Early to clean up. What kind of a friend was that? How was Early able to sleep through all this? Didn't he smell it?

"Tell Chip to get over here. Right now. Tell him he's got to help." My voice was thin, reedy. My hands, I noticed, were shaking a little.

"I can clean it up."

"You shouldn't have to. Call him."

"Really, Mom, it's no big deal. I can do it myself."

Okay. So he wasn't going to call Chip. Then I'd help. No way Early could clean this up by himself.

I felt overwhelmed. Where to begin? For a second, I wished we could just leave, lock the door. Put the house up for sale.

I made myself go down to the laundry room, get the Lysol, plastic bucket, pack of sponges. Back upstairs. Early and I, together, began to scrub. We didn't talk. A couple of times I started to say something, but I didn't want to say the wrong thing. My mood shifted from anger toward Chip to sympathy for Early to sympathy for myself—stuck with this mess—to wondering what Peter would say about this when he got home. *If* I told him. (I decided later not to.)

Over and over, I emptied the bucket of snail-colored water into the toilet, rinsed out the bucket, started all over again with fresh water and a squirt of Lysol. Early worked in the bathroom. I brought in fresh sheets, changed the bed, took the dirty sheets down to the washing machine, got that going. Back upstairs, cleaned around the bed. Then he and I switched. I worked in the bathroom, he cleaned the bedroom. Together, we went through four sponges. We scrubbed until there was not a trace of vomit left.

TWENTY-SIX

M OM." That tone of voice. Even on the phone, I could tell something was wrong. "Everything's okay" came next. I thought of Joy and how she'd said that when someone begins the conversation with *everything's okay,* you can be sure nothing is okay.

"What's wrong, Early?"

"Well, there's been a small accident—"

"You were in an accident? In your car? Are you all right? Early?"

"Wait a minute, Mom, hold on. Chip and I—"

"Chip was driving?"

"Mom, just listen a minute. I was driving and I'm not sure what happened, but all of a sudden my car left the road and we ended up in a ditch. I promise, we're both all right. It just scared me, that's all."

"Are you sure you're all right?"

"I'm positive. The car—"

"What about the car?"

"Well, the car's pretty messed up. It's still down in the ditch. We didn't know what to do, so we left it there."

"Because it has to be towed? Did the police come?"

"No, we didn't call the police. We walked up the street to somebody's house—a real nice lady who let us use her phone. In fact, she reminded me of you. She kept asking if we were all right and she gave us lemonade and homemade cookies. We called Steven Todd and he came and picked us up."

"When did all this happen?"

"After lunch. Around one."

"One? It's almost four now. Why did you wait so long to call?"

"Well, I didn't think you'd be home."

Didn't think I'd be home? All he had to do was try, and if I wasn't home, he'd leave a message on the machine. Anyway, I *was* home. "You weren't driving too fast, were you?"

"I don't think so."

"Where are you now?"

"At Chip's house."

"Why didn't you just come home?"

"Well, Chip wanted to go to his house, so I came over here with him. Listen, the reason I'm calling is, what should I do now? Call a wrecker? Or what? How do I get my car?"

"Don't do anything, Early. I'll handle it. You just take it easy. Rest. You sure you're not hurt? Sometimes these things don't show up for a while, like a whiplash, you know. Nothing hurts? Your neck?"

"No, Mom, I'm really fine. I knew you'd know what to do. And Mom?"

"Yes, Early?"

"Thank you for helping me. I'm sorry it happened. I should've been paying better attention. I'm sorry for what I did."

"Oh, Early, it's not your fault. It could happen to anybody. Really.

I can't count the number of times I've done something careless when I was driving. It happens. Don't be hard on yourself, honey."

"Thanks, Mom." We sat there a few seconds, listening to the silence.

"You'll be home for supper, right?"

"Right."

"Oh, where's the car?"

"On Sharon-Amity, on the right-hand side of the street, past where you cross Central Avenue. Not far."

"Okay. I'll take care of it. Bye, honey."

"Bye, Mom."

I found the AAA number, picked up the phone to call, hung up without dialing. *First, go to the car and see what's there.* I decided to call Peter to ask if he'd meet me at the car, or better yet, come by for me and we'd go together. Then I hung up, again without dialing. *Just go yourself,* something told me.

Driving through the mid-June city, I rolled down my windows to let the magnolia-heavy air enter the car. Sharon-Amity took me past perfectly painted garages, then garages with chipped paint, then small houses with no garages. The operatic sweetness of the air reassured me. What could be bad on a glorious summer day in Charlotte? My favorite season. Three months before Early would begin his last year in high school.

I tapped my horn at a dog that looked like it might dart into the road and thought of my father and the time he'd driven home from the office, late, honking his horn the whole way. Billy and I were playing with neighborhood kids in our front yard and heard the throaty Studebaker horn from when my father turned onto our street, almost a mile away, until he pulled into our tree-lined driveway and turned off the motor. Since he was not the type to lay on his horn for blocks, I was convinced we were in for some kind of special celebration; he would have surprises for all of us. Surely my father was saying, *It's summer! Let's be a little bit foolish! Let's tell everyone in the neighborhood I'm on my way home to my precious children, and life is wonderful!* It turned out his horn had been stuck, and all he did when he got out of the car was wave us off and disappear into the house.

Why is it, when we think of childhood, our memories are usually from summer? Swimming in the Springers' pool next door, doing Esther Williams handstands in the shallow end, feet together, toes pointed, making our legs straight as sticks. The slow trucks that drove through the neighborhood spraying for mosquitoes, how we played in the clouds as if we were wandering into sleep.

I swerved to miss a crushed possum in the street, its body stretched out across the asphalt, drying. *What if I've driven past the car? Will I be able to see it from the road? Surely they didn't go this far out. What could they possibly be doing out here? Am I still in Mecklenburg County?*

I pulled into the next driveway, a short gravel drive. The yard was loaded, I mean loaded, with blooming flowers—like a child carrying a package that was too big. No grass, just an outburst of marigolds, zinnias in every color, purple ageratum, overgrown sunflowers. And everywhere, adolescent-awkward alliums teetering on tall stems.

Even the front porch was filled with plastic pots of all sizes, heaped with summer annuals. I understood. It was easy to buy too many of those six-packs of seedlings, easy to go overboard. Especially in early spring, when winter's over and you're hungry for color.

I backed into the street—Peter would say never do this, never on a street with a blind curve—and I put the car in drive, pressed my foot down hard on the gas.

Look carefully now. Don't miss it this time.

There. On the left. I could see the rear bumper of Early's Honda. The car was almost hidden in a thicket of weeds and collapsed branches. It looked as though it had ventured into a green wall of leaves and stopped, sinking in embarrassment. I pulled off the side of the road into mud, turned off the engine, and opened my door.

When I looked closer, I could see the car was cheek by jowl with a tree. For a minute, I felt I shouldn't be looking. As though I were interrupting something private.

I hadn't even thought to ask if the Honda was locked. I should've gone by Chip's to pick up the keys.

I walked sideways through the crooked tree limbs, with their haphazard claim on the damp slope, down to the car. I had to move quickly; the heels of my sandals kept sinking in the mud.

All the windows were open. Well, at least I didn't have to worry about getting in. Early's gray Patagonia jacket was balled up on the front seat. I pushed the jacket over to the passenger side and got in. The keys—with the tiny blue and white Carolina basketball and the sterling silver R.A. (Randolph Academy) Early had been awarded for soccer—were still in the ignition. Why would he leave the keys in the ignition? I tried to turn on the engine. Nothing. Not a sound. I took the keys, unzipped my purse, and dropped them in—my son's keys suddenly seemed so personal, so intimately his, in among my lipsticks, wallet, checkbook, compact, blush.

I looked around. Everything was okay. Under the driver's seat was a white towel—one of those towels Peter brought home from the Y. Each of us—Peter, Early, and I—kept one under the front seat for emergencies. Stopping for Bojangles, for example, you could use the towel to spread over your lap so you wouldn't get greasy.

I got out of the front seat and opened the back door, checked the floor and the shelf in the rear window, climbed into the backseat on my knees—didn't want to dirty the floor mats—and looked as far as I could under both front seats. Nothing unusual. Coke can under the driver's seat. Burger King cup flattened under the passenger seat.

BK Lounge, Early and his friends called Burger King, located a block from school.

Everything was all right. Perfectly normal. Why had I been so suspicious?

I got back in the driver's seat, dangling my feet—my caked shoes—out the open door. Tried the glove compartment. Locked. I fished through my purse for his keys. Inside the glove compartment, right in front, were two packs of rolling papers. I felt ankle-deep in something—I knew what this meant. Behind where the rolling papers had been—they were now in my purse—was a brass thing that looked vaguely Art Nouveau with its fancy curls (like a design you'd see on an old vase). A roach clip. In the corner, a small pipe. All of a sudden I was aware of the smell in the glove compartment. A wild, reckless smell. Like something burning. Or spices past their prime.

Of course. Pot.

I grabbed everything and crammed it into my purse. I locked the glove compartment. My first thought was that all this drug paraphernalia must belong to Chip. It had been in the glove compartment, which was, of course, on the passenger's side. Chip's side. I found myself furious with Chip. *Why did he leave this in my son's car? What was Chip thinking?*

I realized I was short of breath. And that I was excusing my son for something I probably should not excuse him for. But I couldn't help it. I held on to his jacket for stability, rolled up the windows, locked the Honda, got into my car, and started the engine. I felt like a thief or an impostor who had to flee before getting caught. As though *I* were the one who'd done something wrong. Not my son. I cast a nervous glance over my shoulder—and was shocked—shocked!—to see a patrol car pulling up behind me, blue light flashing. Behind that, another patrol car. His blue light flashing. Two patrol cars! I drew Early's jacket close and thought of what was now in my purse. I looked down to make sure I'd zipped it all the way. Suddenly two patrolmen were standing beside my car, peering in, motioning me to roll down my window.

"Is that your Honda?" one said, the older of the two, the one with the pin-dot eyes and shaggy brows.

"Oh no, it belongs to my son."

"Where is he?"

"Well, he asked me to come here."

"Who was driving that vehicle at the time of the accident, ma'am?"

"My son."

"And he's not here?"

"He's only seventeen, Officer. He was upset, and since it didn't involve anybody else, I mean, another car, he didn't know he was supposed to call the police. He walked up the street to somebody's house and phoned a friend to come pick him up." I didn't mention Chip. I'm not sure why. "My son called the minute he got to his friend's house and asked me to come out here and to please call the police for him. I was just leaving to go home and make the call." *Why had Early and Chip called Steven Todd and not me?*

"Where's the car registration?" the younger patrolman asked. "And the keys?" His hat was at least one size too big, making him look like he might topple over any minute. He pushed in beside the older cop. Their heads filled my window.

I didn't want them to open the glove compartment—the smell!—but I knew that's where the registration was, even though I hadn't seen it when I'd looked before. Peter, Early, and I all kept our car registrations in our glove compartments.

Before I could answer, the same patrolman, the young one, said, "And what about your son's driver's license?" While he was talking, I'd reached my hand inside the pocket of Early's jacket. I could feel his driver's license, the square plastic. For some reason, though, I wasn't sure I should take it out. If it was in Early's jacket, it had to be okay. Still, I pulled my hand out, leaving the license deep inside the linty pocket.

"My son has the keys and he keeps his license and registration in his wallet, so, of course, I can't give you those. I wish I'd thought to get them before I came out here." My old trick. Give lots of details. Make it all sound true. Anyway, why would I have somebody else's license and registration? "I could go get them if you want me to."

The older one said, "You stay right here, ma'am. We need to look around."

They trudged down toward Early's car. I felt the heavy heat of the day on my skin, almost as if I were running a fever. I blew on my upper lip. The older patrolman tried the door on the driver's side. His expression said, *Yes, locked. Just as I suspected.* Then he went around to the front of the car, wedging himself between the broken branches, and disappeared into the shadows. The younger patrolman stooped beside the passenger side, looking underneath the car—what on earth was he hoping to find there? Then he joined the other patrolman. Maybe *I* should have checked the front of the car. I lifted my arms so that air could circulate beneath them.

They were both walking toward me.

"You have Triple A?" one asked.

I said that I did.

He told me I could go home and call a wrecker; looked like there was no reason to charge anyone.

I sat in my car until they turned off their blue lights and pulled into traffic, until they disappeared around the curve. Then I took the license out of Early's jacket. Frank Doar Millett, it said. But it was Early's photograph. Date of birth: September 3, 1965. Not the right month, day, or year. Four years before Early was born. Which would make this person, this Frank Doar Millett person, twenty-one. Drinking age.

I had never considered that Early might have a fake ID. At the same time, I wasn't the type of parent who thought it was a federal crime for teenage boys to take a drink. I believed it was safer for them to do their experimenting while they were still living at home. Under the protection of their parents.

But pot was a different story.

Peter and I had smoked marijuana once, around 1970, a year or so after Early was born. We only smoked that one time because Peter didn't like breaking the law and I wasn't crazy about feeling so out of control. We were spending the weekend in Blowing Rock; somebody in Peter's office had given him a joint (the lingo makes even a middle-aged woman sound like a hippie). We sat in our car outside the restaurant and smoked. By the time we got to our table, decided what to order, then found our way to the salad bar, we were feeling the effects. At one end of the salad bar were small cups and two kinds of soup. At the other end were plates for salad. In our blundery state, we didn't see the salad plates and began stuffing the cups with salad, but because they were so tiny, all we could get in were a couple of olives, a slice or two of cucumber, and a few croutons. There was no way we could fit lettuce in those cups. When the waiter came to the table to refill our water, he just stared at our miniature salads. Peter and I started laughing hysterically and couldn't stop. We laughed so hard we had to leave the restaurant. We never even got to the main course.

But Early. Surely, I thought, he couldn't be making the grades he was making in school and playing varsity sports if he were heavy into pot. Wouldn't I see a dramatic change in his behavior? And anyway, what could I do? Ground him? Would that stop him? I certainly wasn't going to let him get into trouble with the police. I decided to just wait and see. Keep a close watch.

I slipped the license back into his pocket. I definitely didn't want him to know I'd been snooping.

By the time I pulled onto the road and began to accelerate, I knew I would not mention anything about what I'd found in the glove compartment to Early or to Peter. I understood that covering for Early was not such a good thing. But I felt I had to do it this one last time. He was almost a senior. Soon he'd be going off to college. I'd give him the benefit of the doubt and assume this was an isolated incident (like the time *I'd* smoked). I didn't want one little blunder—kids just being kids—to jeopardize his already not-so-steady relationship with his father.

As for Chip, Early would meet new friends once he got to college. He'd forget about Chip. No way I could step in the middle of that friendship now, keep Early away from him. I'd be inviting an all-out rebellion on my son's part. After their senior year, they'd go their separate ways.

I'd go home and call AAA.

Call Peter at the office to tell him about the accident.

Call Early at Chip's to say everything had been taken care of and for him to come home. Almost time for supper.

Go over with him what he'd told me on the phone, casually, without drawing attention to what I was doing, to make sure he and I were in sync.

No need to rile Peter with conflicting stories.

TWENTY-SEVEN

I T'S THE TRUDGING through mud that mothers are good at. We'll go to the ends of the wet, pulpy earth for our children.

Images emerge. Holdovers from the past. They lie in wait until I pay attention. Some are like a dream I wake from, where I believe I can remember everything. But as I think of the beginning and the middle, the end fades. I concentrate, try to remember how it was. Then the moments settle around me and spread out:

The Easter I'm twelve. Mother takes me to Rock Hill Feed and Supply to buy a dyed baby chick. I kneel beside the large wooden box and watch them, rolling about in the sawdust, fluttering awkwardly. Lime green ones, bright pink, lilac, powder blue. I can't make up my mind between lilac and powder blue. Of course, Mother says I can have one of each.

"How would you like that, sugar?" She says those exact words.

"I'd like that fine," I answer.

Easter is early, and by summer, my chicks have grown into full-size roosters, strutting around like kings. They're my pets, like other people have dogs, and I keep them in our fenced-in backyard. Every morning I scatter glassy kernels of corn in the grass for them to scratch up. Afternoons, I carry them around the neighborhood, showing them off, one under each arm, as though they're weightless. Over and over, Billy tells me—and everyone else—how weird it is that I have roosters for pets.

One night a storm blows in. Billy is in his room messing with his camera or practicing magic. My parents and I are in the den, my father reading, Mother and I watching Milton Berle's *Texaco Star Theater*. A magician is rolling around a double-edge razor blade inside his mouth with his tongue; Milton Berle is off to the side, grimacing, those big teeth like rocks. All of a sudden pounding rain and rolls of thunder drown out the background music on TV. I immediately think of my roosters and ask my father to bring them into the house.

"They don't like to be rained on," I say, hoping to appeal to his sense of fairness.

"Not necessary, not necessary at all," he says, folding the newspaper back over itself with a crackle. "The rain won't hurt them a bit."

I look at Mother and know what she's thinking. I always know what she's thinking.

As soon as my father goes to bed, Mother heads for the screened-in back porch (really just a tiny utility room) and reaches over the wooden crate of Coca-Colas on the clothes dryer to rummage through the tool cabinet for a flashlight. She clumps out into the rain; I sit cross-legged on the floor of the porch and watch.

It's raining so hard I have to lean forward, my face pressed to the screen, to keep her in sight. One minute she's hitching up her skirt and crawling under the hydrangea bush, shaking its branches until the blooms, in the flashlight's glow, fall around her like lavender stars. The next, she's bending over the whitewashed stones that line her flower bed, tipping one or two, checking to see if a rooster could be hiding there. She threads her way through the rosebushes, her flashlight flinging strips of light as sharp as the lightning that's cutting the sky.

Finally, she finds my roosters huddled together in the hedge and she brings them in, just as a suck of thunder makes me clap my hands to my ears. My roosters sit so close together on the kitchen floor, they look like one rooster. With the back of her foot, Mother closes the swinging door between the kitchen and the hall, then the door between the kitchen and breakfast room. She grabs a bath towel from the laundry basket and dries her hair and the front of her black-and-white-checked sundress, my favorite of all her sundresses. Finally, she stands still and reaches down to give me a long, slow hug.

I follow her up the stairs. Her black patent-leather flats are sopping wet. They make little suctioning noises and leave puddles on each wooden step. I'm torn between feeling sorry she had to get so drenched and being relieved my pets are safe.

Sometime around the middle of the night, the storm comes to an end.

The next morning, when the sky lightens, loud squawks fill the house. My mother, father, Billy, and I all stumble sleepily down the stairs—my father, in his loose cotton pajamas and leather slippers, taking the lead.

The kitchen is a stir of red. My roosters are skittering around, flying as high as their fat bodies will allow them to fly. Everything from the counters is on the floor, the muddy floor, and everything breakable has been broken: the cookie jar, iced tea glasses from last night's dinner left to dry on a dish towel, our good crystal pitcher, the ceramic canisters that held sugar and flour (making it look like it snowed in the kitchen).

I don't dare look at my father, but I sense the stiffness in his back. Billy stands between my father and me, closer to my father, making them a team. I put my hand on Mother's back, the bumpy ridges of her pink chenille robe soft beneath my fingers. She smells like roses. Then, as though we actually talked about it and decided to do this thing together, she and I kneel at exactly the same instant and begin picking up broken glass—the icy needles, the larger pieces curved like shells. When I see in her face that she's afraid I might cut myself, I hand her the ones I've gathered. I don't want to add to the worry I've already caused her.

Billy and my father catch the roosters and take them outside. I stay with Mother while she picks up the rest of the glass from the kitchen floor and stacks it in a tall, teetery mound in the palm of her hand.

F OR A LONG TIME I believed with all my heart she did not know that at that very minute my father and Billy were stuffing the roosters in the car and driving them out into the country to set them free. I couldn't imagine she'd allow them to do that. My mother was the basket I'd put all my eggs in.

Now everything is up for grabs. If my son and my husband, whom I trusted, could do things I never believed possible—if I was not able to see them clearly—what's to keep me, this many years after my mother's death, from doubting her?

When a hurricane beats down, it can loosen tree roots—even the roots of giant trees that have stood for generations. Of course, no one can actually see this happening. But long after the name of the hurricane is forgotten, a slight wind will collapse a hundred-foot oak.

TWENTY-EIGHT

PETER GOT THE HONDA FIXED—our insurance paid for it—and I was glad I hadn't called unnecessary attention to the accident by telling him too many details. My philosophy, *let a little time pass and things will right themselves,* seemed to be working. I flushed the marijuana down the toilet, threw the pipe, papers, and clip—along with my pocketbook, which smelled terrible—into a Dumpster behind the drugstore. The day after the accident, Early told me in an offhand way, too nonchalantly to be nonchalant, that Chip had left some "stuff" (the exact word he used) in his car and for me not to worry; none of it belonged to him. "I promise, Mom," he said, "none of it." He did not ask whether I'd found it or what happened to it. I knew he wouldn't.

He was now in his senior year. A senior year that had all the signs of being flawless. Life seemed to be back on an even keel, as my mother would say. His applications were in, to Duke, Vanderbilt, Emory, Davidson, and Wake Forest. The varsity soccer team went undefeated and he, personally, had a great season. He was editor of the yearbook. His class voted him speaker for graduation. He was president of the French club. All of his hard work was paying off, and he was finally receiving the recognition he deserved.

Chip was doing well, too. President of New Beginnings. Grades improving. He seemed to be—well, just living a life. Even Peter was aware of Chip's progress, and when he came to the house, Peter acted friendly toward him again.

One afternoon, Chip and Steven Todd were shooting baskets with Early in the driveway. Varsity basketball had begun, and they were all starters on the team. At the last minute, Chip had tried out; it had been a long time since he'd played any sport, but he not only made the team, the coach named him captain.

Steven had to go home early because his grandmother was visiting from Baltimore. I invited Chip for supper.

I fixed everyone's plate and brought them to the kitchen table. Lasagna, garlic bread, tossed salad. I sat down, unfolded my napkin (I'd shaped all the napkins into birds), and looked around the table. "Pull the curtains, honey," I said to Early, and thought how happy I was for my family to be here together and for Early and Chip to be doing so well. I was happy for the sound of forks on china, the bread two shades of gold. Peter was packed with energy even just sitting there, spearing a slice of cucumber with his fork. He wore a white cotton-knit golf shirt and jeans. He'd been playing a lot of golf lately and was tan and healthy looking. I found myself falling in love with his looks all over again.

Early had on a light green Randolph Academy T-shirt and a new pair of jeans. The light green made his green eyes greener. His hair, darker than blond and lighter than brown, the color of peanut shells (exactly my shade before I started turning gray), was straight and longish. Early, like Peter, always appeared so clean. You looked at them and thought of soap and water. Chip's brown hair was short.

He had a cowlick in front, so his hair, over his right eyebrow, sprouted in different directions. He was wearing a white button-down oxford shirt, yellow tie with little fish, khakis. His shirttail always hung out a little.

I asked him how things were going with New Beginnings.

"Fine, Mrs. Smallwood."

That's all he said.

I glanced across the table at Peter, as if to ask if I should try a follow-up question or drop it. Before I could read the expression on his face, he said, "I just saw an interesting article, Chip, about prayer. How they've found it to be a potent healing force. The research shows that people who pray regularly have fewer physical ailments, and when they do become ill, they recover more quickly. People with terminal diseases even live longer. And they fare better during surgery."

I liked the generosity, the graciousness, the Dale Carnegie-speak-in-terms-of-the-other-person's-interest of what he'd said. Peter at his best.

Chip brightened. "That's exactly right, Mr. Smallwood. But the real reason you pray is to stay close to God. You have to serve God in the ways He expects. Confess your sins. Or else be damned for all eternity."

Early pushed his chair maybe an inch away from the table. For a second I could picture him, millimeter by millimeter, pushing himself farther and farther from the table and the conversation—until he was finally in the den.

"Y'all should have heard Chip at the game," Early said. "He gave the opening prayer. He wrote it himself. It was great. He's a great writer."

"Anybody want more lasagna? Plenty left." I was right there with Early. Get Chip off the religion thing. I definitely didn't want to hear a sermon at my kitchen table. I stood up, ready to reach for some-one's—anyone's—plate. "Chip? How about you?"

"No, thank you, Mrs. Smallwood. It was really good, though. You're the best cook!"

"Thank you, Chip. Early? Peter? More?"

No's all around.

"How about salad? More milk? Water, Peter?"

They were all fine.

"You know, Mr. and Mrs. Smallwood, I've told Early this and he's finally coming around to my way of thinking. You don't want to disappoint God. Eternity lasts a long time."

"But prayer is so personal," Peter said. "Each person has to make his own decision where religion is concerned. Speaking of religion, I overheard a conversation the other day—one of my partners was asking a woman who'd just moved to Charlotte what church she went to. Her answer was, 'I don't actually go. I'm doing home-churching.' I thought that was pretty good!" Peter laughed. Early and I laughed, too. Chip smiled. The best he could do.

Early pushed his chair a little farther from the table. Then he got up and began clearing the dishes. I was at the sink now, rinsing and fitting everything into the dishwasher. Let Peter handle Chip.

"We have to keep praying until we get it right, Mr. Smallwood."

"As long as religion is a comfort," Peter said. "As long as it's not based on fear. As long as it's your own personal choice."

"I disagree. Religion *has* to be based on fear," Chip said. Amaz-ing, I thought. The nerve he has to contradict an adult! To think he knows what we don't. "Our fate in the hereafter is determined by what we do in this life. If we fear God, we don't have to fear death."

"It seems to me, Chip, that religion is a reaction to our fear of death. It's how we deal with anxiety about our own personal demise."

By this time, I was smashing whole shelled pecans between

sheets of wax paper with the flat end of a butcher knife. I stopped just before everything turned to powder. Then I dug out the chocolate ice cream and plopped big muddy scoops in four glass bowls. I tried to sprinkle the nuts over each serving, but they were so pulverized they stuck to my fingers. I decided to drown the desserts in chocolate sauce.

Early took two—and I took two—to the table.

"Dessert, everyone! Dig in!" I said cheerily.

As soon as I sat down, I asked Early about French Day, which the French club was sponsoring—if they were able to find the French tapes they'd been looking for and who was going to make the croissants. It was *not* my imagination that a look of relief spread across Early's face.

By the time we'd finished dessert, it was after nine. Chip said he had to go home to make phone calls for New Beginnings. He thanked me for dinner, gave me a kiss on the cheek, shook hands with Peter, thanked him for "a good discussion." Chip was so polite at the end, I wondered if I'd overreacted to what he'd said about religion. Early headed up to his room to work on his term paper on Buddhism. Peter went into the den, flicked the remote. I finished the dishes.

Over the following months, I noticed Early beginning to sound a little like Chip. Not on the subject of prayer. Or religion. But on doing good in the world. It was the stridency that was similar. Chip's perspective was conservative, narrow. Early's was, of course, liberal and compassionate.

One night, late, Early started a conversation about how Peter and I had an obligation to make the world a better place because we'd had so many advantages. Naturally, Peter and I agreed. Then Early brought up Phyllis and how he'd been shocked I could be so heartless and fire her just because she'd taken a few bars of soap, knowing how badly she needed the money and how many years she'd worked for us. Before I could remind him that she was now receiving money from us monthly, he turned to Peter and began criticizing Turning Point, the project Peter had been involved in at the Y, a citywide program that paired low-income families with "successful" families who served as their mentors. Early asked Peter why the Turning Point office was in a white neighborhood, which meant that poor families would have a hard time getting there. Peter was scratching in cottonseed meal around the roots of a bonsai crab apple and didn't answer. Didn't even look up. I thought of my own father and the times he hadn't answered me. I decided somebody had to say something. I told Early that maybe he (Early) was tired and needed a good night's sleep; he should probably just go to bed; he'd had a lot on him lately, with his term paper, tests, the yearbook, basketball.

My thinking was that his edgy behavior was simply a result of fatigue. When a child talks back or stays out past curfew or leaves his wet towel on the carpet in his room after his parents have told him not to, he probably just needs nine hours of good solid rest. Not so different from my own mother's belief that low hemoglobin was to blame for everything. The one time I'd raised my voice at her, accusing her of telling me what to do every minute of my life, that I couldn't put one foot in front of the other without her showing me how to do it, she'd taken me to the doctor, convinced I had "low blood."

TOWARD THE END of the school year, we had a party for the yearbook staff at our house. The yearbook had won a statewide award for creativity—the theme was "Once Upon a Time." Everyone had gone home but Eddie Jackson, who was business manager. I collected the dirty glasses, chip-and-dip bowls, Coke bottles, balled-up paper napkins, and took them into the kitchen, then stopped to chat for a minute with Eddie. I asked how his mother was. I'd gotten to know her at soccer games and liked her very much. She was what I'd call a toucher. She reacted to whatever you said by touching your arm—a soft tap when you said something funny, a caress when she agreed with you or wanted you to know she understood, yes, she understood exactly what you were saying. Eddie said she was doing fine and that she'd taken a second job—secretary in the upper school office—to help with his college expenses. (He'd already been awarded a math scholarship to Stanford.) She'll be a great addition to the staff, I said. More chitchat. I said good night, went into my bedroom, closed the door, and decided to call Peter at the office to find out how late he'd be. It was already ten o'clock.

I could hear Early and Eddie talking in the den. I put the phone down, without dialing the last two numbers. Early was showing Eddie a photograph of my grandfather, one of the family pictures on the staircase wall just outside my door. The studio shot of my grandfather, wearing a dark suit and matching collared vest and bow tie, was framed in braided antique gold leaf with bubble glass. My grandfather's stubborn jaw was like my father's and my brother's. Early was pointing out to Eddie how dark-skinned his great-grandfather was and then he said that he suspected the man may have been part black. I couldn't believe what I was hearing. Where'd he get an idea like that? Sure, people discovered this sort of thing about their ancestors, and if this were true about ours, there'd be nothing wrong with it. It'd be interesting, in fact. But my grandfather was just a suntanned Italian immigrant. If Early wondered about his great-grandfather, why hadn't he asked me? Was he trying to prove to Eddie he was like him? I thought of Dr. Kusz, the child psychologist I'd taken Early to when I was trying to get him into Willow Open School, how he'd said that Early was so highly attuned to other people. How far would empathy take a person?

On a sleepy Saturday morning, two days before graduation, I was in bed, trying to talk myself into getting up. I rolled over on my back, stretched until one hand brushed Peter's pillow and the other lay across my bedside table. Peter had just left the house for his Saturday morning golf game, and Chip had picked up Early for a graduation rehearsal at school. The run-through was called for 8 A.M. because the day was supposed to be hot.

Then I heard Peter back in the kitchen: "Kathryne! I think you might want to see this!"

I couldn't imagine what I might want to see at seven forty-five on a Saturday morning, but I slid out of bed, found my robe, and went into the kitchen.

"Out here," he said. He was breathing quickly, audibly.

I followed him out the back door, into the acid-sharp sunshine, down to the driveway.

The trunk of Early's Honda was open, and inside were at least a dozen cases of beer—all different brands—turned this way and that.

"What were you doing in his trunk?" I asked, still a little groggy from sleep.

"That's what you say? 'What was I doing in his trunk?'"

"Well, I mean—"

"What do you think about all this beer? That's what you ought to be reacting to. Not what I was doing in his trunk!"

"Surely there's a good explanation," I said, rubbing my eyes.

Peter slammed the trunk shut and the car trembled. It snapped me wide awake.

"I'm late. We'll talk about this when I get home," he said. "Don't say anything to Early if he gets here before I do. I want to be in on *this* conversation."

"What do you mean by that?"

"Never mind. Just wait for me so we can talk to him together." He said this more matter-of-factly.

The day did turn hot, temperature above ninety, which, in early June, when you're not used to it, feels hotter than it actually is. I spent the morning on the screen porch, ceiling fan on high, just sitting there, watching the light drain out of the sky. It was too hot to eat, too hot to do anything. I dreaded what was coming.

Around one, Peter and Early walked into the house. I couldn't believe they got home at the exact same time. I came in from the porch when I heard Peter's car in the driveway and then Chip's, dropping Early off. And there we all were, standing in the den, arranging ourselves into a triangle.

"Early," Peter said, pointing his thumb at him. Was he going to dive right in, without the two of us discussing it first? Not what I had in mind. I wanted to prep him before he said anything. "I opened your trunk because I needed your jumper cables—Adam Lobell called this morning to say his battery was dead. He wanted me to pick him up for our golf game and then afterward help him start his car—"

"Dad, I can explain—"

"How do you explain having enough beer in your car for the entire Randolph Academy student body?"

"It's not my beer, Dad."

"It sure looks like your beer. It's in your trunk, son." Peter did that chin-wiggling thing, easing his shirt collar away from his neck.

"I know, I know. But you've got to believe me. It's not my beer." Early was downright relaxed, smiley.

"How much are you drinking anyway?" Peter asked. He was standing very close to Early. He looked like he wanted his son to *feel* his words, not just hear them.

"Why are you asking me this?" Not so relaxed now. Or smiley.

"Because I'm concerned."

"Okay, here's the truth, Dad. I've had beer a few times, but that's all. I know it may be hard to believe, but I'm not that wild about drinking. I don't like feeling out of control. I don't even like going to those big parties at people's houses when the parents are out of town and everybody gets drunk. It's just a bunch of people being loud and crazy, and it's not that much fun. I'm not saying I've never taken a drink. Because I have. I'm just saying I don't like it that much."

"Who does the beer belong to, then?" Peter said.

"I don't want to tell you."

"You don't want to tell me? I'm your father and I find ten cases of beer in your trunk and you don't want to tell me who it belongs to? What else is going on that you don't want me to know?" Peter made a light snorting noise. I eased myself down onto the arm of the sofa. They were still standing. It felt like the heat of the day had overtaken our air-conditioning system.

"I *will* tell you this: I have a fake ID. I admit that. Chip and I made them on the copy machine at the library. And some of my friends gave me money to buy them beer. I was just helping them out. The beer's for a party after graduation. A party I'm not even going to. I'm going out with Amy after graduation. But that's all I'll say. I won't tell you where the party is or who I bought the beer for."

"Are you telling me the truth?"

"Yes, sir."

"Do you understand the legal ramifications of what you've done? Buying this beer? First of all, you're underage. You're using a fake ID. And you're giving the beer to people who are underage. I can't *believe* your judgment!" Now Peter was yelling. I didn't know his voice could make it up to that pitch. "All that needs to happen is for something to go wrong at that party and *you're responsible!*"

"Don't scream at me!" Early was yelling now—and he seemed on the verge of bursting into tears. Everything in my body hurt.

"You're breaking the law!" Peter shouted back.

"People do it all the time! It's not so unusual!"

"I'm not going to argue with you." Peter's voice turned dispassionate, lawyerly. "I don't have to convince you that I'm right."

"You're *not* right!"

"Early, go to your room."

"I don't *want* to go to my room! Let's finish this right here and now!" Did Early actually bump Peter with his body?

"Early," I said, standing up, squeezing closer to him, placing my hand on his arm. "Peter," I said, reaching across for him.

Peter stayed put. "Move, Kathryne," he said.

Move?

"Stay out of this, Mom. It's none of your business." Early's neck was wet with sweat. He swallowed, and his Adam's apple raised up like a flag.

"Son, don't talk to your mother like that."

"Don't you tell me how to talk! You come in here and start throwing your goddamn accusations all over the place and don't even give me a chance to explain, and then when I do explain, you tell me I'm lying and you want me to betray my friends by telling on them and then you talk to me like I'm a criminal and now you think you can tell me how to talk to Mom? Who the hell do you think you are? Just *who the hell* do you think you are?" Early was yelling and crying and pointing his thumb at Peter. And it was that gesture—that mocking gesture—that almost-grown-up thumb, pointing, a gesture similar to the middle-finger gesture, but in these circumstances more bristling, more bruising. It was this gesture that seemed to break something loose in Early. His face shifted. His whole body shifted. I saw it. Peter saw it. Before Peter could say anything, before I could say anything, Early stomped out of the room, into the kitchen, grabbed his keys from the counter, slammed the back door.

Peter and I could hear the engine start, then the radio (he must've rolled down his windows), the car backing out, scraping—no, hammering—the low spot near the bottom of the driveway. A gasp of gears and a screech all the way up the street.

Peter turned and walked upstairs to the guest room. He stared down at his own steps the whole way.

When Early finally came home—after about an hour—he took the stairs by twos up to the landing, walked heavily down the long hall to his room and closed the door.

I cat-padded up to the guest room—I'd taken off my shoes—and eased the door open. Peter was sitting on the side of the bed, staring into the closet. I stood over him. "You know, you're the one who used to say a temper tantrum is normal," I said. "No wonder he's grouchy; look what he's going through. Graduation. Leaving home. Leaving us. His friends. These are big things. And he's probably exhausted. Let's try to be understanding. Besides, I believe what he told us about the beer."

"Of course you do," Peter said. "That doesn't surprise me. I did not like the way he talked to you. Or to me. And I'm not sure what he's up to."

I sensed someone else in the room. Early. Standing in the doorway.

"I'm sorry," he said. "I was wrong to talk that way. Really, I'm sorry." The expression of off-key pain on his face, the sheepish way he held his shoulders—he looked used up. As though he would accept anything we might dish out.

"It's all right, honey," I said quickly. "We all got a little excited. Let's just forget it." I so wanted to mend the rifts—between Early and me, between Early and Peter—that I wasn't thinking about the rift between Peter and me, which I was prying wide open. I wasn't thinking—period. Over and over, I've wished I could go back to that afternoon—all those afternoons, mornings, evenings—and think, think, think. This was my husband I was flicking aside. This was our child I was dreaming away.

Peter didn't say a word.

By the next day, it was over. The weather was back in the low eighties and everything in our house, including the air-conditioning, was humming along. Like normal.

TWENTY-NINE

GRADUATION NIGHT, the sky was royal blue. Rows of white wooden chairs filled the quad. The ceremony was to be at eight. As early as seven-thirty, eager mothers, fathers, sisters, brothers, and grandparents had claimed their seats. The wooden dais was draped with starched white cloths and decorated with baskets of feathery ferns. Candles fluttered everywhere, like white flowers caught in a sudden light.

My brother, Billy, with his wife, Lily, and their twin daughters, Lee Ann and Lila, had driven down from New York the night before. The six of us sat in the third row off the center aisle. I'd gotten there early—around seven—to save seats. Peter, Billy, Lily, and the girls came later. All of us, including Early, had had dinner together at five-thirty at the Pewter Rose, Early's favorite restaurant. Billy, of course, took pictures. We started out with champagne toasts—even allowed Early, Lee Ann, and Lila to have a glass—and ordered plenty of good food. Caesar salads, carrot and ginger soup, crabmeat dip and pita. Pork tenderloin stuffed with spinach for Peter and Billy. Salmon for me, mushroom ravioli for Lily and the girls. Early had steak. There were lots of laughs and easy conversation. Lee Ann and Lila, fourteen years old, orange hair and orange eyebrows like their mother's, talkative, giggly, were wild about Early, and the feeling was mutual. Whatever story they told, he was mesmerized. He loved hearing them tell about life in New York City. Billy joked that Manhattan was like an opera, with people walking around in all kinds of costumes! We talked about the possibility of Early spending a summer with them, maybe after his freshman year. Peter said he could get Early a summer job or internship with a top New York law firm.

When Billy and Lily got married, there'd been a million jokes, of course, about the rhyme their names made. Lily grew up in the midwest. St. Paul. She's quieter than Billy, very genuine; she smiles that kind of slow smile where you don't part your lips. The most remarkable thing about her is the close attention she pays to whoever's talking. She doesn't take her big brown eyes off the person's face. The first time I'd met her—while I was living in New York—I'd told her how pretty I thought the name Lily was. She said she'd picked it out of the phone book. "You named yourself?" I asked, astonished. She said her relationship with her parents had been so bad that when she graduated from the University of Minnesota she renamed herself, which was the best way she could think of to start her life over. A life, she said, that did not include her mother and father. Later, when I asked Billy about this, saying how hard it was for me to imagine children not being close to their mothers, he shrugged. "All that's ancient history now," he said. I wondered how much understanding he was able to give Lily. When we were young, he'd leave the room if there was any kind of emotional upheaval. Up to his room he'd go. He'd stay there for hours, pasting his photographs in albums or doing his magic.

Graduation night, the weatherman called for seventy degrees and seventy degrees it was. Dragonflies were out late over the pond that separated the middle-school building from upper school. I wore a new chocolate-colored linen sheath with matching cropped jacket. Peter looked crisp and cool—pressed—in khaki pants, red print tie, navy blazer. Ninety percent of the fathers wore khaki pants, red ties, navy blazers.

Then that familiar graduation music, and those innocent boys and girls—graduating seniors!—began their walk down the grassy aisle between the chairs. I used to think that I could go to graduations and weddings every single day. There's just something about those bright, brimming, hopeful young people marching to music.

Some seniors were wearing sunglasses, which, of course, the administration had specifically asked them not to do. But everyone knew, in the spirit of the evening, consequences would be ignored, both by the students and the faculty. Surely, I thought, Early wasn't going to break that rule, regardless of the presence or absence of consequences.

I saw Chip before I saw Early, since Dunham comes before Smallwood in the alphabet. When Chip came sauntering down the aisle in oversize, aviator-style sunglasses, I knew Early would be doing the same. And there he was, my son, handsome and dignified in his light green mortarboard and white tassel, white collar and dark tie neatly folded into the V of his light green robe, wearing a wide grin and sunglasses.

The invocation was given by the class president and Morehead Scholar, Brian Shipley Coddington (this was the night every child was called by his full name), followed by a welcome from the headmaster, Mr. Bucy. Then Mrs. Houser, head of upper school, her voice sweet and southern as gardenias, introduced the speaker for the class of 1987: Earl David Smallwood. Peter draped his arm around the back of my chair. I patted his hand and sat up straighter.

I was relieved that Early had taken off his sunglasses before he walked to the lectern. He'd worked on his speech for weeks, writing a first draft, then reading it to Peter and me, asking for our feedback (I'd said it was fine; Peter gave a number of suggestions), then working on it more. Mr. Hamrick, his Advanced Placement English teacher (the same Mr. Hamrick Early had had in eleventh grade for Clay Matters), helped him with the content and delivery. At home, I'd walk by the bathroom and Early would be in his boxers in front of the sink, toothbrush in one hand, speech in the other, mouth full of toothpaste foam, his words rising and falling with the rush of water. Long after we'd turned out the lights, I could hear him practicing in his room, voice low and earnest, muffled in the darkness.

Now, with one bright light beaming in his direction, like the sun shining only on him, he spoke to the senior class, their families and friends, and the faculty:

I'm sure we can all still remember our first day of high school. Every first is accompanied by some degree of apprehension and that first day was no exception. Tomorrow will be full of first times and it's only natural that the prospect of everything we'll face in the future elicits a certain sense of fear. Along with that fear is an inkling of hope—a knowledge deep down that we have learned enough to face tomorrow and that we will learn enough in the course of tomorrow to face every day after that.

I have learned a lot in the last four years. After three years of chemistry, I can finally balance a redox reaction. I can conjugate a French verb. I understand the symbolism in Macbeth. But most of what I've learned wasn't taught in a classroom. What we've been preparing for all these years is not a final exam—it isn't pass or fail. Life isn't pass or fail. I've learned that a person cannot be quantified. Who we are is not a GPA or an SAT score, the number of goals we make in soccer, the number of pounds we can bench, or the number of pounds that we weigh. Let's not get hung up on numbers.

Who we are is who we are when no one is watching. It is not the image of ourselves we try to project so that we look good to the outside world. We must make sure that who we appear to be on the outside is the same as who we are inside. And that means we must be honest with ourselves and with others.

Who we are is also who we surround ourselves with, the friends we make who know us better than anyone else in this world, friends we can count on. Of course, in friendship we always run the risk of getting hurt, but I've learned that the rewards of caring about a person—standing up for that person, no matter what—are well worth the risk. Our hearts are the greatest tools we possess.

We need to seek out every opportunity to love others, regardless of the color of their skin, regardless of whether they are similar to us or different from us in big or small ways. I am grateful to my parents for teaching me this. Thank you, Mom and Dad!

Stop for just a moment and think about where we are right now. Some may dread this day as the beginning of an era when we will have to fend for ourselves. Some of us may even have to do our own laundry, a scary thought! I prefer to look at our graduation in more optimistic light. We must appreciate this moment for what it is worth. We are bound by nothing. We can do anything.

Good luck to the class of '87!

A standing ovation. Early just stood there, behind the lectern, nodding, smiling, graciously acknowledging the applause. I marveled at his poise. I could feel everyone's eyes on Peter and me. Early hadn't shown us the part in the speech where he thanked us. I knew people were thinking what a wonderful job we'd done raising our son. I adjusted my jacket, straightened my sleeves, held in my stomach. I felt as though we were in a parade—no, a dream. This was what all three of our lives, and the years, had sifted down to. And the grains in the hourglass had turned to pure sugar.

The rest of the ceremony was a sweet drift of faces and words. Amy Whitley presented the class gift, a redwood bench to be placed outside the senior lounge. Amy's mother, Janet, had had a tasteful bronze plaque engraved *from the Class of 1987* for the back of the bench. The glee club's choral presentation was a song written by Chip called "Talking to God," the melody actually pleasant, the lyrics gently stressing the importance of taking time out of the day to be still and pray. The refrain: *We all must learn the art . . . of saying to the Lord what's in our hearts.*

Mr. Bucy introduced the main speaker, Mayor Oliver, a golfing buddy of Peter's, who talked way too long and was extremely boring. Every time he made a point, he nodded emphatically, as though he were congratulating himself on his startling insights. I kept my face raised and tried to appear as if I were listening, but I let myself get lost in the memory of Early's speech. His good values. The ease with which he'd spoken to this large audience.

Mr. Bucy presented the Teacher of the Year award to a surprised and happy history teacher, Mrs. Yeager. Then the presentation of diplomas by the chairman of the board of trustees of the school. Finally, the benediction and recessional.

Afterward, everyone milled around outside the cafeteria. Homemade refreshments from the Parents' Council filled tables crossed with ivy garlands wilting in the waxy heat of candles; unruly groups of seniors clowned for the camera, balancing cups of frosty green punch, programs, diplomas bound in leather; grandparents kissed grandchildren; younger siblings tried on older siblings' mortarboards; senior girls hugged senior girls, and cried; white-robed teachers were thanked, or ignored.

Peter and I stayed late, chatting with Early's classmates and their parents, introducing Billy, Lily, and the twins to everyone we'd known all those years at Randolph Academy. Billy snapped pictures. "Stand over there, together," he'd say. "Keep talking, don't look at the camera, just act natural." People complimented us on Early's speech. Joy was there, wearing a suit the shade of lime sherbet. She had to leave mid-reception for her daughter's birthday dinner. Chip's parents, Thomas and Barbara, walked over, and we laughed together and said things like, "Well, they finally made it!" and "Can you believe it's all over?" Barbara wore black linen with a silver, black, and green pin at the neckline. Thomas wore a tan tweedish sport coat that was probably silk. Billy, Lily, and the girls said their good-byes to everyone and left; they were driving to Wrightsville Beach for a week's vacation, then heading back to New York. When Billy had told me their plans, I couldn't believe they were only spending one night with us.

Thomas and Barbara Dunham said they were getting a group together to go out for coffee—the Whitleys and the Booths had said yes—and did we want to join them? About that time, Early and Chip walked across the grass. They had their big, swooping arms around each other like two bear cubs. Amy Whitley ducked away from a group nearby and joined us. Early pecked her lightly on the cheek and they stood there, holding hands. A crowd of girls came over and whisked her away. Early looked in her direction, told us he'd be home late, not to worry.

Then he turned to Peter. "Dad, I promise, I'll be fine."

Thomas Dunham and Peter joked back and forth about the "I'll be fine" part, about how the boys were on their own now—no curfew tonight!—and the parents were finished worrying.

Chip gave everyone hugs—his parents, Peter and me. The affectionate side of him I'd seen lately. Early kissed me, shook hands with the others, including Peter. He and Peter held on to each other for several seconds, though, I noticed, each with both hands.

As we walked through the restaurant, we saw people we knew at almost every table. Other parents who'd just come from graduation. Steven Todd's parents and grandmother. Eddie Jackson's parents, two brothers, both sets of grandparents, his aunt. Betsy Green's mother and stepfather, her two older sisters and their husbands. The Heywards. Kirklands. Coddingtons. After we walked past the Coddingtons' table, Peter leaned forward and whispered in my neck, "If Early had applied himself, he could've been the Morehead Scholar." I didn't answer. I felt Early *had* worked hard, but it was the school's fault. Apparently, they hadn't nominated him because of an incident back in ninth grade, something about his looking on another student's paper during a test. They'd never even bothered to tell us. His adviser just happened to mention it, after Brian Coddington was awarded the Morehead, when it was too late for me to do anything. She acted as though considering Early for the award was the most remote thing in the world. I remember thinking how unfair it was. Small-minded. I'd wanted to say to them, You know Early would never cheat.

We had a wonderful time. The eight of us were telling stories involving our kids over the years, teasing one another about being old enough to have kids going off to college, and making jokes about the empty-nest syndrome. Of course, the Whitleys still had younger children at home, but the Dunhams and the Booths were like us— our one and only child would soon be leaving. Early had been accepted at Duke. Chip at UNC-Charlotte. He'd applied to Chapel Hill, but did not get in; UNC-Charlotte had been his last choice. Amy would be at Harvard, Ellen at Furman.

It was Barbara Dunham's idea to order every dessert listed on the menu board over the bar, put them in the center of the table, everyone sample different ones. She had an opinion, albeit a stylish opinion, about everything. That night it was easy to be accepting of her, in the way that we can afford to be generous when we're overflowing, when our own shelves are well stocked. We ate too much lemon-almond pound cake, chocolate pecan pie, coconut pie, pistachio ice cream, cheesecake.

Peter and I left the restaurant around midnight. When we pulled into the driveway, I saw that both the front and back porch lights were on, with their wispy halos of insects. This meant that Early had come home during the evening and turned the lights on before he went back out. Not unusual. Early was thoughtful like that. Before we got out of the car, before Peter twisted the key in the lock to open the back door, I sensed Early wasn't in yet. You can tell when a house is empty, even before you enter it.

As Peter locked the dead bolt from inside, he said he was tired. I was, too. We turned on the light in the back hall, in the kitchen, in the den, leaving a string of bright rooms behind us, like a gold necklace, as we headed toward the bedroom.

In bed, we said a few words about the evening, kissed good night, fell into the deep, satisfied sleep that parents of the star senior at graduation would naturally fall into.

During the night I woke several times, glanced at the clock, wondered if Early was in, forced myself not to check. After all, he'd soon be leaving and I wouldn't know if he was in or not. Good practice for me not to check. I finally did get up, though, and tiptoed upstairs. His door was shut, which meant he was home.

The next morning I heard Peter in the shower. Then he was in his closet, pulling clothes off hangers, then in the kitchen, opening the refrigerator for orange juice, then going outside for the paper. I looked at the clock when he came back in and sat at the kitchen table to take his vitamin and blood-pressure pill. Seven-thirty. I knew he had an eight o'clock appointment at the bank. I flipped my pillow and turned onto my stomach to go back to sleep. At that moment, I felt that life was good and our family was truly fortunate and I was lucky in a million different ways. When I was little, I used to count as one of my blessings the privilege of being able to sleep on my stomach, imagining that if I were in the hospital with a tonsillectomy or appendectomy, I'd have IVs and tubes everywhere and would have to sleep on my back.

The next thing I knew, the doorbell was ringing. Two solemn chimes. The front door. Ten o'clock. I couldn't believe I'd slept so late. It wasn't Joy; she'd use the back door. Had I scheduled someone and forgotten? The man from Patterson Heating and Air to do the early-summer check? Had Peter called a plumber to unclog the drain in our shower and forgotten to tell me? As I tied the sash of my robe and smoothed it down my thigh, I caught a glimpse of myself in the dressing-table mirror, saw my "morning face," puffy-lidded eyes, how old I looked. I combed my hair with my fingers and went into the front hall.

I peered through the brass-rimmed eyehole. Blinked the sleep out of my eyes. Two policemen stared back. I could see a cruiser behind them, at the curb. Of course they had the wrong address. I opened the door, ready to help them find the house they were looking for.

"Mrs. Smallwood?" one policeman said, flicking his eyes over my face, following my hands, looking to the left and right of me. They both stood back from the doorway, as though it were the respectful thing to do. But they appeared stiff and somber. Angry almost.

Suddenly it struck me. Early! Was he okay? Was he home? I hadn't actually opened his door. Why hadn't I made sure? Had he been in an accident?

Before my legs gave way beneath me, the policeman spoke again. "I'm sorry, Mrs. Smallwood. Real sorry. We're here to see your son, Earl David Smallwood."

"He's here?" I stammered. "Is he all right?"

"You better go get him, Mrs. Smallwood. We need to see him right away." He wasn't sounding sympathetic at all. Why was he so angry?

"But what—"

"Mrs. Smallwood, we need to see your son."

I backed away from the door as though, if I didn't keep my eye on the two of them, they might do something I wouldn't like. When I got into the den, I turned and sprinted up the stairs, across the landing, down the long hall to Early's room. I opened his door without knocking. His graduation robe lay over the back of the armchair, cap and diploma and presents (still wrapped) in the seat. Books, Gatorade cans, pens, notebooks, baseball caps, leafy copies of *Sports Illustrated*—all the things he'd cleared out of his locker at school— covered the quilt on the other bed. The window over his bed was open; the sun was already blazing away. He looked like a choirboy, sleeping on his side, his face resting on two hands pressed together.

Things started coming back to me. The brown thrasher he'd tried to save in the driveway years before. How he'd held my sleeve in his tight little fist when the teacher had tried to pry him away from me the first day of nursery school. The note he wrote (age four) when he was having a tantrum, running away from home: *I am going away from yoe.* The time I ran half bent beside him, my hand holding the seat of the two-wheel bike he was learning to ride. When I couldn't run fast enough, he started riding wild without me, the front wheel dipping left, then right, until he laughed himself straight and steady down the street, as far as I could see.

I leaned down and touched his cheek with my lips. I thought of the game we used to play when he was small, "the world's gentlest kiss" game. Each of us would kiss the other on the cheek, the goal being to give a lighter kiss than the other person had given. He'd kiss, I'd kiss, each kiss gentler than the one before. The winner's kiss would be so light, the other could barely feel it.

He didn't move. I shook his shoulder, softly, then more insistently, until he opened his eyes. He didn't seem to have any idea where he was. I thought he must have been dreaming one of those dreams that hold you in its grasp even after you've awakened. I wanted to touch him again, so I ran my forefinger up his sleep-warm arm and down again, as though I were touching my mother's pearl necklace. Then I combed his matted hair away from his forehead with my fingers and said in a voice that sounded more scared than I'd ever heard myself sound, "Wake up, honey. Somebody's here to see you."

THIRTY

ERE'S THE ACCOUNT Early gave his attorney on July 1. The statement will be admitted into evidence when he pleads guilty to murder tomorrow morning, October 6, in Mecklenburg County Superior Court:

A WEEK BEFORE GRADUATION, Steven Todd, a boy in my class at Randolph Academy, told Chip Dunham, my best friend, about some people that wanted to buy some marijuana. Chip said he could get his hands on an ounce. Chip and I had some that I meant to throw away but didn't. In fact, I hid it in the rafters of the toolshed and forgot about it. I smoked pot once the summer before my senior year and ended up wrecking my car. I didn't like the feeling of being out of control and never smoked again. Chip smoked a lot, but not around me. He stopped sometime during our senior year. When he told me about the guys who wanted to buy it, I told him it didn't sound like a good idea, but he said it was a way for us to get rid of the stuff and make a little money. I said I'd rather throw it away. He said throwing it away wouldn't do anybody any good and we might as well sell it. I finally said okay.

The afternoon of graduation, June 1, Steven Todd called Chip and said it turned out those guys just wanted to look at the marijuana. They wanted to check it out before they bought it. Chip called me to say something might be up and those people might be thinking they'd try to steal from us, so we better be careful. I wanted to tell him let's just forget it, but I didn't want to sound like a total wimp. I figured we'd gone too far to back out.

When I got in Chip's car after graduation, he said we were going to meet the guys at one of their houses, and when we finished there, we'd go to the party some seniors were having out at Lake Norman. I wasn't planning to go to the party because I had a date with Amy Whitley, a girl I've been with all during high school, but I told him this would be a good time for me to go to my house and pick up the pot since my parents were out. I'd catch Amy later.

First, we stopped at Chip's house for him to change clothes. Then we went to my house. Chip pulled up in my driveway, and right before I got out of the car, he told me to get the gun. I couldn't believe he said that and I asked why. He said he had a good reason and just to get it, he'd explain later. Chip used to like a girl named Julie Cauthen, who didn't like him. He was going through a bad time and he got this man in his church to buy a 9mm pistol for him by telling the man he wanted to do some target shooting. Chip didn't want his parents to know about the gun, so he asked me to keep it at my house. I told him I put it behind some old board games on the top shelf of my closet, but really, I hid it in the rafters of the toolshed. I was afraid he might come over sometime when I wasn't home and take it and do something crazy.

I went up to my room and put on jeans and a T-shirt and a

button-down shirt. Then I went in the toolshed, pulled out a ladder, and got the marijuana and the gun and put them in my pocket. I pulled my shirttail out to hide all that stuff.

Chip drove to Cherry, back behind Midtown Square. I asked him why he wanted the gun.

He said, "Just in case."

I said, "Just in case what?"

By this time, he'd pulled up in front of a house and was getting out of the car. I went with him to the front door.

After he rang the bell and I saw who was there, I felt better about everything. I knew Eddie Jackson and Allen Marshall, whose house it was. I didn't know the third boy, although he looked familiar. They said his name was William.

I said, "What's up, Eddie?"

Eddie said, "Nothing. Whatcha up to?"

Eddie and I had known each other a long time, on different sports teams at Randolph Academy and on the yearbook staff. Allen didn't go to school with us. He went to public school but he and I had played select soccer together when we were little, so I sort of knew him.

William was holding some car keys and said, "Let's go. I got my mama's Mazda. It's next door, at my house."

Allen got in the passenger seat next to William. Chip and Eddie and I were in the back. I sat behind William. Chip was in the middle. Eddie sat behind Allen.

I gave the bag of grass to Eddie. Allen asked to see it and Eddie handed it over the front seat to him. William stopped the car for a minute and made a big thing about looking for something under the seat. All of a sudden Allen jumped out of the car with the bag and started running. He disappeared into the woods beside the road.

I couldn't believe it. The whole thing was a setup. Chip looked at me and I looked at him. Eddie was staring straight ahead, not looking at Chip or me. It crossed my mind Eddie might be in on this.

William told Eddie to get in front with him and we'd drive back to Allen's house in Cherry to wait for him.

"We'll get that motherfucker and get you back your pot," William said. I could see him looking at Chip and me in the rearview mirror.

We were only about two blocks from the house. If what Allen was doing was taking a shortcut through the woods to go back home, we'd all get there at about the same time.

William parked the car in front of Allen's house, and he and Eddie got out of the car and went to the front door. They opened the door and went inside. Chip and I were by ourselves in the car. I told him we ought to get in his car and go home, I didn't like the idea of hanging around. I didn't want to admit to Chip that William was scaring the hell out of me.

Chip said he just wanted to get the pot back and we should stay a little longer to see if Allen was going to show up.

William and Eddie came back out and got in the car. Chip told William to drive to the street where Allen had disappeared and to keep driving around the neighborhood until we found him. Chip's voice sounded like he meant business. I couldn't believe his guts.

William said he thought he knew where Allen might be, and he drove to an area I'd never been before. I had no idea where we were. There were a few houses, but mostly it was just woods. There were no streetlights and it was pitch-dark. William pulled over in front of an empty lot and turned off the motor.

I didn't know what William was getting ready to do, but I knew we couldn't trust him. He seemed like the kind of guy who would screw you in a heartbeat.

Chip said something like, "I know you set us up, William. Find Allen and get our fucking pot back. And don't try to pull any shit. I'll call the cops and you can be sure they'll believe a guy from Myers Park before they'll believe a punk from Cherry."

I couldn't believe Chip said that.

William turned all the way around and yelled, "Don't you be threatening me, honky! I oughta kick your fucking ass right now!"

At that exact minute, I knew who he was. His name was William Campbell and he was Eddie's cousin. A couple of years ago he and I got in a fight in a pickup basketball game. He punched me in the face and broke my tooth. I wasn't sure whether he recognized me or not.

Before I could do anything, Eddie grabbed William's shoulder and said, "Okay, William, calm down. Everybody calm down. Let's all just go home and forget about this. Nobody has to get hurt. William, start the car."

But William threw Eddie's hand off him and shouted right in his face, "You ain't no better than these white motherfuckers! You ain't nothing but a Randolph Academy pussy!"

Then he turned and looked right at me and shouted, "Ain't that the truth, you little pussy? Ain't that the truth?"

Then he did something really crazy. He looked like he was going to unzip his pants. He didn't actually do it. He was just making the motion and laughing this awful laugh. He said, "I bet you pussies at Randolph fucking Academy don't even have dicks. You all got little pussies like your mama. Maybe I'll show you what a real dick looks like."

Eddie turned all the way around, and his face and the way he was holding his head said it all. How scared he was. He was stiff as a board.

Chip said in a totally calm voice, "William, do what Eddie said. Turn around and start the car and take us back. Come on now. Let's go."

At first, William turned back to the front like he was going to do what Chip said. But then he jerked all the way around fast and lunged halfway over the seat. He had his gigantic hands out toward Chip. Chip started screaming. William kept coming. He was yelling, "Don't you tell me what to do, motherfucker!" The top half of his body was in the backseat and his upper arms were huge. I was scared out of my mind. Chip was trying to get out of the way, but William hit him in the face. Blood spurted from Chip's mouth and nose all over everywhere.

I tried to grab William's hand, but he pushed me away.

Eddie was screaming, "William! Stop it! Stop it!"

William was swinging like a wild man. Chip fought back, but William was too strong. William grabbed Chip by the throat and it looked like he was going to strangle him. Eddie was still screaming at William, trying to get him to stop. Chip was coughing like crazy and gagging, but I heard him say these words: "The gun. Get the gun."

I took the gun out of my pocket and pointed it at William's head.

All of a sudden I wasn't scared anymore. "Let him go!" I said. That asshole stole from us and now he was trying to beat up my best friend. I wanted to beat the living crap out of him. It was like something hot started running through my veins. Like I wasn't myself.

William took his hands off Chip and looked right at me. He was just staring. I pushed the gun into the side of his face and held it there.

He yelled, "Get that fucking gun out of my face!" And then he went for me and that made the gun actually knock him in the head. He smacked the gun out of my hand and yelled, "You ain't got the balls to use that gun."

Out of the corner of my eye I saw Chip scrambling to get out of the car, but his face was bloody and maybe he couldn't see what he was doing and his hands were shaking so bad. Anyway, he couldn't get the door handle to work.

William saw Chip trying to get out of the car and he grabbed him around the neck again. Chip was fighting back, but his breathing was loud.

I saw the gun on the floor. I picked it up.

Chip was saying, "No, no, no, no."

The next thing I know, the gun went off.

The sound exploded through the car and all of a sudden I was deaf. There was blood spewing everywhere and flesh flying all around—it looked like pieces of ripe fruit or something like that—and I could see Eddie was screaming but I couldn't hear him and Chip was crying and the whole car was full of blood and William jerked back toward the front seat and everything in him was squeezing out these horrible twitching motions and then he was still.

Weird rattling sounds were coming from his chest. His arm was twisted all the way around like it had come out of its socket and was hanging between Chip and me, all the way in the backseat. Just hanging there, swinging a little.

I said to Chip, "You all right? You all right?"

"Why'd you shoot him?" Chip said. He was crying like a baby. "I was telling you, 'no, no,' *not* to shoot him!" His neck was red, his face was red, his nose was still bleeding. He looked terrible.

"I thought you were saying 'no, no' to him."

"Are you nuts? I just meant for you to scare him, that's all."

Eddie was saying, "Oh, my God! Oh, my God! You shot William!"

Then I heard myself crying and saying, "What did I do? What did I do?"

I felt like I'd gone crazy, like I'd literally been out of my mind. I didn't know what I'd done and I didn't know what I was going to do next. I never meant to kill him. It was like something outside of me made the gun go off, like it had nothing to do with me. I could've been a million miles away.

I realized I was still holding the gun, only now it was pointed at Eddie. In a panicky voice, he said, "We're friends, Early. We're friends."

I stopped crying, but held the gun in his face.

"If you're my friend, why'd you go in on this?" I heard myself say. Now I knew exactly what I'd done and I was convinced it had been necessary. If Eddie and those guys hadn't tried to steal from us, none of this would've happened. If William hadn't been choking my best friend, none of this would've happened. But they *did* steal from us and William Campbell *was* choking my best friend. I had no choice but to do what I did.

Then it was like I couldn't feel the gun in my hand, and in that instant, I lost the power I'd felt inside myself, that certainty, and I panicked again. I don't know why things kept going back and forth inside me. All I know is I got really scared again.

Chip said, "Early, Eddie's a good guy. He didn't do anything. Leave him alone. For God's sake, don't shoot!"

"I didn't know those guys were going to do this. I swear to God I didn't know," Eddie said.

Then Chip was saying my name over and over, crying, just my name. Early. Early. Early.

Now it was like I was holding the gun but it wasn't attached to me, it was a separate thing, something that had huge power, all by itself. Suddenly, I thought, what if the gun goes off again, this time in Eddie's face?

I pulled the gun back and stuck it in my own face.

Chip wiped his eyes on his sleeve and said, "Give me the gun, Early."

"What did I do? What did I do?" I said. I opened my mouth and put the gun inside.

"Lay the gun down, Early. Please, lay it down."

I pushed the gun farther back in my mouth.

"Early," he said. He didn't reach for the gun or anything. He just looked at me. I kept the gun where it was.

"Early," he said again.

I laid the gun down, on the seat, beside my leg.

Then it was like all that panic I'd been feeling disappeared and I felt fearless again and I was totally clear about what I had to do next. Everything inside me changed all over again. I had to destroy the evidence. Make it like it never happened. I didn't tell Chip and Eddie what I was going to do. I just told them they were going to have to help me.

I put my finger on the trigger.

"Help you do what?" Chip said.

I told them to help me put William's body in the trunk of his car. They didn't answer. I could hardly see their faces. It was like a haze everywhere or thick dust or maybe there was just something wrong with my eyes all of a sudden and there were blotches I couldn't see through. I managed to get out of the car and go around to the driver's side. I was still holding the gun and I pulled William back a little and then toward me. Blood was everywhere. Chip and Eddie were standing behind me. They helped me drag him out of the car and put him in the trunk.

All this time, Chip was crying off and on and mumbling, "Christ Almighty, Christ Almighty."

None of it felt real. Like I was observing everything that was happening, but I couldn't do anything about it. I was shaking all over. I got in the driver's seat and Chip was beside me and Eddie was in the back. The gun was in my lap. My foot was shaking so bad I could hardly press the gas pedal, but somehow I managed to get William's car back to a part of town I knew. Chip's lips were moving the whole time I was driving. He was praying.

I drove to a gas station at the corner of Monroe Road and Wendover Road. I parked next to the pay phone and put the gun in my pocket so nobody could see it, except Chip and Eddie knew it was there. I told them I was going to call Steven Todd.

"Why are you calling *him*?" Chip said.

"Because he was in on this. He's my friend, and he should not've been in on it," I answered.

"No, he wasn't. And anyway, it doesn't matter. Let's just go home. Let's go home," Chip said.

At that point, I knew two things. The only person I could trust for sure was Chip. But I had to make my own decisions.

I got out and dialed Steven's number. The line was busy.

I got back in the car and drove to Steven's house in Montibello. Chip and Eddie were not saying a word. I wanted to tell Chip, "Don't worry, everything will be all right." But the words wouldn't come.

At Steven's house I told Chip and Eddie to get out of the car with me. I was still holding the gun in my pocket and they knew it. I knocked on Steven's bedroom window, which is in the back. Nobody came. Then we went around to the screen porch. It was hard for me to walk because my legs had lost all sensation. I pinched them and hit myself on the knees with my free hand, but I couldn't feel anything. Steven was on the phone in the kitchen and saw us and motioned for us to go to the front door. But then I saw his mother come in the kitchen, so I told Chip and Eddie to run like hell back to the car.

By this time, Steven had come out of the house. I called to him to follow us, that we needed another car. He said he could get his mother's station wagon. He went back in the house and came out with the keys. We pulled out, and he followed us. I thought maybe he knew what had happened and was coming to help us. I remember thinking, Good! Steven ought to have to do some of the dirty work. He started this whole mess.

I drove out into the country, almost to Waxhaw, and Steven stayed right behind us. I drove the Mazda into a field on Harper Church Road and turned off the engine. How I found that field, I have no idea.

Chip said, "Early, please, let's go home. I want to go home." He sounded real sad. I felt sorry for him.

Eddie said, "Yeah, Early, we've got to go home and tell somebody what happened. We've got to go to the police before it gets worse. We've got to tell our parents. Please, let's go home."

I told them we'd be going home soon but to get in Steven's mother's car with me first, that we had one more thing to do.

When we got in Steven's mother's station wagon, I told him about William stopping the car and Allen running off with the pot and William going berserk and doing what he did to Chip. That's all I said. Nothing about me shooting William. Chip and Eddie didn't say a word. I was surprised they were so quiet. I know Steven could see we were covered with blood, but he didn't ask any questions. Maybe it was too dark in the car for him to see us good. Maybe he was just shocked at what had happened. Maybe he was scared. I don't know. All he said was that he could get money for Chip and me tomorrow to cover the loss of our pot. I asked him if he knew where we could get a gas can, and he said there was one in the back of his mother's station wagon. Then he drove us back to Charlotte.

By now we were on Providence Road, heading toward town, and Chip said, "Early, we're a block from Amy's. Don't you want to talk to her? She'll know what to do. Come on, Early. Let's go see Amy."

I didn't say anything.

Chip said, "Steven, pull in Amy's driveway and let's go talk to her. All right, Early? All right?"

"All right," I said.

Steven slowed down in front of her house and was getting ready to turn in, but then I saw the Whitleys' lights were off and I said, "We better not. They're asleep."

Chip said, "It doesn't matter. She won't mind."

"Yeah, Early, she won't mind." Eddie was talking to me but looking at Steven. I could see that.

"Keep going, Steven," I said. "Don't stop."

"Steven, pull in," said Chip.

"Listen to me, Steven," I said. "Go."

Steven pulled away from the curb and drove up Providence Road.

By now it was after midnight. I told Steven to go to the gas station near Presbyterian Hospital.

When we got there, I told Chip to pump the gas in the gas can. Steven voluntarily paid for it. That showed me he'd been in on the setup and was feeling bad about it.

I directed Steven back to that field where we'd left William's Mazda and we all got out of the car. I had the gas can and the gun. I told Steven and Eddie to walk over to the Mazda. Chip and I were behind them.

Chip whispered, "Early, I don't know what you're getting ready to do, but if you stop now, you can explain to the police that William was trying to kill me and that's why you shot him. All you've done at this point is kill this black guy who was trying to choke me. Nothing will happen to you for doing that, I promise. But stop now. For Christ sake, stop now."

I guess what he was trying to say was that I'd killed a guy who was trying to kill my friend and that might get me off. Sort of like self-defense. But at the time I thought he was saying nobody would care about what I did since it was only a black guy. That really upset me. I did not believe there was a difference between shooting blacks and shooting whites. I'd been raised to believe we were all the same. Anyway, this wasn't about black and white. This was about protecting my best friend, regardless of the color of William's skin. And it was wrong for Eddie and Steven to be in on this. They were supposed to be our friends.

For the first time since the gun went off, it occurred to me Chip was afraid I might do something to him or Steven or Eddie. He didn't have to worry about that. It's not what I had in mind.

I poured gas all over the car, inside and out, and threw the empty gas can on the backseat. Chip and Steven and Eddie started running down the edge of the field, near the fence. I stepped back and struck a match and tossed it at the car and then I started running. There was a huge explosion and flames were shooting everywhere and I barely got out of the way fast enough. You couldn't even see a skeleton of the car. It was just this gigantic fireball that lit up the sky.

"Stop!" I yelled. Chip, Steven, and Eddie all stopped. I could see their faces as clear as if it was the middle of the day. That's how light it suddenly was. Above the blaze was all this thick black smoke that made everything in the light show up more. I told them to walk back to Steven's car with me and for Steven to drive us home.

On the way to the car and in the car driving home, Chip kept saying to himself, "Dear God, dear God."

They dropped me off first. By this time it was around three in the morning.

My parents were asleep and didn't hear me come in or go by their room on my way upstairs.

I washed up and put on a clean pair of boxers. I wrapped my clothes and the gun in my Patagonia jacket and took it out in the backyard and buried it under the pine trees way in the back.

I went up to my room and fell into a hard sleep.

The next morning, my mother woke me up and said the police wanted to see me. They took me to the Mecklenburg County Jail.

THIRTY-ONE

T HURSDAY, OCTOBER 7, 1987, after the sentencing, Peter and I pull out of Courthouse Parking into the autumny street. We drive past the black students from Johnson C. Smith University picketing across from the courthouse, their signs big and awkward. Those young people, so close to Early's age. Their determined faces. Quiet anger. They turn to stare—no, glare—at us as our car splashes water in the potholes. They know. They know who we are.

Maybe they were in the courtroom. Maybe they heard Andrew Wheeler, the district attorney, ask Donald, "How does your client plead to the charge of second-degree murder?" Maybe they heard our lawyer's answer: "He tenders a plea of guilty." Maybe they heard Judge McDermott sentence Early to fifteen years.

I wonder if one of these young people picketing threw the brick through our bedroom window the only night this past summer that Peter and I went out for dinner. I wonder if one of them is the person who keeps calling the house and hanging up. Attaching a face to the threat makes it feel even more threatening. Could it be the young woman in the baseball cap, the one who has stopped walking back and forth and is just standing there, her elongated face raised, staring at me? Her sign reads IF A BLACK TORCHED A WHITE, HE'D GET DEATH! Maybe it's the young man with the mustache, the one fidgeting with a cigarette and holding RACISM RAMPANT IN CHARLOTTE.

After the sentencing, William Campbell's mother was crying and talking to reporters. I couldn't help but hear her: "That white boy shoulda gotten sent to the gas chamber." Donald pushed Peter and me out of the courtroom, our heads down.

How did I end up on the wrong side of a race issue? I'm still the same person who taught in the first integrated high school in Georgia. The same person who gave money to Phyllis after she stole from me. Who made sure Eddie Jackson could go to the prom with a white girl. How different I must appear, though, to William Campbell's mother, to those young people marching back and forth in their lonely line. How *other*.

The three of us—Peter, Early, and I—believed we were the kind of people who cared about others. How can there be such a gap between how we see ourselves and the harm we're able to do?

Up ahead, AME Zion Church. Huge, handwritten banner across the entire yard: BLACKS WHO KILL WHITES GET DEATH! WHITES WHO KILL BLACKS LIVE! JOIN THE PROTEST!

In yesterday's paper, the headline story was about the citywide demonstrations being organized by black churches all over town, in anticipation of Early's sentencing. Mayor Oliver (he spoke at Early's graduation) called for "restraint and calm."

Peter and I are not talking. When he first turned on the motor in the parking garage, the radio came on—a talk show, a woman who'd written a book about her son being kidnapped in some Central American country. Peter hit the button and the car went silent. Now he's watching the road. I look up, at the sky, suddenly riddled with blackbirds.

At the end of the sentencing, our lawyer made this statement: "Early Smallwood was raised by loving parents and had every privilege you could ask for. There are no easy answers here."

Peter and I have always been private people who don't go around baring our souls. Now we're being discussed on the evening news and the front page of the local paper. Just before I went to sleep last night, long after Peter had gone to bed, I picked up the *Observer* and read until the printed words began to lose their detail. Soon I couldn't see at all.

A block from the courthouse, at the traffic light, a girl and boy, maybe in their twenties, are crossing the street, heading toward the courthouse. His arm is around her waist. He's holding her so tight, she has to walk sideways. Now I see that she's gripping a bouquet. A bridal bouquet? Are they going to the courthouse to get married? He's wearing dark blue pants and a white shirt, both unpressed. He probably thought if he took them out of the dryer the minute they were dry and hung them on hangers, they'd be fine. The shirt looks like he slept in it, the collar not just curled, crushed. She's wearing a long filmy skirt. A tiny floral print, the color of strawberry jam, *that* bright. And a white, cap-sleeved knit shirt. I can't help but be drawn to them. I can't turn away, in fact. I feel as though I could be sucked out of my seat, through the window, right to them. The expression on their faces says, This is the most glorious day of our lives.

Chip, Eddie, and Steven were charged as accessories to the crime. Early was allowed to speak in court. I'll never forget the speech he gave at graduation. And I'll never forget what he said in the courtroom. Nor how he sounded—young, frail, a hard shyness: "I am sorry. I am truly sorry. I hope one day William Campbell's family can forgive me for the horrible thing I've done. I've created a nightmare for everyone that won't go away, and I take full responsibility. One thing, though, I want the court to know Chip Dunham is innocent. He had nothing to do with the murder. Please, Your Honor, spare him."

Peter taps the wheel with his forefinger, quick little thumps. The light turns green, but the couple is still making their way across—step by slaphappy step. I hear a horn blow behind us. Halfway across, in the middle of the intersection, the young man stops and turns to look at us. He crosses his arms and puffs out his wrinkled, white-shirted chest. Then he lets out a howl—a piercing, joyful-for-all-the-world howl. "I'm getting married today!" is what he shouts. I can hear his words through our closed windows. The young woman puts her face in his, molding herself to his body, and kisses him flat on the lips. They are nothing but themselves, young people so in love with promises that they pay no attention to the traffic all around them. The cars could be puppies nipping at their heels.

At the sentencing, Peter asked the judge if he could address William Campbell's mother. Peter's voice was quiet, but composed. "I do not have the words to express how deeply, deeply sorry I am. My heart goes out to you, Mrs. Campbell. Your tragedy is profound and there's no way I would even begin to compare it with ours," he said. "Yet, you and I have one thing in common. We have both lost our sons."

He then asked permission to speak to Early, who had been hiding his face in his hands.

"I could never imagine something like this happening in our family or in any family I might know," said Peter. "I am devastated by your actions and at a total loss to explain them. However, since the day of your arrest last June, you have taken full responsibility for what you did and that makes me extremely proud of you." At that minute, Early looked up at Peter. "As you've heard me say many times, son, it's not so much what happens to us in life as what we do with it."

Judge McDermott allowed me to hold Early. He was crying in my arms, but I forced myself to remain dry-eyed. *Don't cry,* I said to myself, *don't dare cry.*

And then they led him—his legs in shackles, the cold sound of that—from the courtroom.

"I'M LEAVING," Peter says, pressing his foot on the gas, gunning it through the intersection as soon as the couple is on the opposite curb. Is this the same Peter who stops at yellow lights? Who slows down when the light is green?

"You're leaving," I repeat slowly. As I say the words, I realize he doesn't mean he's leaving the spot where he waited for the couple to cross the street. He means he's leaving. Me.

He reaches for my hand. "Kathryne, you mean . . . you mean everything to me. For a long time you've meant everything to me. When I married you, I felt like the luckiest guy in the world. I remember thinking the day of our wedding, I'm marrying the most beautiful girl I've ever known. I couldn't believe you wanted to spend the rest of your life with me."

But he said he was leaving. And why is he holding my hand?

"Then we had a son and he was . . . well, he was smart, kind-hearted, everything anyone could ever dream of a child being. But that wasn't good enough for us."

Here it comes. The blame. Of course. My fault. If I weren't so overprotective, Early would never have had all this trouble. He'd be calling from Duke, talking about rush, deciding which fraternity he should pledge, telling hilarious roommate stories.

"I'm not blaming you, Kathryne." His fingers stroke the back of my hand. "We're both responsible for what happened. That's not to say we're to blame. It's . . . it's too late for blame."

My hand curls up to meet his. Our silver Volvo is passing slowly through Charlotte, the one-way streets crisscrossing downtown. It feels like we're floating above the traffic. Like a blimp. Going so slow it would appear we're not moving at all.

"Of course we made mistakes," he goes on. "As parents of a newborn, we had to respond to his every need. When he couldn't let us know what he needed, it was our job to try to guess. That's what parents of infants are supposed to do. But we never stopped. We were there, at every turn, telling him what he needed and making sure he got it."

I open my mouth to speak, but no words come. Words are—what?—unnecessary? That's what they are. Useless. The same as wearing a big, heavy raincoat with a zip-in lining when the sun is bearing down.

"I know I put a lot of pressure on Early to excel. The same kind of pressure I put on myself. And then I promised to lighten up. But I didn't. To demand the best of yourself is one thing. To demand the best of your child is a whole other thing. I pushed too hard."

Again, I open my mouth to speak.

"Something else I've been thinking about. Remember the tantrums he had when he was little? Remember how abruptly they ended? Where do temper tantrums *go* when they disappear?"

Underground is the word that comes to my mind. Instead of speaking, I close my mouth.

"When I say I have to leave, it's not that there's anybody else," he says. "I know you're wondering if that's it. It's not."

Wondering? That's the last thing I'm doing. If I started wondering, I wouldn't know where to stop. Too many things to wonder about. The past. The future. I want to speak. Peter glances over at me. He's waiting for a response. I shake my head, all I can manage. There's no way I can say anything. I'm like a stroke victim.

"I just need . . . I need to get off by myself for a while and think." He takes his hand and places it on the wheel. I want it back. *Put your hand on my hand.*

"I plan to . . . to move out tonight," he says. "I've taken an apartment downtown. At Eighth and Poplar. Close to the office. It's a month-to-month rental. I know this is too much to ask, but I hope I can come back to you. I realize that's the most selfish request I can make."

I roll down my window. People are walking to the park. Some park. In the middle of high-rise bank buildings, the city set aside a piece of land the size of my front hall, stuck a few Bradford pear trees on it and a bench, and called it a park. People are chatting with one another, telling jokes, strolling, carrying canvas bags filled with belongings, rushing to glassy restaurants for lunch, jogging by—a whole city of people doing the same things they did yesterday and the day before that. They have no idea the world just ended. They have no idea the world just ended twice.

"Kathryne, are you listening? I wish you'd answer me. 'I love you' is what I'm saying. And I don't want to hurt you. Especially now. We've been through so much. But I'm not sure I even know how to love another person. For a long time there's been a discrepancy between how we appear to others and what it means to be us. We've been living a lie, Kathryne. Acting as though we're the perfect family. The only way I can even begin to love another person is to know the truth about myself. And about us."

What I hate most about what he's saying is that we've become a cliché. How many couples have you heard about who experience the trauma of losing a child—whether to death, drugs, or prison—and each spouse is desperate for the other to take away the pain? When they each fail to make the other person feel better, they turn on each other. They separate. Divorce. It's so predictable.

Worse than a cliché, we're a bad joke. *They stayed together until the children went off to prison.*

If I had a pad and pen, I could scribble a response. Yes. You can leave. And yes, you can come back. Or not come back. Whatever you decide. It's okay. Because I know where Early is and I can see him every Sunday. I have Early. He's my baby. I'll take care of him. Whatever he asks for, I'll bring to him—surprises, things he might not *think* to ask for but I know he'd like. It's okay if you go away for a while, Peter. You can come back when you want. Or you can stay away forever, if that's what you want. Whatever. I'll concentrate on my son. There'll be no distractions. I've got Early.

My heart is throbbing in my throat. It hurts. More than I can stand. Finally, I cry.

I cry until I'm sobbing. Until my face and hands are wet and my nose is running and my ears are stopped up and I can barely hear the animal sounds coming from the back of my throat. The thought occurs to me, This must be what we mean when we say we're crying our hearts out.

Peter doesn't know what to do. He looks at me, looks back at the road, both hands on the steering wheel. He runs one hand through his hair, then sets both hands on the wheel again. He reaches across me and punches open the glove compartment. His gesture is so deliberate and purposeful I make myself stop crying to see what he's after. He takes the last Kleenex from the box in the glove compartment and places it gently in my lap.

THE NEXT TWO SUNDAY MORNINGS, Mayor Oliver and a group of civic leaders visit the major churches in town, in black and white neighborhoods. Normally, Peter would be right there with them. The men pull the city together and keep it from drifting toward riots.

THIRTY-TWO

I HAVEN'T SLEPT a full night since the day they took Early away and Peter left. Around eleven every night, the dark closes in on me and I fall into an exhausted sleep, but then at three in the morning I stop grinding my teeth and snap awake. The pillow beside my pillow is still plump and unwrinkled from when I made the bed, no hollow left from a husband's head. I lie awake for hours, until the rising light of morning fills my window, until I'm in the groggy mist of sleep again. Then I slip into my dream, the same dream every time:

Peter, Early, and I are entering a building, an institutional kind of place, a government building or maybe a university. It's a vast, echoing entrance area with a high ceiling, dark-veined marble floor, and wide, carpeted staircases on either end, the kind of staircases that judges in black robes or scholars wearing mortarboards descend.

A woman off to the side, a visitor like us, recognizes Early and waves enthusiastically. "Early!" she says. "Hi!"

It's his third-grade teacher, Mrs. Poe. He smiles back at her but doesn't speak or lift his hand to wave.

Then he turns to me and says, as we enter a long, broad corridor, "I can't believe she remembered me after all these years! Amazing that she was able to think of my name so quickly!"

I'm thinking, *But why weren't you friendlier? You didn't even speak to her.*

We walk through one of the many doorways off the corridor and find ourselves in an auditorium filled with people apparently assembled for a program. Early goes right up on the stage, props himself on the corner of a table, and begins delivering a speech. I'm proud that he can be so casual and relaxed in front of such a large audience. But then I notice his shirt is unbuttoned down to his belt buckle, revealing a hairy chest, like a Las Vegas entertainer.

Why is he dressed like that? So cheesy, I think. I'm embarrassed by the way he looks.

He begins telling a story I've heard him tell before. I feel proud again—and forget my embarrassment—because when I heard him tell this story another time, I thought what a wonderful storyteller he is.

But he begins rambling, and suddenly his thoughts don't really connect or make sense. As if that weren't bad enough, in his story he refers to someone as a "prick" and then mentions "S and M." I can't believe he's using those words, that he even *knows* those words.

Such terrible, terrible judgment, I think.

People in the audience are walking out. In droves.

Only five or six people remain. I whisper to a woman seated next to me, "Why is everyone leaving?"

"Well, to begin with," she says, "he was supposed to start speaking at one-thirty and he didn't even get here until two . . ." In the middle of her sentence, *she* gets up and leaves.

Then I notice Early and Peter walking back up the aisle. I hurry to catch up with them. Early is sobbing. I'm trying to decide what I can say to him that will make him feel better, but everything that occurs to me sounds wrong.

You were great. It's just that this audience wasn't smart enough to understand what you were saying. No, that's not true. More important, Early will never believe me if I say that.

Why didn't you tell us you were supposed to be here at 1:30? No, I don't want to be blaming him at this point. It will only make him feel worse.

He's very upset. Nothing I can think of to say sounds right.

WHY MUST I transform Early's enormously successful graduation speech into this nightmare of a speech? Why dream over and over about his imperfections and the consequences of his imperfections? Why can't I just do what I'm good at? Make things okay.

THIRTY-THREE

MECKLENBURG COUNTY CORRECTIONAL CENTER #4535 in Huntersville, North Carolina, thirty minutes north of Charlotte. My first visitors' day. The road leading in, dry gravel and dirt. My car bounces recklessly as I roll over the uneven holes. In my rearview mirror, a loaf of dust rises, blotting out everything behind me.

Through the gates into the parking lot. Full. Pickup trucks everywhere. Half-crumpled cars. I drive up and down the rows until I find a spot near the razor-wire fence on the far side, in front of a row of mammoth Dumpsters. The prison is a cluster of concrete-block buildings beside the parking lot, zigzagging close to the Mount Holly–Huntersville Road. I wonder if the people who travel down that road every morning on their way to work look at the inmates, wave to them, roll down their windows and call out hello. I wonder if the inmates watch the workers as they head home at the end of the day, if they see familiar faces.

I bend over the steering wheel to peer out and up. A guard in the watchtower is looking down in my direction. He stands so still he could be a World War II statue in a town square. I think of an article I read in *Parade* in which people described what they do all day. One man stands guard in a prison, "armed with a thirty-eight-caliber pistol and a gas canister in case you catch one trying to escape. You use it to bring them back down off the fence." His comments startled me when I read them. Today they take hold of me; they're an undertow.

I have to keep my spirits up. I've brought fried chicken, biscuits and fries from Bojangles (Early's favorites), and Coke and paper cups. I baked a mocha cake, which is on a round tole tray on the floor of the front seat. Every year, for as long as I can remember, I've baked a mocha cake for Early's birthday. He's not a sweet-eater, but he loves the taste of coffee. Today is not his birthday, but I couldn't *not* bake for him. Melting the marshmallows, stirring in the coffee, whipping the heavy cream are as close as I can get to tucking him in at night.

I haven't seen him since the trial, since they took him away. Two weeks ago.

I've also brought a book of poetry written by a young man in prison. Honest poems, so broken and scary that when I took the book home from the store, I could only bear to read one poem at a time. I sat at the kitchen table, read the first poem, got up to empty the dishwasher, sat back down to read another poem, got up to stuff wet towels in the dryer. Each word is an ache.

I get out of the car, holding everything close. As I walk away, I hear the hood ticking.

Inside the prison building, I join a long, snaky line. When I finally get to the counter, I sign my name, along with Early's full name and the date and time, on a smudged pad of paper attached to a clipboard. My knit shirt is wet under the arms and across my back. I rummage in my purse for a Kleenex and fan my face, then wipe under my eyes, my neck. A guard in the far doorway is shouting—there's so much noise here!—that no food can leave the visitors' area and the main thing is to keep the inmates from taking leftover food to their lockers, which will cause problems with bugs. He's a stocky man, sturdy, looks like he lifts weights, probably in his twenties. I wonder if he's a college graduate. Can you major in prison work? He yells his same message over and over about leftover food. The line is no longer a line. It's a throng of desperate people, too eager to get from here to there. Someone could get trampled.

"I've found whole roasted possums in inmates' lockers after Sunday family visits!" the guard is shouting. Pockets of laughter. It's obvious he enjoys an audience.

I finally reach the doorway and am face-to-face with him.

"Cakes go in the kitchen, ma'am," he says, looking at my breasts. "Prison workers have to cut them. Leave it on that table, in the corner. I'll get to it when I can."

I make my way to the table and wedge my tray in beside a stack of different-size cardboard boxes that could easily tumble. On my cake.

"Next time," he yells across the room at me, "bring cupcakes!" He laughs as though he's cracked the funniest joke in the world.

I bump along with the crowd in his direction, a movement that seems to have its own slow, jerky flow, and when I face him again, he says to my chest, "Hardcover books are not allowed, ma'am. Go put it next to the cake. Your purse, too. You'll have to come get me after visitation so I can give them back to you. If you want, you can put your things in one of those lockers where you signed in."

I turn around, stepping on a woman's sandals, nearly knocking over a little girl holding a stuffed animal—a striped orange-and-yellow bee with orange felt antennae and wings. I push against the sweaty crowd, saying, "Excuse me . . . excuse me . . . I'm sorry . . ."

I move two of the boxes to the back of the table—another falls on the floor—to make room for my book and purse, but a sharp corner of my purse pokes the cake and some of the ladyfingers end up leaning, pointing in the direction of the exit.

I get in with the crowd again, behind a woman carrying a marbled watermelon the size of a small chair. How will they cut *that*? I notice she doesn't have a purse. None of the women have purses. How did they know to leave them in the lockers? Maybe I should just go back and put my purse in a locker. It's not going to be safe where I left it. But if I go now, I could miss seeing Early. Sunday visitation is from two to four. It's already two-thirty.

Everybody seems to be carrying a newspaper. The guard unfolds each one, shaking out the pages. He also checks the food and gifts people bring in. Why would so many inmates ask for newspapers?

I leave the outer office and push with the crowd through a set of massive iron gates.

I'm inside the prison!

This could be a scene from one of those movies where newspaper reporters are finally allowed to cross the border into a war-torn country. I stand still, let everyone rush past me, try to take it all in. The gravel surface. The trees, cut down, amputated. Gray-brown stumps left to rot. A few trees remain: all dead. What else beside weeds could live in gravel? Concrete tables with benches are everywhere, bolted to square concrete slabs. The place *smells* like gravel and concrete. And heat. Nobody ever expects October to be this muggy. Plastic umbrellas stick up out of holes in the middle of the tables, creating the illusion of shade. But the sun is a bulldog and has no intention of letting up. Everyone—inmates, mothers, fathers, grandparents, wives, sons, daughters, grandchildren—is grabbing a seat at a table, squeezing in. Too many bodies per square inch.

Never, even in my most tangled dreams, have I seen a time when the details of my son's life are so foreign to anything anyone in our family has known. For a split second, I yearn for the luxury of worrying about the garden-variety things other mothers worry about. Is he buckling his seat belt? Keeping his nails clipped? Writing thank-you notes?

But I'm just beginning my visit and I need to concentrate on Early—Early now. I can't think about how unnatural this feels. Focusing on my emotions is the last thing I need to do. This is not about my feelings. Concentrate. Concentrate on my son. Concentrate on his being all right.

Does the instinct to guide our children—to reach over and steady them—ever go away?

The area is cut in half by a fence, and on the other side, inmates are playing basketball. Do those men have families? Maybe their mothers and fathers are so disappointed in them, they won't have anything to do with them. Maybe their families live in California or Arizona. I think of Phyllis. Where are her boys now? I make a mental note to call her when I get home. She's the only person I know who will understand what this day was like.

On my side of the fence, the yard is teeming with children. The next population boom is right here. High-pitched, childish *Daddy this, Daddy that* fills the air like piped-in mall music. Some of the inmates seem to be giving small gifts to their visitors: shower caps, plastic bottles of shampoo and conditioner and hand lotion, miniature soaps. I remember hearing about a woman in Davidson who visits the prison and brings motel toiletries, which her friends have brought home to her from trips. Why didn't I ever think to do something like that?

Fright is draining out of me and a deep, steadying sorrow is left. Sorrow for myself—what am I doing here? How did we come to this? How in the world did we come to this? Sorrow for Early, sorrow for all the young men who'll live out the better part of their lives here. For the women visiting them. For the children too young to understand that their fathers are in prison and will stay in prison until after their own childhoods vanish.

I sit down at an empty table and immediately pop up. The bench is scorching! I look around. Everyone is sitting on newspapers. I pull out a wad of paper napkins from the box of chicken and biscuits. The napkins are yellow with oily patches, but I peel off four or five and tuck them under my legs, then unfold the rest for Early. There's no breeze, so they don't move.

How will he be able to find me in the middle of all this? Should I go look for him?

At the next table, a woman has brought a pair of shoes for the man she's visiting. Black loafers with square toes. I remember seeing the guard out front examine them. The inmate is pleased with the shoes. He reaches over the shoe box, open between them, and hugs her neck. One shoe is still wrapped in tissue in the box. The other is on its side on the table; it looks like a dead thing lying there. The man is so much bigger than the woman, she almost disappears in his arms. He must be seven feet tall and at least three hundred pounds. She's not so small herself, but next to him, she looks tiny. Beneath them, on the ground, two boys are sifting gravel through their fingers, trying to make one tall pile, but the gravel keeps collapsing on itself. The boys could be at the beach, building sand castles, digging tunnels with yellow shovels, a plastic pail of seawater between them. When they look up, a knot of sunlight is in their eyes. They hold their hands to their faces—gritty palms twisted up—to block it out.

"I been in this place for fifteen years." A mulchy voice behind me. "Don't know if I'd even know how to drive anymore. I used to drive my sister's blue Ford Mustang to school. I'd sit back and just drive that thing."

I turn around to see where the voice is coming from, but then I hear, from the opposite direction, a woman talking: "My nine-year-old brother, he was sitting in the street with his legs tucked under a manhole cover and a car drove by and hit the cover and it cut off both his legs."

"Bet it made him tough," the man she's visiting answers.

I feel a hand on my shoulder, and without thinking, jump. The last thing I want is to appear nervous. I consciously take a breath and look up slowly.

It's Early. It's a miracle—and a horror—to see him.

He's wearing a dark olive cotton shirt, pants the same color, rubber thong sandals. Like the other inmates. *This is a mistake,* I want to yell. *These are not his clothes. Give him back his khaki shorts and that old washed-out blue T-shirt and his running shoes and the socks he pushes down around his ankles.*

His face is his face, though. The scar from the corner of his mouth up to his eye appears normal here; everybody has scars.

He's looking down at me as though he's a doctor and I'm a patient who needs and deserves compassion. That face. The face I've known as well as my own for eighteen years. There is good in his face that has nothing to do with where he is.

"Hi, Mom." The voice. The voice I used to hear when I was at the kitchen sink putting supper together and he'd come in the back door after soccer practice, dropping his muddy cleats beside the heat vent in the back hall.

Hi, Mom.

Nothing unusual happened today.

We had to run laps because some guy forgot his uniform. Boy, I felt sorry for him. He really caught it.

Coach told us what we did wrong last game and what to look out for in the tournament. We're ready!

Hi, Mom.

Nothing new at school.

Algebra midterm.

Made an A.

Finished my notecards for my term paper. All I have to do is write it.

Hi, Mom.

"Early," I say. Because that's what I've been dreaming of saying since they walked him out of the courtroom. I've dreamed of saying his name and looking into his face at the same time. I stand, raise myself up on my tiptoes, put my arms around his neck, and we stay like this for a long time. I feel him crying. His shoulders are moving, small rhythmic shudders in my hands. I'm crying, too, without making a sound. We hug as though we could spend the entire visitors' day like this, and still, it won't be enough. There'll never be enough time to show my son how much I love him. How much I miss him. Crave him.

We pull apart and wipe our eyes with the backs of our arms, already wet with perspiration, and sit down next to each other on the bench. He sits on the napkins I spread for him.

Wordless, I take out the chicken, biscuits, and fries, pour the Coke, and we begin. Always, no matter where you are, no matter what the circumstances, you eat. At times, it's the only way to say, *I can get through this. This is not so catastrophic that I am not going to eat.* When your mother dies, when your father dies, when you visit your son in prison, you bring out the food and eat because you *can* eat and you're surprised you can still swallow, but this says that nothing is so bad you give up nourishment.

"How are you, honey?" I ask.

He looks at me but doesn't answer. He seems tired. I understand. If he tried to speak, he might well up again. He just shakes his head. Which could be a *not good.* Or maybe a *no, I can't even begin to answer that question.*

After a long silence, he finds his voice. He has a friend, he says, and they jog every day. They talk about what their life was like. Before prison.

His voice is raw when he says that last part. As though something has taken him by the throat.

It's amazing how alike we are, he says. His voice picks up; he doesn't want me to worry. "The guy is from Wilmington, Mom. I wish you could meet him. But he's over there. Playing basketball with the guys who don't have visitors."

For a minute, I think this could be visitors' day at camp. Children in rowboats off in the distance sing their familiar rounds. My son tells me he's met a nice boy from Wilmington and maybe they'll write to each other during the coming school year, arrange to visit next summer, maybe even decide to be roommates in college, end up partners in a successful law firm in downtown Charlotte.

But these are not camp pals. They're big and tough, most with scars—none from dog bites, I would bet.

The emergency room of the hospital. That's where you see these people. They're there at night with gunshot and stab wounds, T-shirts crudely wrapped around bloody body parts. Some brought in on stretchers, in handcuffs, accompanied by policemen, not family.

Early is saying he goes to the prison library and checks out books. He plays basketball. "Over there," he says. "Where my friend, Robert, and the others are shooting hoops.

"As long as you do what you're told," he says, his voice flat again, like he's reading instructions for a childhood board game, "the guards aren't too bad. You learn which guards you can talk to, which ones to trust. Some are just normal guys. A few you don't want to notice you, so you don't make eye contact with them. You do what you have to do to blend in."

I hear an argument behind me, men's loud voices, cursing, scuffling. Early immediately says, "Don't look. It's none of our business. Two inmates."

I can feel the gravel and hard-packed dirt beneath my feet. My shoes are socked in with dust. The fight is over; without turning around, I can tell the men have been taken away.

I ask Early what his cell is like, although I don't actually use that word—I say "room"—and he answers that it's about eight by ten with a bed, a toilet, a sink with cold water, two metal lockers, a plastic chair. I think about that one summer he rode the camp bus to Y camp, how difficult it was for me, not having actually seen where he was sleeping, where he was waking up every morning. I used to believe that if you could just lay eyes on your child's room so that later you could visualize him in it, you'd be able to adjust to his absence.

"Mom," he says, "have you seen Chip? Do you know how he is? Do you think he'll come see me?"

I tell him that I haven't seen Chip or heard anything about him. "I'm sure he'll visit, though," I add.

He bites into the thick meat of a drumstick, his favorite part of the chicken. Steam rises from the moist, pink flesh inside the crust. After all the hours of travel and waiting, the food is still hot. I'm glad, at least, for this. Food still hot and fresh is a small thing, but a good thing.

A LL THE WAY HOME I ask myself, *What if he gets sick? How can I leave him alone in that place? He'll die without me.*

I WALK INTO THE HOUSE, and the phone is ringing. It's Phyllis. I haven't talked with her since the day I went to tell her about the money I was going to deposit in her account every month.

"Oh, Mrs. Smallwood, I just heard about Early and I'm calling to say I'm here if you need me," she said. "If you want to talk."

If I need her. If I want to talk. It suddenly occurs to me I never asked her what it was like visiting her sons in prison. Sure, I knew the logistics of her driving to the different prisons in all those different towns, and yes, I knew that her car sometimes didn't make it and she couldn't see them that day, and I knew that she thought her boys were imprisoned unjustly. But did I ever try to understand how she *felt* having the sons she'd diapered, put down for naps, carried on her hip, in prison?

"Oh, Phyllis," I say, "please call me Kathryne."

"Well, that's not easy to do, after all these years," she says.

"But we're not employer and employee, and"—I hesitate because I know I'm getting ready to say something I've never said to her before— "we're not just black and white." I'm winded, trying to catch my breath. "I want us to be more than that." I didn't plan to say any of this. I didn't even have any idea that Phyllis would be calling. If only I'd had a chance to think this through, figure out the right way to say what I want to say.

"We're two mothers, Phyllis, talking about our sons," is what I manage to say. My voice sounds jagged. I can taste tears.

For the first time since I've known her, for the first time since I became aware that people have different-colored skins, I understand. I get it, almost in a snap. Perspective, I mean. She's not here to take care of me—the black woman's role in a white woman's world. She no longer irons my blouses and scrubs my oven. And I'm not here to take care of her—the white woman's role in a black woman's world. I no longer give her my hand-me-down sweaters and chipped dinner plates. This woman and I are simply two mothers. Two mothers without our sons, having to endure the daylight and the dark of night. I'm thankful we can have the conversation we're about to have—about razor-wire fences and surly guards, about weak moments, about the things we used to take for granted.

THIRTY-FOUR

I T's BEEN SEVEN MONTHS since Early was sent away.
Today is his birthday. He's nineteen. I mailed him a card.
Standing there, in that crowded, senseless Hallmark store
in SouthPark Mall, I wept. What kind of message do you look for?
Have a happy birthday? Here's to a great year? I found a card with a
photograph of a child on the front, his eager face turned up like an
urn. The card was blank inside. I wrote: *All my love to the most wonderful son in the whole world, Mom.*

Then I wrote *P.S.,* but scratched it out.

I have given up trying to find a formula. If I pray before I go to
sleep, wish hard, if I'm patient with boring people, if I let the other
car cut in, if I donate old coats to Crisis Assistance Ministry, Early
will miraculously be released from prison, ring the doorbell in the
middle of a gray afternoon carrying a sack of belongings (comb,
toothbrush, not much more than that), which I'll throw into the
trash because I'll want him to start again with everything new.

I haven't missed a single Sunday visiting him. Sometimes I don't know what to say when I'm with him, and I cannot believe this is us. I never dreamed there would be a time when I'd watch every word I say to my son. We were so close. There was nothing we couldn't talk about. But if I tell him about my day-to-day doings (running errands, paying bills, washing clothes, renting movies, cooking a scant dinner at night), it feels as though I'm pointing out what's missing in his life. It's been so long; he doesn't have any connection to the people he used to know or to the life he led. He was just a child when he left. If I ask about his days—and he tells me—I'm barely able to breathe. I want the old him, the old me, the old us, back so badly, the wanting is a heaviness in my chest.

All those years I worried about keeping him from harm. When his fever would rise with the flu or strep and I'd press my cool hand to his eyes. When that tornado careened through town and he insisted on walking up and down the driveway, his arms open to the swell. I want to feel the winds, he'd said. I tried to bring him in, but all I could do was watch from the back door, my calls lost in the air whipping by.

It never occurred to me to worry about keeping him from *doing* harm.

Now I'm back to worrying about—no, I'm terrified of—his receiving harm. Murderers. Rapists. Burglars. Threat of violence. Arbitrary and cruel. Guards. Locks. I realize I'm squeezing my eyes shut. If I ask him if he's safe, he might answer. Too much to take. Visualize what goes on when I'm not there? I can't. Details turn vague. The bitter clarity blurs. If images do worm their way in, the day divides itself into minutes, seconds, half seconds. If images get in, my day won't end.

It would be less painful if he'd been hit by a car (a drunk driver swerving onto the sidewalk where he's walking after having pizza with friends) or if he'd drowned (dived off a huge rock in a quarry, never came up for air) or if he'd become ill (leukemia, the bad kind, they did everything, no luck). Even though I'm not sure I believe in heaven, I like to think he'd be there with the angels. Protected. Taken care of. Instead, he's living with—eating and sleeping with— the most menacing men you could conjure up; you'd roll up your car windows and lock your doors if one crossed the street in your direction.

This many months later, it's a fresh assault every day to remember all over again where he is. Like the first year your mother dies— every morning you have to remind yourself that yes, it happened and she's not here. Mornings, you finally get moving, and that's relief. I still wake and for a second, forget where Early is. The blessed dumbness doesn't last long, though. The day is cold water in my face.

I'm very aware of the arrival of each season. *So now I've gone through an autumn with my son gone. Now I've gotten through winter. If I can make it past spring. Summer, that long and lazy one. Autumn again, the season he was sent away.*

Those first months I was stuck in a cycle of relentless self-observation. I stopped reviewing movies or serving on committees and boards, so I had all the time in the world to observe myself. I would answer the phone and say in a nasty voice, no, I don't want to buy a time-share in Myrtle Beach. I'd change the place mats on the kitchen table, all the while watching myself, too conscious of everything I was doing. Observing, judging. You picked the wrong place mats, I'd say to myself. Besides, who even needs place mats when nobody comes to dinner? And how could I have been so rude to the telemarketer, who only wanted to offer me a new TV if I'd come to the beach for a ten-minute presentation? She's probably like me, trying to keep a life from flying off. It's as though I couldn't stop myself from doing everything wrong. Which is how I saw the way I'd been for years—all those mistakes I kept making with Early and Peter, how I justified my mistakes.

Now I'm wondering why we go from viewing our actions as totally innocent to blaming ourselves for everything. Why do we swing from one extreme to the other before we can finally settle in to *yes, I did some things wrong and some things right and that's the reality*.

All that self-observation and judging. It was as though I was watching myself through one-way glass. Like at Early's nursery school, where the mothers could huddle in the side room and observe our children without their seeing us as they hung their coats on hooks by the door, snapped open their lunchboxes, unfolded their blankets for naps. One morning, a mother accidentally flipped the wrong switch and the light came on in the observation room. Suddenly the children could see us. They just stood there, motionless, their mouths twisted in amazement.

PETER NEVER CAME BACK. He left town, moved to Atlanta, went with a law firm headquartered in Chicago with offices around the country. I heard he moved in with Ann Cole. They'll marry when our divorce is final. Other than resolving, through our lawyers, the simple details of our settlement (he gave me everything I asked for), I have not spoken with him since the night he moved his things out. He took so little.

His leaving was the aftershock that followed the earthquake of Early's sentencing.

We all want to believe we live miles from a natural disaster site. The state that has to apply for federal relief is always at least three states away. Alabama has floods. California, fault lines. Florida is famous for hurricanes. We would never live in those places. Divorce, murder happen on other people's soil. We read obituaries and search the details to uncover an explanation. Oh, he smoked. No wonder he died of lung cancer. She ran out of gas on I-85 at 3 A.M. No wonder she was kidnapped. Nobody drives alone on the expressway in the middle of the night. She was asking for trouble. Of course that family's house caught fire. Faulty wiring. We would've had it checked. We want to separate ourselves from the people who are suffering and dying. The truth is, we're all only a hair away.

P ETER'S BUSINESS TAKES HIM to the Research Triangle almost every week. He's worked out an arrangement to see Early on weekdays, instead of during Sunday visitation. I don't know whether their relationship has changed. I do know he told Early that if he had an "exemplary disciplinary record," he'd be moved into the "honor unit." In the beginning, I asked Early for details about Peter, my bitterness barely caged in my pointed remarks. "So your father has to have his own special visiting hours? Can't just come when everybody else does?" Early would answer by talking around my questions. Then he told me—flat out—not to bring up his dad. I'd ask Early if he'd heard from anybody, thinking this would get him talking about Peter. He said he'd received letters and photographs from Billy, letters from Lily, from Joy, cards from the twins. I'd say, "How's your dad's blood pressure, does he ever mention it? I guess his new life is less stressful, huh?" Sometimes I'd get more direct and ask if his father talked much about Ann Cole. Finally, Early refused to answer. Refused to answer! At the time, I was shocked by his attitude. So unyielding, I thought. So different from the way he used to be. But I stopped asking.

Every now and then, I run into Chip's mother in the grocery aisle. We say hello but don't stop to talk. She becomes intent on selecting a papaya or jicama with the perfect ripeness, or some other exotic fruit or vegetable the rest of us haven't discovered yet; I concentrate on turning the twist tie an extra notch on my bag of apples. I haven't seen Chip's father. I heard that a mole on his arm was diagnosed as melanoma and he's gone through several rounds of chemotherapy. I don't call. What is there for any of us to say to one another now? Too many months have passed. We knew each other in another life.

Chip was given probation and community service. The fall Early was sent away, Chip started at UNC-Charlotte. Just before Christmas, he came to see me. When I answered the door, I was shocked. He hadn't called to let me know he was coming; he just appeared. Like the morning I'd opened the door to the two policemen. With this visitor, though, I hadn't bothered looking through the eyehole. For months, things like that haven't mattered to me—who comes, who doesn't. I don't worry about checking before I open my door. Sometimes I think I would welcome an intruder. An interruption, something jarring—a floorboard rotting and giving way beneath my feet, wiring in the house chewed down, suddenly igniting—would feel better than this termite hill of numbness.

Chip and I sat in the den—such a familiar room for him!—drinking Cokes, talking. Not about what he and Early had gone through. Just surface things: his classes, his acceptance into the honors program, his plans for the future. He wants to be a youth director in a church. Will settle somewhere in North Carolina. Maybe Raleigh, he says. He's going with a girl from Virginia, who's also interested in making the church her career. He asked about Early in a way that let me know he did not want details. He said he couldn't bring himself to visit Early because it would be too difficult, but he was praying that God would forgive Early, have mercy on him.

While he was here, a million what-if voices tunneled through my mind: *What if he had listened when Early said that selling the marijuana was a bad idea? What if he hadn't told Early to bring the gun? What if they'd left when Early first told Chip he wanted to leave, before anything happened? What if Chip had been as good a friend to Early as Early was to him when he, Early, told the judge that Chip had nothing to do with the murder and to please spare him?*

After about an hour of both of us working to keep the conversation alive, Chip stood to leave. He gave me a hug and I wished him luck.

And Eddie Jackson and Steven Todd and Allen Marshall? I realize this might be hard to believe, but I don't know if they were given probation and community service, like Chip, or what. By the time Eddie and Steven were in court (I don't know if Allen Marshall, the boy who took the marijuana and ran, was even charged), I was too tired to pay attention. I could not bear to read the newspaper. And of course, no one dares mention their names. No one mentions Early's name either; it's as if he's a nonperson now. But that's okay. I don't seek out conversations with people anyway. Opening the café curtains in the kitchen to let in the day is about all I can manage at this point.

After Early went to prison, he told me that Eddie had written him a two-page letter. Here's the part he showed me:

I'm very sorry for the way things turned out. I hope you believe me. I just happened to be hanging out with William after graduation. I had no idea anything was up. William and his mother moved to Charlotte from Mississippi when William was fourteen. He was always getting in trouble, and to be honest, I didn't much like him, but my mother and his mother are sisters and my mother wanted us to be close. I think she was hoping I could help him turn his life around. William's parents got divorced when he was two and his father once broke down the front door of their house and held William and his mother at gunpoint for hours until a neighbor called the police. My uncle got off by saying my aunt hit him first.

Later Early told me that Eddie had come to see him, not long after he'd sent the letter. Eddie is the only friend from high school who ever comes. Not Amy Whitley. Not Steven or Brian. Of course, not Chip. Eddie visits whenever he's in North Carolina. Fall break. Thanksgiving. Christmas. Spring break. He's doing very well at Stanford. Plans to go on to graduate school, teach in a university.

FOR MONTHS, Joy and I haven't seen each other. She keeps calling, inviting me for a bowl of soup or afternoon tea. I say I'll come, but then don't. Sometimes I turn her down right off; sometimes I accept and at the last minute call to say it's not convenient. Once, she asked me a very simple question: "Kathryne, do you think maybe you're putting your*self* in prison by not seeing anyone or going anywhere?" I gave her a nothing answer, then hung up the phone and thought about it. What she doesn't understand is that I'm busy—learning how to live without hope.

THIRTY-FIVE

EARLY IS NO LONGER in Huntersville. Huntersville is a minimum-security prison. He was there for eight months, awaiting permanent assignment. Now they've taken him to Central Prison in Raleigh. Maximum security.

Central Prison is not what I wanted. When I say the words, "Central Prison," my lips stick on the *P*. My mouth does not want to form the syllables.

He's being housed in a section for violent youthful offenders—age twenty-five and under. Years ago, Phyllis told me about this unit. One of her boys was there. She said it's the worst group you could put together, that the younger inmates are often more difficult than the older ones because they're trying to prove themselves—they start fights, cause trouble.

I'm in my car. Making the three-hour drive from home for my first visit.

Through Raleigh. Past North Carolina State. The mannerly brick

buildings and hedges softly blend into the surrounding neighborhood. (In Charlotte, I make it a point never to drive down Selwyn
Avenue. I can't bear to pass Queens College—the students lying in
the damp grass, their backpacks pillows for their well-groomed
heads.)

Stop for the red light at the prison entrance. Turn left into Visitors' Parking. No gate or guards. I could be going to see my insurance man at an office park in southeast Charlotte. But the lot is half
paved, half dirt.

On the other side of Visitors' Parking, a tollbooth-style guardhouse lifts a stiff arm to admit one dusty car into a nice, paved area.
The lot for prison employees.

Adjacent to the guardhouse, the Welcome Center.

Fifty yards down, the main prison complex.

In the sadness of the afternoon, I push open the double glass
doors of the Welcome Center, go to the long counter, wait in line,
show my driver's license to the guard. Without raising his face to me,
he shuffles papers, scribbles my name on a card, hands me back my
license along with the card, which he says is my pass. He points to
where I should go, not once looking directly at me. If you asked him
the color of my hair, he wouldn't be able to tell you.

I walk back through the double doors. In the bright sun, my face
is so hot it feels cold. I hurry along the sidewalk to the main entrance
of the prison. An older man in a white T-shirt and olive pants kneels
in the flower bed beside the front doors. An inmate? He's picking
each individual weed so carefully, so delicately, it makes me think of
the time I pulled Early's baby tooth, which I'd let hang by a thread
too long.

This entrance could be the entrance to a school. There's no chain-
link fence, no barbed wire. I push through two sets of doors. Like a
library. Or a store. But inside, an officer in a blue uniform—a *correc-
tion-officer* uniform—sits in a booth of thick glass. (Bulletproof?)

There's a phone beside him. The booth is surrounded by a bank of closed-circuit TVs.

Ahead of me in line is a small elderly woman with white hair and a large bandage covering her throat. She's pushing a baby in a stroller and holding a teddy bear and diaper bag. The baby is around eight or nine months old. The officer says to her, "Lady, you know you can't bring that stroller in here. It's against the rules. And leave all that other stuff in your car, too."

"I'm not the one in prison," she says. "And neither is my grand-baby." But she wheels the stroller around and heads for the outside. I watch as she struggles through the two sets of doors.

The officer slides out a drawer for my driver's license and pass and gives me a steady, over-the-glasses look—at least he looks at me! But he quickly goes back to my driver's license and pass. He grimaces at them as though he suspects I'm guilty of some crime myself. Then he slides the drawer with my IDs back to me and motions for me to wait.

I stand at the booth. I can almost feel the people in line behind me shift from foot to foot. He pulls out a *Stock Car Racing* magazine and begins to read. He crouches around the pages. If Peter were here, this would not be happening. This man would not keep us waiting while he sits there reading. *If they treat visitors this way, how must they treat inmates?*

I glance over at a display case filled with trophies. A sign says they were won by the prison guards in their sports leagues. Around the room are photographs of the governor, warden, various officers, all hung too high. Past the last stern photograph is a closed door. Loud, cracking noises from inside. Almost like drums. Or cymbals. Sharp striking sounds. Blows.

The officer looks up at me sleepily, gestures with one hand—a motion halfway between a wave and a dismissal—and says, "Through those doors. Take the elevator. Do not touch any of the buttons outside or inside the elevator."

I move through the automatic sliding door, which he seems to be operating from across the room. The opening is so narrow, if two people were trying to pass through, we'd have to walk single file.

I'm now in a small lobby crowded with people. We're all facing two elevators. No one presses the button. We wait for an elevator to arrive, wait for the button to light up and the door to open. The elevator fills. Wait for the next one. It fills. Wait. Finally, enter. Three buttons—first floor, second floor, third floor. We don't touch the buttons. The door closes. A camera is mounted in the upper right-hand corner. I hold my hands out, palms up, elbows bent—pocketbook dangling from my arm—to show that I'm following the rules. Third-floor button lights up. The officer—the one in that last booth, the one with the magazine—is controlling the elevator, too!

Third floor. Spotless. Not one bit of debris. Clean, ammonia smell. Why do I have such a strong desire to wash my hands?

Beside the elevator, a water fountain. I drink in large thirsty mouthfuls.

Ahead, a semicircular arc of doorways. In the center of the arc, an officer sits at a small, plain desk. Thirteen numbered doors on either side of him: 1–13. 14–26. I hand him my pass. He lines it up with a name on his list, makes a crooked X beside the name—my name, I can see now—and hands me back my pass.

He picks up the phone: "I need number DU-104 to come up to visitation."

He twists the receiver into his neck to speak over it to me: "Go to eleven."

I turn the doorknob of solid metal (steel?) door number 11, walk in, pull the door shut behind me. I'm aware that another officer standing outside the floor-to-ceiling glass behind me can see every inch of me.

The booth is divided into two sections. On my side are two stools bolted to the floor, each round seat perched atop a steel column, like mushrooms. The stools are about six inches apart and maybe six inches from the wall.

I sit so lightly on the stool my bottom barely touches the vinyl. I place my purse on the narrow ledge in front of me. Above the ledge is a metal grate, perforated like a large cheese grater. Above the grate, a double pane of glass. Between the panes are steel bars, painted white. Thick bars.

The booth feels airless.

Early enters on the other side of the bars and glass. He's wearing a yellow jumpsuit. He sits down in a plastic chair, digs both elbows into his ledge, leans right into the grate. I find myself searching his face for bruises.

"Hi, Mom," he says. "How *are* you? How are you holding up?" His voice is the same. But different. A mother can tell these things right off. His voice is opened up. Clear. It has—it has Authority.

We talk back and forth, how I am, whom I've seen back home, my drive here.

"Oh, Early," I say, "that noise coming from inside the room with the closed door in that area downstairs, you know, next to the trophy case. What *is* that noise?"

"It's a lounge for prison employees."

"But the noise."

"What you heard is pool balls being struck. There's a pool table in there."

I start to ask how he knows, but an inmate, behind Early, yells through the floor-to-ceiling glass on Early's side. Early jerks around quickly; I notice he reacts to the slightest noise.

"Hey!" the inmate says. "You drive the silver Volvo!"

He's talking to me!

"Don't worry, Mom," Early says. "His cell looks out on the visitors' parking lot. The guys with windows on the front spend all their time staring out. They memorize the cars the visitors drive."

I wonder if the young man has memorized my license plate. I button the top button of my cardigan sweater.

One of the two single lightbulbs on either side of the grate is out, so the light is dim. But I can see an officer watching us through the glass behind Early, on the inmates' side.

Every now and then, an inmate walking by the officer recognizes Early, knocks on the glass to gesture at him—a blocky wave or an index finger pointing, as if to say, *You're the man!* One young man, his hair in a tight ponytail, raps on the glass so many times Early has to turn completely around to wave so he'll stop. I take in the back of Early's head, think of the times I stood at the kitchen sink, my hands lost under suds, watching him leave the house for school.

"Why are some people wearing those yellow suits and some, regular clothes?" I say. "There was a man working outside in a T-shirt and pants."

"Well, everybody, even the guys on death row, we all wear white T-shirts and green pants on the block. But here we have to wear these jumpsuits. The guys you see around, who've earned privileges like delivering the mail, working on the grounds, in the library, stuff like that, get to wear regular clothes. T-shirts and green pants."

"What does 'on the block' mean?" I ask.

"In the cell."

He studies me, without blinking. The yellow uniform next to his face changes the color of his eyes. "Mom," he says, "I've got something I want to talk about."

"Okay." I draw the "kay" out.

"It's something that's been on my mind." He looks away. He looks back at me. "Remember when you fired Phyllis?"

"Sure I do. When I let her go, you mean."

"Well, I've been thinking about how you were dealing with the question of right and wrong, and you felt so strongly that what she did was wrong. At the time, I thought you were really being unfair. I couldn't understand why you would do that to her."

"Well, there are things that have happened since that time, things you don't know about. She called me—"

"It's the right and wrong part I'm talking about. What I want to say is, what happened with William Campbell and me is similar, in a way, to what happened between Phyllis and you. He stole from me and was after my best friend. Phyllis stole from you. Neither one of us could let them get away with what they did."

"You're comparing—"

"I don't mean to say that what you did was the same as what I did or that what you did was bad. I mean that we were both dealing with the question of right and wrong. In fact, I've had so much time to think about all this that now I can understand what you were going through. I was so quick to judge at the time. I was really critical of what you did. What *I* did, I know is wrong. I'm very ashamed. I can't get past the shame. But that's how I'm supposed to feel. Look at what I did. I took somebody's life."

"Early."

"And I brought so much shame to our family."

"Honey."

"I wrote to William Campbell's mother."

"You—"

"I wanted to ask for her forgiveness."

"Did you hear back from her?"

"No. I probably won't. Even if she did forgive me, I could never forgive myself. But that's okay. I'm okay, in fact. I am. I'm figuring things out little by little. I still don't understand what happened that night, why I went so far, but I'm working on it."

"You seem okay. I'm, I'm surprised at how okay you seem."

"In some ways, maybe I've never been better."

"Never been better?"

"Well, in the sense that I'm my own person in here, yeah. It's rough, plenty rough, and there's a lot to be scared of, but for the first time in my life I know I have only myself to depend on." He stops talking. I start to say something, I don't know what. "You know, you never hear your name spoken in prison. Because nobody knows it. Not the other inmates. And for sure, not the COs. Corrections officers, Mom. Nobody ever starts a sentence with, 'Early, this . . .' or 'Early, that . . .' There's not one soul in here who really cares about me. Not a single person who would help if I needed help. If I make it, it's going to be up to me."

There's no self-pity in his voice. What is it I hear? That he's serious, earnest? No, he's always been serious and earnest. Is it that he appears more muscular, his body looming large above me? Actually, he's been growing and maturing and filling out for some time now.

"I got a book from the library," he says. "By Walker Percy. It's called *Lancelot*. I've memorized one part."

He doesn't take his eyes off my face.

"'Come into my cell,'" he recites. "'Make yourself at home. Take the chair; I'll sit on the cot. No? You prefer to stand by the window? I understand. You like my little view. Have you noticed that the narrower the view the more you can see?'"

Full-fledged, is what I see. And what I hear. Where does that leave me? I've been his mother for a long time; do I even know how to be anything else? His door doesn't have a knob inside, yet the way he holds himself, the way he's speaking, the tenor of his voice—it's the body and voice of someone who has—the word that comes to me is: escaped.

I want to fix his hair on the left side, just push it in a little.

Because of the glare from the floor-to-ceiling glass behind him, I can hardly make out his face. I lean to the right, to the left, back to the right. The thick bars I have to look around don't help. And the two panes of glass sandwiching the bars refract the light like a prism.

Ghostlike voices from the other booths drift up through the metal grate: inmates and visitors talking to one another, inmates and visitors yelling at one another. It feels like I'm in my own little world and Early is in his. I'm trying to get to him. But I can't touch him. I can hardly hear him. I can hardly see him.

All I want is to hold him in my arms, rock him until the inmates, visitors, guards disappear and this cracked concrete floor gives way to sculptured carpet and the concrete walls soften. The smell of ammonia turns into baby powder and I hold that little boy, his head snug between my shoulder and neck, and I tell the story:

The day you were born, there was an article on the front page of the Local section about the unusually large number of baby boys at Memorial Hospital, ready to be claimed. I still remember the headline, I say: BUMPER CROP OF NEWBORN BOYS! COUPLES INVITED TO CHOOSE BABIES!

So, all the parents rushed to the hospital. Your dad and I drove so fast he ran a yellow light. Can you believe that? When we got to the hospital, the parking lot was full. And it was a big parking lot. We had to park blocks from the hospital, on a side street, but that was okay. We got out of the car and ran to the columned front entrance; we didn't want to be late.

The lobby was filled with excited parents, calling out to one another, talking loudly, laughing. The crowd turned into one big festive mass—all those jostling bodies—moving through the halls of the hospital, like teenagers at a rock concert.

In the nursery, rows and rows of babies formed Os with their mouths, as though they were singing opera. Their eyes squinted in that bright, artificial light. At first glance I thought, They're all so adorable, how can I possibly pick? But it was not difficult. One baby was by far the most wonderful, the smartest, the most gentle. I gathered up that loose bundle of baby—you, of course, Early—your shell-colored blanket falling over my arm with a soft tickle. And I held you. That's it. End of story. I held you. For hours.

Around midnight, I looked up at the window high over the bassinet where I'd found you and motioned to your dad to pull down the shade, reducing the outside dark to a sliver. Then we closed all the doors to the nursery, and we kept those doors closed the rest of the night, against whatever might want in.

THIRTY-SIX

I HAD A SOLID FAITH in my mother. We delighted in each other and in our unspoken agreement: she saw no wrong in me, I saw no wrong in her. I was perfectly content to be a miniature version of her.

When I was pregnant, she told me a newborn brings good luck. I remember thinking, Giving birth must be like buying a lottery ticket. Suddenly there are endless odds. Unlimited possibilities.

Of course she failed to say that at no time after the instant that baby is born—after the lottery ticket is tucked in a purse or in the visor of the car to keep it from being carried away by a violent wind—is anything ever again so clear or so sure.

Mothers think that a newborn is a chance to create a perfect person, with all our best qualities and none of our flaws (we want so desperately to do it right), but we soon find the certainties we counted on breaking apart. The child will grow as if driven by a restlessness; his face, at first taken from the mother or the father, in the end will hold no trace of either. It will appear he's dreamed himself into a stranger. Which is when we learn that what we believed in was merely a promise that can dissolve, like a lozenge on the tongue.

THIRTY-SEVEN

THERE'S SO MUCH you watch go by, saying, "It'll turn out all right." Then a few years pass and it doesn't turn out all right at all. A million different signals you should've paid attention to, markers you sped past like street signs framed for a split second in the car window. Everything ran right by you and you didn't notice until it was too late.

THIRTY-EIGHT

EARLY THIS MORNING, just before the sun came up, I saw a luna moth fly out of the unmowed grass beneath the kitchen window. I watched the quick flick of its green wings. Waving to me as it rose. As though it were a marionette and the moon were pulling its strings. As though a magician were turning a long string of silk scarves into something that flies. Into a son so far away his mother can only watch the sky, the one thing left they have in common.

There should have been an instant of breaking. A time when Early cut loose. When I allowed it. For eighteen years he submitted, and then one night he found a way to make himself distinct from me.

Like Geppetto with Pinocchio, I thought I wanted a real boy, but what I really wanted was someone made in my own image. When the paint was barely dry, when the wood was softening to flesh, I held on to the strings for dear life.

THIRTY-NINE

T HE PERSON I REALLY AM is difficult to catch, although I'm beginning to see her. Like an optical floater—that ragged speck or thread that hovers vaguely on the periphery of vision, which you can see only when you're not making an effort to see it. If you turn your head for a closer look, it vanishes. You have to concentrate, hold still, not turn from side to side. I understand now how I tried to alter my world, refine it until there was no trace of repair. How my life was an illusion. A movie. A cinema fantasy. A series of frames to be edited—delete this, expand that—for the sole purpose of presenting to the world a happy conclusion.

Mothers everywhere are making the same mistakes I made, and yet their sons do not end up committing murder. Maybe their sons only cheat other people in business. Maybe they marry girls who are spoiled and self-centered. Maybe they drink too much. Drive too fast. Overeat. How much room is there for a mother's imperfect behavior? We cannot possibly know what the consequences of our parenting will be, whether we'll come away clean. Some mothers seem to naturally know to do the right thing, and their children, not surprisingly, turn out well. Other mothers are not so skilled—they may think they're doing the right thing, but what they're really doing is following their own hungers. In spite of that, in many cases, their children turn out well.

Then, of course, there are the mothers who make dreadful mistakes and whose children make dreadful mistakes.

Did I make dreadful mistakes? I don't believe so. Did I make mistakes? Yes. Peter made mistakes, also. You're looking at two decent people who made mistakes. If only he and I would have confronted the fact that our good family was sliding into bad. If only we could have confronted Early—as a team, as husband and wife—instead of the two of us pushing and pulling at each other. Early was an exceptional and sensitive child, and we agonized—individually, not together—over what to tell him, what not to tell him.

Too much. Too little. I was excessive when I should have held back, Peter was stingy when fullness was needed.

Beneath it all: anger. Anger in control, anger out of control. Stifled anger, expressed anger. Appropriate anger. Inappropriate anger. Neither of us knew what to do with our anger. So we weren't able to teach Early what to do with his.

What it all comes down to: I have to accept the justice of a prison sentence, the injustice of life.

I have to let go because I have no choice.

I have to keep my eye on a fixed point, look straight ahead, so that what I couldn't see all those years—the person I am—will come clear. That person has known the worst, and suffered for it, but can still turn her life around.

FORTY

I T'S BEEN THIRTEEN MONTHS since Early was taken away. I call Joy to ask if she can come over. In less than half an hour, she's here. We talk. She asks me questions nobody else would dare ask, about Early, Peter, me. I answer in sentences, paragraphs, long paragraphs. She encourages me to go deep. It feels like I'm carving out a mine with a pick or an ax.

She says she's been writing to Early. All this time. Visiting him, too. I'm surprised she's stayed in such close touch with him, but she tells me that because I was refusing to see her, she'd asked Early not to say anything to me about their visits; she didn't want me to feel any pressure to see her.

Her voice fills the house like a pastel balloon. Through the French doors, I can see a bird balancing on the feeder, fanning its wings. The feeder is empty. Has been for over a year. I remind myself to go by Myers Park Hardware to buy seed. Maybe I'll stop at the nursery and buy pansies for the bed beneath the lamppost, see what other small bright things they have that I can bring home.

I'm on the sofa, Joy is in the leather chair. I leave the room to get my copy of the account Early gave our attorney, Donald Sanders, not long after the arrest. All this time, I've kept it in the bottom drawer of my dresser, hidden in the folds of my scarves. I read it only twice, when Donald first gave it to Peter and the night before the sentencing.

I hand it to Joy.

"What do you think was going on in his mind that night?" I ask. She reads. I wait.

"You know, Kathryne," she says slowly, "graduation is a key transition in life. Think about it. Here, Early's going through this important rite of passage. Plus, he's the center of attention all evening. It's the height of everything for him." She moves next to me, leaving the papers in the chair. She sits so close I can smell her skin, the sweetness. "And then within hours he is as frightened as he's ever been in his whole life. Confronted by an aggressive black kid. A black kid confronted by an aggressive white kid would feel the same terror. Knowing Early and his sense of justice, so typical of bright kids—anyway, he's Peter's and your son—I can see him doing whatever he had to do to protect his best friend. Feeling such panic, there was no way he could interpret the cues correctly. I can understand his overreacting, even overreacting to that degree. He snapped, Kathryne. Our precious boy just snapped."

"We could've been better parents—"

"Well, we all could've been better parents. But we have to make sure that our guilt over what we did or didn't do for our children isn't just allowing us to carry the burden for them. Anyway, Kathryne, they come into the world with their own set of traits and then they surround themselves with friends of their choosing and—this is the main thing—chance weighs in. Children emerge slowly. Along the way, there are accidents, illnesses, influences beyond our control, things we can't possibly know. Once that child leaves our lap, anything can happen."

Her face is serious and almost smiling at once.

"Remember what I said about Phyllis? When I told you her husband broke her wrist? Remember how I said that she's a strong woman? Well, you and she have a lot in common. You're both going to outlive your problems. More than outlive. You're going to be okay."

I nod at the link between Phyllis and me. I'd like to think I have Phyllis's strength. I make a mental note to call her, go see her.

I find myself feeling something like happiness, just for a moment. Knowing that the feeling won't change anything, but it's a reminder of what it means to be alive.

I think of the offer a few years ago from my editor to become managing editor of the magazine. That still doesn't feel right to me, but maybe I could get back my old job at the *Observer* as full-time movie critic. The woman who's been reviewing movies there is pretty old; maybe she's ready to retire. I make another mental note for tomorrow, to call the paper.

"I'm glad you asked me to come over. I've been waiting," Joy says.

"I just wasn't ready—"

"Oh, I know. I was fine with that. In fact, I can't believe you called today. It's perfect timing. Early asked me to discuss something with you. See, I was there on Sunday—"

"Early asked you—wait, I didn't see you."

"I know. I got there after you left."

"I didn't stay very long. I had a bad sore throat. I barely made it home before my fever hit a hundred and two."

"Kathryne! Are you better now?"

"I'm better. But Early—what did he say?"

"The truth is," Joy says, "I always try to go at the end of visiting hours. I would never want to cut into your time with him. Anyway, Early asked if I would tell you this whenever you're ready to see me. He said it doesn't matter when that is."

"I can't imagine! What?"

"Kathryne, he's been transferred into the honor unit."

"Oh, God! But why wouldn't he tell *me*?"

"Wait. There's more. After I tell you everything, you'll understand why he was unsure about saying this to you himself. There are a lot of wonderful things about his being in the honor unit. First of all, he said the guys in the unit are pretty decent. It's safe there."

I put my hands on my knees to try to steady myself.

"And," Joy says, "he's working in the library. Spends just about all day there every day, studying law. Isn't this amazing?"

"Studying law?" The news of his transfer is so big, the fact that he didn't tell me is so big—I can't take it all in. Easier to focus on one detail.

"He says he's going to file motions for inmates who've been wrongfully convicted. He's planning to write letters to attorneys, law schools, newspapers, and news shows to drum up support for them."

So like Early, finding ways to help others, I say to myself, almost reflexively. I don't want to take it to the next step, ask the important question: Why isn't he trying to help himself?

Joy takes my hand and rubs my palm with her thumb. I feel something running between us. "I asked him if he'd ever consider looking into his own situation."

I search her face for his answer. She's still holding my hand.

"He said he's been thinking about it, that he stumbled across something called a law of self-defense and defense of others—I believe I'm remembering it correctly—and he feels Donald Sanders misled him, that he should have pressed for voluntary manslaughter, which would've resulted in a much lesser sentence. Early said it was a case of imperfect self-defense, that he didn't initiate the problem that night and he had a reasonable belief that what he did was necessary to save Chip's life. Early also told me something very disturbing about Donald. Did you know that at the time of the sentencing, he had a teenage son who was heavy into drugs?"

"No! I never knew that!"

"Early told me that the first time he met with Donald, right after he was arrested, Donald said, 'This is all about a drug deal, son, and there's not a lot I can do for you.' He also told Early that, yes, he tried to defend his friend, but unfortunately, he used excessive force. 'You don't bring a gun to a fistfight,' he told Early."

"I can't believe that! Donald had such a good reputation. We thought we'd hired the best. It sounds like he decided it was over before he even investigated the facts."

"But here's the most important part. Early is thinking about filing a motion for appropriate relief—he said it's called MAR—to see if they'll set aside his plea. He said the heart of his motion would be ineffective assistance of counsel. In other words, he's hoping that because his lawyer didn't advise him correctly, he can essentially start over. The court will have a hearing—"

"Start *over*?"

"They would go back to square one. He said there's a strong possibility he could get a new sentence for voluntary manslaughter and he'd get credit for time served—"

"How long? How long?"

"He *could* be released right from the courtroom. But he says we shouldn't get our hopes up. Not yet. The judge will have to evaluate the nature of the case, and he'll have wide discretion. Early kept repeating that he, Early, has to do his homework on all this first."

"Oh, God, we've got to get him a good lawyer." My voice won't go any higher than a notch above a whisper. "We've got to get him the very best lawyer in the country."

"Early used the term 'pro se.' Which, he explained, means he plans to represent himself."

I can tell she wants that to sink in. Neither of us speaks for a few seconds.

"Listen," she finally says, "this is why he wanted me to tell you. He asked me to help you understand why it's so important for him to do this himself. This is more of a graduation than graduation itself. Do you know what I'm saying?"

"I know, Joy. I know." And I do.

"Kathryne, I wanted to ask him a thousand questions, but he didn't want that. I just let it go. All we need to know is he's in charge. In fact, he quickly changed the subject and started talking about how he's also going to tutor inmates who are studying for their GED tests."

"Well, should we at least—"

"Kathryne." Joy lets go of my hand and holds my face.

I try to call up my mother's face. And think suddenly of what she used to say about Early when he was little. *There's nothing that boy won't be able to do, if he puts his mind to it.* I hold on to that thought. It's an iron railing. Hold on.

P.S.

Insights,
Interviews
& More . . .

About the author

About the book

Read on

Meet **Judy Goldman**

JUDY GOLDMAN was born and raised in Rock Hill, South Carolina, where she attended Winthrop Training School, a laboratory school for Winthrop College—kindergarten through twelfth grade in one building. She and her husband have lived in Charlotte, North Carolina, for thirty-seven years and have two children and three granddaughters. She received a bachelor of science in education with a concentration in English from the University of Georgia. She has worked as a high school English and journalism teacher in Atlanta, an advertising copywriter in New York City and Charlotte, and a teacher of creative writing workshops at Queens University, as well as at numerous writers' conferences. Her book reviews have appeared in the *Washington Post* and the *Charlotte Observer;* her commentaries have aired on public radio. Her work has been published widely in such journals as the *Southern Review,* the *Kenyon Review,* the *Ohio Review,* the *Gettysburg Review, Shenandoah, Prairie Schooner,* and in many anthologies.

Judy is the author of two books of poetry (the most recent the winner of the Gerald Cable Poetry Award, the Roanoke-Chowan Poetry Award, the Zoe Kincaid Brockman Book Award, and the Oscar Arnold Young Award) and two novels. Her first novel, *The Slow Way Back,* won the Sir Walter Raleigh Fiction Award and the Mary Ruffin Poole First Work of Fiction Award, and was short-listed for the Southeast Booksellers Association's Novel of the Year. *Early Leaving* was called

Judy Goldman

Laurie Goldman Smithwick

2

"masterfully written and fast-paced . . . highly recommended" by *Library Journal* and "brutally honest . . . a provocative read" by *Booklist.* She has been the recipient of a grant from the North Carolina Arts Council, has received the Beverly D. Clark Author Award, and was given the Fortner Writer and Community Award for "outstanding generosity to other writers and the larger community."

For more information visit the author on the Web at www.judygoldman.com. ∾

A Conversation with
Judy Goldman

Early Leaving unfolds through the perspective of Kathryne Smallwood, who probes every detail of her son's past in an effort to uncover what she could have done to save him. She shoulders much of the blame for his actions. Is your book a cautionary tale for parents?

I didn't set out to write a cautionary tale. I don't believe we should write a novel because we think we have something important to say. We write novels because we have questions. Can a mother love her child too much? How much of a role do parents play in how their children turn out and how much is due to larger forces? I tell beginning writers to write about what keeps them up at night. These are the questions that occupy my mind at three in the morning. All that protective worry—does it ever go away?

A recent New York Times *column by David Brooks discussed how the parents of Dylan Klebold, one of the Columbine killers, acknowledged the horrible crime their son had committed but were still fiercely loyal to him. Brooks asked a question you confront head-on in* Early Leaving: *"If your child commits a crime like that, what do you do with the rest of your life?" How would you respond personally to that? How would Kathryne?*

What do any parents do with the rest of their lives after their child does something that goes against all of their values? Our children can become disappointingly "other." They can fall

> 66 Can a mother love her child too much? How much of a role do parents play in how their children turn out and how much is due to larger forces? 99

into error suddenly, a single event irrevocably leading to a new fate.

Whether our children are taking their first wobbly steps or walking down the aisle, our job as parents is to put ourselves out of a job. We must prepare our children for life without us. And we must prepare ourselves for life without our children. It's a delicate balance— letting our children know we're there when they need us and not letting *our* happiness depend on *their* happiness.

Near the end of my book, Kathryne's friend, Joy, tells her, "Well, we all could've been better parents. But we have to make sure our guilt over what we did or didn't do for our children isn't just allowing us to carry the burden for them."

My husband used to say this wonderful thing when our children were going through hard times: "It's okay. Here's their chance to have a rough go of it and see that they can come out on the other side. It's how children gain self-confidence." Kathryne finally decides she must let go because she has no choice. She says she has known the worst and suffered for it, but realizes it's not too late to turn everything around. Her future is no longer tied to her son's future, and she can now become an active participant in her own life.

In Early Leaving *and in your previous novel,* The Slow Way Back, *you explore the complex themes of love, loyalty, trust, and betrayal within a family. What compels you to write about family relationships?* ▶

66 We must prepare our children for life without us. And we must prepare ourselves for life without our children. 99

A Conversation with Judy Goldman
(*continued*)

What interests me about family relationships are the ways we connect, disconnect, and reconnect. I love how resilient families are, how anything is possible, how change can take place, change we never thought could happen in a lifetime—both within family members and between family members. My basic feeling about family is hopeful, optimistic.

Before you turned to fiction writing, you were an accomplished poet with two published books of poetry. How does your background in poetry affect the creative process of your novels?

It makes writing a novel very slow going! Poets-turned-novelists tend to pick. We look for the rightness of every single word; we study a word or sentence or paragraph a hundred or two hundred times as though that huge gorilla of a novel we're trying to wrestle down is merely a two-stanza poem.

Being a former poet also means I'm page-obsessed. The length and breadth of a novel scare me to death. When I started my first novel, acquaintances would stop me in the grocery store and ask what I was working on. I always said, "I'm writing a two hundred six–page novel." I had checked the *New York Times Book Review* several Sundays in a row and found the shortest novel that could still be called a novel was two hundred six pages. This is how I made a daunting task appear less daunting.

66 What interests me about family relationships are the ways we connect, disconnect, and reconnect. 99

You were born in South Carolina and now live in Charlotte, North Carolina. Do you consider yourself to be a southern writer? How do you see yourself within the tradition of southern writing?

If it means I'm keeping company with Eudora Welty and Flannery O'Connor, then yes, I'm a southern writer! That's like being born into a family that's absolutely stellar and even though you had nothing to do with the facts of your birth, you use that connection for all it's worth.

Because I have great affection—and nostalgia—for my hometown, I make sure at least one character in every novel I write is from Rock Hill. It's my way of paying tribute to the town in South Carolina where I was born and raised—which means I get to indulge myself with all those sweet and tender memories of childhood.

I love being southern. I never want to lose my soft vowels. But I don't want the fact that I've lived here all my life (except for two years after college in New York City) to limit me. Plus, I'm not sure there's even such a thing as a southern writer. Isn't it true that regardless of whether we claim the Carolinas or the Dakotas as home, we're all just writing about what Faulkner called the "human heart in conflict with itself?"

You teach writing workshops all over the country. What advice would you give beginning writers? ▶

7

A Conversation with Judy Goldman
(*continued*)

Each of us has a story. If we're truly lucky, maybe we even have more than one story. Your job is to find the one only you can tell. Find that story and begin.

What advice would you give people your age?

My first novel was published a month before my fifty-eighth birthday. I had decided to try writing fiction when I was fifty-three. That's old! As the years passed and I was still working on that novel, I clung to a quote from the writer Fred Chappell: "You have to write as though you have all the time in the world." I remember thinking, Will I be able to take my laptop to the nursing home? Can I still write if I become incontinent?

Here's what keeps me going: I believe it's important for all of us as we grow older—but particularly women—to keep taking on new challenges. Whether we're thirty-three, fifty-three, or seventy-three, we must force ourselves to try new things. We have to decide what we want to do next and try. It's the trying that counts. ❧

> 66 I believe it's important for all of us as we grow older—but particularly women—to keep taking on new challenges. 99

Judy Goldman on
Writing *Early Leaving*

A TRAGIC EVENT close to home, a throwaway remark, and a personal trait I'm not especially proud of led me to write this novel.

About six years ago, the grandson of my mother's best friend shot two fellow teenagers at point-blank range, tossed their bodies in the trunk of a car, and set the car ablaze. My mother is no longer living and I've lost contact with her friend. But I can tell you this—that young man is from a lovely, loving family. Our families knew each other for years; the young man's uncle was my ninth-grade boyfriend. The news grieved me—and terrified me. If something like this could happen in their family, I knew it could happen in any family.

We all want to distance ourselves from tragedy. We read obituaries and search the details to try to uncover an explanation. No wonder this happened to those people, we tell ourselves. They're different from us. That man died from lung cancer because he smoked; I don't smoke. That woman was kidnapped because she ran out of gas on I-85 at three in the morning; I'd never drive alone on the expressway in the middle of the night. Their house caught fire; we would've had the wiring checked. But when something happens to a family that is so like our own, we realize we're only a hair away. We're *all* vulnerable.

I did not tell that family's story. I don't know the young man who committed the murders, or his mother—and I haven't seen his father since we were children. I invented a family for my book, and my fictional family ▶

> 66 We all want to distance ourselves from tragedy. 99

told me their fictional story. But my emotion over what happened in that wonderful family fueled the writing of my novel.

While I was working on my first novel, a sentence popped into my head. I knew it didn't fit that novel, so I stored it away in my notebook. The sentence was "Everything in my house has been broken and glued back together." A friend had admired a white porcelain pitcher on my kitchen table and I told her it once belonged to my mother and that if she looked more closely, she'd see it had been broken many times and glued back together. "In fact," I added, "everything in my house has been broken and glued back together."

I decided to invent a family for whom that sentence would be true. It became the opening of my new novel. Later it was moved to the middle of the novel. Then it was bumped to the end. Ultimately I deleted it altogether. But that's okay; it served its purpose. It gained me entrance into my novel.

Early Leaving is the story of a woman who is so protective of her son—overinvolved, suffocating—that the only way out for him is to disappoint her profoundly. And he does. At eighteen, Early Smallwood kills someone. The novel opens the night before his sentencing. His mother, Kathryne Smallwood, begins to probe the past, to see if she should have seen the end coming. Was there any point where she might have come between her son and what lay in wait for him? Or was it just fate and its random consequences? Was she the cause?

> **"** Everything in my house has been broken and glued back together. **"**

All she ever wanted was to keep him safe and happy. Isn't that what every mother wants?

Kathryne Smallwood is the mother I might've been if I hadn't reined myself in. She is obsessive in the extreme—my own worst nightmare of myself. I wanted to explore that overprotective tendency—the part that smudges the line separating my children from me. I hope the emotions will be recognizable to other women. ᗃ

> 66 Kathryne Smallwood is the mother I might've been if I hadn't reined myself in. 99

If You'd Like to Write a Novel . . .

THE MOST IMPORTANT thing I have to tell you can be boiled down to two words: Show up. This is what separates the real writer from that person you're always sitting beside at a dinner party who tells you someday he's going to write a book. Everybody wants to have already written something. Not many people want to do the writing. People yearn to wear black turtlenecks and tweed jackets with worn-to-a-shine elbows. But who wants to do the actual work?

We get brilliant ideas—those sparks that ignite us in the middle of the night, when we scramble for paper and pen, knocking to the floor everything on our bedside table. Inspiration? Talent? They're only the beginning. Perseverance is what it's all about.

I wrote my first novel in three months. I didn't have the confidence to believe that if I stopped to revise, I'd actually finish. I was like an arrow—my aim was to go from beginning to end as quickly as possible. When I look back on that time, I see myself in my bathrobe and furry slippers. I'd go to my computer first thing in the morning—when I was closest to my subconscious, to my dreams—and begin. Then I'd hear my husband down in the kitchen calling up to me. It was already the end of the day and he was home from work—and I hadn't even brushed my teeth yet.

Leaving all those clunky sentences and paragraphs—without stopping to fix them—felt like I'd had company for dinner five nights

> 66 Show up. This is what separates the real writer from that person you're always sitting beside at a dinner party who tells you someday he's going to write a book. 99

12

66 If you want to
write a novel, just
write it. Don't
stop to revise
along the way. 99

in a row and left the dirty dishes piled in the
sink: the opposite of my normally tidy self. But
this is the second most important tip I have to
offer: If you want to write a novel, just write it.
Don't stop to revise along the way. At this
point, perfectionism can be a form of
procrastination.

How do you begin? Keep a notebook.
This will help you become a great noticer.
Curiosity is part of the job description for a
writer. Write down ideas the minute they
occur—memories that float up, dreams,
newspaper items, words whose texture
appeals to you, overheard conversations, and
so forth. One morning my husband, my son-
in-law, and I were having breakfast at Honey's
in Durham, North Carolina. At the table next
to us was a family—a man, his wife, and their
son, who was about five years old. The little
boy was talking when we sat down and he
continued to talk throughout the meal. All
of a sudden, the father got right in the boy's
face and yelled, "You know what your
problem is? You're hardheaded and you talk
too much!" Now I didn't like what the father
said to his son, but I did appreciate the
rhythm of his sentence. I whipped out my
notebook and wrote down exactly what
he'd said. If you look on page eleven of *Early
Leaving*, you'll find the beginning of an
entire chapter that is wrapped around those
thirteen words I overheard eating eggs and
bacon in Honey's.

What are you thinking about right now?
Something that happened to you in the ▶

fifth grade? A conversation you overheard in the hardware store yesterday? Last night's dream? Pull out that notebook and start writing. You're on your way to page one of your novel. ༄

Have You **Read?**

THE SLOW WAY BACK

This exquisitely written, remarkably crafted first novel traces three generations of a southern Jewish family. It is a story about deeply rooted family secrets, the complex love between sisters, and the constant human struggle to keep one's history alive.

Finding her mother's wedding dress, ten-year-old Thea was sure she had discovered a treasure. Trying the gown on, she easily envisioned the beautiful bride her mother must have been. But when her mother discovered her with the dress, the sight unleashed a shattering rage—the sting of her slap across Thea's face lasted a lifetime. Her mother's irrational anger, coupled with Thea's already strong feelings of disconnection with her father and her only sister, Mickey, caused Thea to feel like an outsider in her own family.

Married to a non-Jewish man, unable to have children, and with her parents now dead, Thea acquires eight letters from her grandmother to her grandmother's sister, written in Yiddish in the 1930s—just before and after Thea's parents' wedding. The cache of letters promises to answer some of Thea's life-long questions and resolve her ambivalence toward her family, but Mickey urges her not to have the letters translated, to "let sleeping dogs lie." Thea decides to trust her own instincts and have the letters deciphered—and indeed begins to unravel the perplexing and disquieting secrets of her family. In the end, Thea faces sadness in her life, as well as a multitude of questions ▶

raised by these letters—questions about marriage, sisters, and what it means to belong.

The Slow Way Back is a love song to family: this family's—and every family's—ability to confront the most difficult parts of its past and face the future with hope. The story will move you deeply; the ending has a fullness of spirit you will not easily forget. ❧

> ❝ *The Slow Way Back* is a love song to family: this family's—and every family's—ability to confront the most difficult parts of its past and face the future with hope. ❞

Don't miss the next book by your favorite author. Sign up now for AuthorTracker by visiting www.AuthorTracker.com.